AMERICAN BLUE BLOOD

AMERICAN BLUE BLOOD

The Challenge of Coming of Age in Upper-Class America

by Tom Lightfoot
Edited by William C. Codington

iUniverse, Inc.
New York Lincoln Shanghai

American Blue Blood

The Challenge of Coming of Age in Upper-Class America

iUniverse books may be ordered through booksellers or by contacting:

iUniverse
2021 Pine Lake Road, Suite 100
Lincoln, NE 68512
www.iuniverse.com
1-800-Authors (1-800-288-4677)

This book is a work of fiction. Names (including names of businesses and non-profit entities), characters, places, and incidents are either products of the author's imagination or are used fictitiously. Any resemblance to actual events or locales or persons, living or dead, is entirely coincidental.

ISBN-13: 978-0-595-31611-3 (pbk)
ISBN-13: 978-0-595-76424-2 (ebk)
ISBN-10: 0-595-31611-5 (pbk)
ISBN-10: 0-595-76424-X (ebk)

Printed in the United States of America

To Carol

INTRODUCTION

This is the story of someone trying to connect with other people socially and professionally, but who has difficulty doing so because of Article 1, Section 9 of The Constitution of the United States, in which it is stated: "No title of nobility shall be granted."

If it was necessary to sell Article 1, Section 9 to the American people, Alexander Hamilton did it in *The Federalist, No. 84*, in which he wrote: "Nothing need be said to illustrate the importance of the prohibition of titles of nobility. This may truly be denominated the corner-stone of republican government; for so long as they are excluded, there can never be serious danger that the government will be any other than that of the people."

Despite the law of the land, shades of a European aristocracy have, nevertheless, come into being in America at certain times and places. Indeed, it is a natural trait of most men and women to want to create something of permanence, something that will continue when they are no longer. It is natural to want to pass along hard-earned economic and social capital to future generations. There is the assumption that those few individuals who do successfully establish dynasties will fear their mortality less.

But the American families that have amassed the trappings of aristocracy over many generations must ultimately come to terms with Article 1, Section 9 and the vast culture that has sprung from it, not the least of which are the many laws and government policies.

This book is the autobiography of Tom Lightfoot, an American blue blood. He has difficulty connecting with the world because our democratic society prefers the self-made man. He is the product of a family that is largely defined by the success of previous generations, but in a country whose existence is defined by the rejection of inherited privilege.

In the 1970s I was a schoolmate of Tom Lightfoot's, and for the past ten years his partially completed, autobiographical manuscript has been sitting on my shelf. His is the voice of a generation, and for this reason during all those years I've harbored the goal of getting his memoir into print. Now I finally have. To spare the reader, I've edited out many lengthy passages that went nowhere, though their wandering was symbolic of Tom's coming-of-age years. There were also numerous gaps. I've filled them in with the help of my own memory, with the help of letters left behind, and by extensively interviewing members of Tom's family, co-workers, and acquaintances.

Throughout the autobiography we find that the challenges faced by other members of the Lightfoot family spring from the same source as Tom's: the family's aristocratic heritage, unwelcome in a democratic country. To find acceptance, three generations of Lightfoots, each in his or her own way, attempt to reconcile that heritage with the democratic social currents of the late 20th Century. In the process family schisms have opened wide. Tom's grandfather descends from American nobility: the Lees of Virginia. He is obsessed with Robert E. Lee as an ideal: the dutiful public servant, warrior, and educator. In contrast, Tom's grandmother is of ancient Quaker heritage, and with it has come tolerance, liberal politics, the fear of vanity and the desire for harmony and peace. Her prize possession is an Edward Hicks *Peaceable Kingdom*. Over the decades the gap between grandfather and grandmother has widened, and we find that the younger generations have taken sides.

In Tom Lightfoot's autobiography he and his family are confronting Article 1, Section 9. Tom himself is a voracious reader, and we see his search to make sense of the Lightfoot family's place in America in the quotations he selected to begin each chapter. Many come from *Democracy in America*, a book Tom was drawn to because it is the perspective of another blue blood, Alexis de Tocqueville.

In *The Federalist* Alexander Hamilton called the prohibition of nobility the "corner-stone." Indeed, the Lightfoot family story is at the heart of the American experience.

—William C. Codington, 2004

*   *   *   *

In his original autobiographical manuscript Tom begins by introducing the reader to his world with the passage below. It does not fit easily with the first chapter, but because there is much in it that is symbolic of what is to follow, I've chosen to place it here rather than eliminate it altogether.

When I was in boarding school, I knew a woman who could recite complete sentences spoken by George Washington that had actually never been written down and then published for later generations. Rather, they were sentences uttered by the great man 200 years before when he had visited her family's manor on his way to that terrible winter at Valley Forge, and various members of succeeding generations had committed them to memory.

This woman was in her early seventies when I knew her, and she may be still alive today in the decade of the nineties. A "grande dame" was the way Mother had described her, and after our meeting I finally understood the meaning. She was slender and tall and elegantly dressed, with very high cheekbones and squinty blue eyes under silver hair. When she spoke, I was reminded of the brisk, refined accent of Katharine Hepburn.

She was a trustee of an early Georgian mansion that I visited on an autumn afternoon away from boarding school. Built of fieldstone in 1746 in Pennsylvania's Schuylkill Valley by her ancestors, a father and son whose surname had become the name of the surrounding industrial town, it had been her family's seat for over two centuries. In colonial times my friend's ancestors had accumulated thousands of acres on which teams of men cut wood and made the charcoal to fuel the family iron furnaces along the Schuylkill River. As large landowners they had remained prominent well into the twentieth century.

My elderly friend's father had inherited the house, and his two daughters had ultimately presented it to the local historical society. When I met her I was doing research for a term paper. She was an old friend of my grandmother whose telephone call had brought the two of us together.

I was tall and thin and the target of considerable abuse for my pretty-boy face around the dormitory in those days. Visiting an old lady the afternoon of a varsity football game was an activity my peers were not at all surprised I had done, and it further fueled the case against me.

Dressed in school tie and blazer, I rode my bicycle to the large house where the grande dame met me at the front door, greeting me with the words George Washington had apparently spoken when he first stepped into the house in 1777. What these exact words were I do not recall, but as we walked through the house she quoted him numerous times, mostly compliments paid to her family for their hospitality. He had also apparently encouraged the manor lord's daughter to end her shyness.

My host took me from room to room and to two floors that the public never saw. Built in symmetrical early Georgian style with an expansive center hall, and trimmed inside with exquisite woodwork and cabinetry, the home was full of antiques of the eighteenth century. In the dining room hung the ubiquitous head and shoulders portrait of Washington by Gilbert Stuart. In the bookshelves were China-trade plates, saucers and cups, along with leather-bound books. Among them a sizeable collection of the Romans: Livy, Horace, Virgil, and Marcus Aurelius. My host handed me The Republic, *by Cicero, explaining that George Washington, himself may have once held it, or Alexander Hamilton, or another of the Founding Fathers. I told her excitedly that I had spent a good portion of my fall term struggling to read it in Latin.*

We walked outside among the ancient boxwoods, under even older scraggly oaks, to view the formal garden. But we were forced to raise our voices, for only one hundred yards away lay a major interstate, and an entrance ramp was even closer. A service station was across the street and a fast food restaurant next door. We paused in our conversation to briefly watch some commotion in the restaurant parking lot.

"Such indifference!" exclaimed my host bitterly. "Trespassers!" She turned to me and mumbled: "I've been robbed by democracy…this country has no rudder…we insist on forgetting our proud history, always wanting to start over…don't we need to know who we are? It particularly saddens me that even my own children and grandchildren don't know! They say their friends will call them snobbish for knowing. That's why my sister and I gave the house away—to an institution that we hope has a loftier vision. We gave it away so that there would be a monument, however small, to continuity and to our family…and to the nation."

CHAPTER 1

▼

Among nations whose law of descent is founded upon the right of primogeniture, landed estates often pass from generation to generation without undergoing division,—the consequence of which is, that family feeling is to a certain degree incorporated with the estate. The family represents the estate, the estate the family,—whose name, together with its origin, its glory, its power, and its virtues, is thus perpetuated in an imperishable memorial of the past and a sure pledge of the future.

—Alexis de Tocqueville

There is something to be said for government by a great aristocracy which has furnished leaders for the nation in peace and war for generations; even a democrat like myself must admit this.

—Theodore Roosevelt

My first visit to Posey Hall in Maryland was during the steamy June after my freshman year in the mid-seventies. I, Thomas Williamson Lightfoot, was in college in Lexington, Virginia, and my roommate for the coming year asked me to stop by his home on my way north to Philadelphia.

Clay Ludwell had never given me the details of how his family lived. He was humble and had led me to believe he lived on a simple family farm in the backwoods of Maryland. I soon found my vision of his family domain hopelessly inadequate.

The property was southeast of Washington, D.C., along the Potomac River where there is still a subtle tide. The heat was oppressive and the woods alive with chatter as I crossed the bridge from Virginia. The trees were old and tall and the undergrowth impenetrable. On the Maryland side I swerved to avoid a snake half the width of the road.

I am a Northerner from a wealthy suburb. When I stopped at a gas station to get directions, the attendant and his crew were tough and intimidating. They chewed tobacco and spat and most of their local slang was unintelligible. If I would have been best cast as the pink-cheeked schoolboy in blazer and gray flannels with beanie, they would have been best cast as cavalrymen riding with J.E.B. Stuart. If I had fought in a war, I might be able to talk to such people—so I thought then.

Fifteen minutes later I stopped to read a historic marker on the side of the road: John Wilkes Booth had crossed these fields on his flight from Washington.

At this marker white fences—"horse high, hog tight," Clay called them— began in parallel on both sides of the road and undulated in tandem to the horizon. Clay had told me that when the white fences start, look for the driveway. When he said this I should have guessed that I was in for something grand.

The gates came shortly: white columns connected by an arch. An American version, I thought, of the entrance to an English country house. Discreet, black script read: "Posey Hall 1681."

I turned in the gates and drove the half-mile, red-gravel driveway between another pair of undulating white fences. Where they ended stood a brick house crowned by four chimneys, three stories high in the center, with a one-story wing on either side. The land behind sloped down to the Potomac River.

"My God, I can't believe this place!" I yelled at Clay as he opened the front door. It was set beneath a massive Palladian window.

In his humble and casual way Clay avoided acknowledging my excitement: "Tom Lightfoot! Welcome to Posey Hall. How were my directions?"

From the outside the house looked very old and a little crumbly. But this crumbly look authenticated its long and interesting history. The grounds had been planted in a formal colonial style but decades before, and they had aged like wine ages in the humid depths of an ancient cellar, taking on a character uniquely their own.

The house inside matched the exterior's Old South grandeur: a wide, semi-circular stairway glided downward under a high ceiling, past drooping portraits and landed on a massive but faded Oriental. Musketry and engraved shotguns hung above tall double doors and windows. The moist air of mildew and dogs' breath left a sheen on the plaster walls. An occasional snake, I was told, had been found in here.

Dinner at Posey Hall was ready when I arrived, and we sat at the well used but highly polished cherry table in front of a wide, calming view of the Potomac Valley. Like a nineteenth-century scene of unspoiled nature, like a landscape painting of the Hudson River School, ancient trees of enormous size leaned over the wide river, and all craft moved slowly, some by oar, most by sail.

It was Clay, his brother Lang, his father, mother and myself at the table that night. Mary served us dinner. Her verbal exchanges were only with Lang, and the two maintained an amusing banter for our entertainment. The boys' mother never had to speak to Mary about what was expected. But Lang liked telling Mary how to wait on the table, and Mary relished even more telling Lang about his manners and general deportment. This give-and-take grew ever more loud and amusing every time Mary entered with a new dish or to clear plates, until Lang was baiting Mary with his foot on the table picking the dirt from under his toenails. Then, finally, Mr. Ludwell ended the silliness.

It seemed a carefree and lively household compared to the disciplined, introspective world of my upbringing. The apparent lack of tension was a pleasing relief, and I suddenly wanted to be a part of this family!

The Ludwell men were casual country aristocrats. There was a rural wholesomeness about them and what their good friend Mr. Randolph called an "aristocratic decency." By that he meant they displayed a generous dose of paternalism. This paternalism was made evident by the Ludwells employing more than their "share" of black women to clean the house and black men to work the farm. And there was the phenomenon of Joe Buck, the family cook.

Joe Buck was the son of a Ludwell groom and the grandson of a Ludwell slave. "When my grandfather died, the 1939 will left the orphaned, five-year-old Joe Buck to Dad," Clay told me. Joe Buck (we never called him just "Joe") was somewhere between an older brother and a second father to Clay and his brother Lang.

I was finally witness to what my grandfather had referred to as the "special relationship between the Southern white and the Negro."

"I grew up a Southerner," Grandad often reminded me, "and I can say that you'll find pockets of a special relationship down there—the two races bound by history and the spirit and love of the land."

This view was highly controversial in my own family and contributed to the pervasive Lightfoot schism. "*Special* lets us off," my grandmother had said.

As a Northerner who had spent less than a summer in the South, my older brother refused to recognize the existence of *any* shared warmth and humor between the two races, even after my telling him that I thought I had now witnessed it first hand. He responded with his usual refrain, insisting, "the American Dream has been nothing but a nightmare for African-Americans." He enjoyed telling me that at Mt. Vernon there were tales of incest that would rival anything out of Faulkner. "Your idol, George Washington, worked his slaves hard to make his farm pay. He divided slave families for efficiency and punished by whipping or selling them."

*   *   *   *

The original Ludwell house had been burned by the British on their way up the Potomac to attack Washington in 1814. In 1832 the "new" house was begun on the same site overlooking the river valley. It was three years being built.

The source of funds for the new house was the same that had supported Ludwells for generations: tobacco. The land had been granted to Clay's father's ancestor in 1681 by patent from the third Lord Baltimore, the wording of which was identical to the standard, centuries-old English baronial grant complete with the right to appoint clergy.

The family had once owned thousands of acres. They were now down to their last fifteen hundred. Some distant cousins of the name Fitzhugh owned a neighboring parcel but lived upriver in Washington.

Tobacco was still the plantation's primary crop, and I assumed the family's primary source of income. After dinner, watching the sunset over the Potomac, we sat on the screened porch smoking pipes full of tobacco grown on the property. We stuffed it in white clay pipes of the sort used in colonial days—long stemmed to allow the smoke to cool before taking it into our mouths.

Clay's mother retired early with an announcement: "We are expecting a visitor sometime tonight." Her two sons and husband seemed to know whom she meant. I didn't think to ask Clay when we were finally alone several hours later.

Unlike Mrs. Ludwell, the men in her family were voracious readers. The four of us sat up late discussing history: we all shared it as a college major. The Ludwells knew little of science beyond the agricultural science necessary to oversee the professional farmers who ran their properties. "Science is without class," Clay had announced with youthful authority when he told me his major. "History is for people who pay attention to their roots. I don't mean just their genealogies; I mean the regions and communities from which they spring. And I'll also minor in English. Great literature is written and studied by people who know the land and its history."

Mr. Ludwell was serving his twentieth year in the Maryland legislature. Like *my* grandfather, he was a member of the Society of the Cincinnati—that quaint shred of primogeniture still alive in America.

Around midnight our lights were out. "Dad's such a pillar in this county that most elections go uncontested," Clay rambled with a yawn from the four-poster next to mine. "He says he wants me to take his seat when he retires. Someone in the family has represented this part of Maryland since before the Civil War...."

*   *   *   *

The first sign of light had me up, as I couldn't wait to look around the house and explore the farm. I postponed a shower and dressed quickly.

The cool, nightly reprieve from the remorseless heat was already ending as I quietly descended the stairs and walked out the back door toward the river. The route down was a winding, red-gravel path between evenly planted oaks, each with perhaps a ten-foot girth. One hundred yards down the slope I spotted an ancient burial plot nestled in the woods. Parting the undergrowth, I made an extra long step over a fallen tree—ever paranoid of snakes—and walked in among the mostly toppled tombstones.

There were eight stones, and, of those that were legible, three were nineteenth-century and two eighteenth-century. I scratched below the leaves into the forest floor and scooped up clumps of moist soil. One of the stones had a lengthy inscription, and I rubbed the clumps along its surface until enough humus had collected in the indented lettering such that it could be read:

CLAY FITZHUGH LUDWELL
Born November 11, 1793—Died November 2, 1862
He loved Posey Hall,
Deeming his possession of it
A sacred trust to be handed on
To his successors in a like manner.

A pre-dawn gray was on the water when I arrived at its edge. I sat on the sand imagining British men-of-war sailing up the river in 1814 to burn the house and then Washington.

"My Great Aunt Posey," Mr. Ludwell had said the previous evening at dinner, "born and died here, never married and lived to one hundred and one. Was playing on the beach down along the river when a Yankee gunboat put men ashore. They looted this house!"

When the gray had left and the water was a navy blue under a cloudless sky, I rose up to head back. I wandered quietly up the red-gravel slope, enjoying the solitude of the woods. But as I emerged from the cool shade into the already hot sun, I was startled by the distant sight of a young woman of perhaps sixteen in a flowing nightgown walking under the fat columns on the backside of the house. The low-lying sun made visible a slim figure through her silky white gown.

A bit shaken by the sudden appearance of this mysterious person, I hesitated to intrude upon her solitary walk. She disappeared into the boxwood maze, and I moved quickly to the house. There I slipped quietly back to bed.

I slept soundly, and Clay's bed next to mine was empty when I went to the shower. The sun was high and the morning coolness long burned away by the powerful Maryland heat. I was pulling up my tennis socks when some soft feet came to the door, and it cautiously opened.

She was about five and a half feet tall with dark hair to the middle of her back, dark eyebrows, a fine bone structure and a reckless smile. Her slim body was wet with perspiration, and its shapely form was discernible through the same white gown of the early morning.

"Oh, Clay's not here! Sorry!" she gasped and immediately shut the door.

The house felt empty when I descended the sweeping front stairs. Breakfast was long over. A breeze from the river blew up the curtains. It took all thoughts with it of any other world but this. I wanted to be a part of this family. So unthreatening, so secure, so beautiful. I was ready to stay all summer!

I heard the pop of the tennis ball and went out to make a fourth with Clay, his brother and father. But by midday the heat was too much, and we were soon down on the river swimming and waterskiing.

*   *   *   *

Jackets and ties were expected for Saturday dinner as the Ludwells' best friends, the Randolphs, would be joining us. Clay considered the Randolphs genteel poverty. Apparently they had depleted most of their capital maintaining an *ante bellum* farm and on financing their two sons' private educations.

Drinks were served on the screened porch but, disappointingly, only the men were present.

The mysterious girl of my morning walk was Clay's sister, Posey. I hadn't seen her since morning when she had opened the door to Clay's and my room while I was dressing. Before lunch I was disappointed that she hadn't joined us out on the tennis court. In the afternoon I had hoped she would wander down to the river where we were skiing. Fantasies of her had crowded my thoughts all day. Meanwhile, Clay had made no effort to arrange an introduction! Wouldn't she now be at dinner?

Joe Buck had prepared a cold soup and had sliced a smoked ham. It was spread over the side table on silver platters under candlelight dancing across the walls and ceiling with the rising river breeze. There had never been a light switch or socket installed in this dining room—the Ludwells had no intention of yielding the wonderful antique light to electricity.

We men helped ourselves around eight thirty. But still no sign of the women! Clay didn't find it unusual.

Sometime into the second course I heard the feminine hum of conversation, and they finally emerged—from the library, the only air-conditioned room in the house. Clay's mother and Mrs. Randolph went to the side table for soup, but the girl of my fantasies went up the stairs! The other men were in serious conversation and didn't even notice.

The talk was again mostly of history, as Mr. Randolph, a gentle scholarly man, courtly and sentimental, seemed to be a descendent or cousin of every Randolph who had done anything in Virginia during the past 300 years, including Thomas Jefferson. I asked him if he knew a classmate of Clay's and mine at college.

"No. I don't know this friend of yours. His name is *John* Randolph? Whereabouts in Virginia does he live?"

"He doesn't live in Virginia, he lives in Michigan."

I had taken notice of this John Randolph around campus in the past year, my eyes of their own volition picking him out from groups of anonymous students. I had mentally tagged him because of the preposterous and futile reason he had put forth in response to a question once posed by an upperclassman at a fraternity rush party: "Why have you come to college in Virginia all the way from Michigan?"

"Because," Randolph enthusiastically responded, "I'm a direct descendent of the great Virginia statesman of the first quarter of the nineteenth century, John Randolph of Roanoke, and my family wants to close the gap between us and the Randolphs still living in Virginia."

The upperclassman had collapsed on the couch in hysterics.

"You have to earn the right to your heritage," mumbled Mr. Ludwell with a full mouth after hearing why the Michigan Randolph had come to college in Virginia. He was looking at his two sons when he spoke. "It's not God given. It's a question of doing your duty. You'll look like a fool if you try to lay claim to it without at the same time living up to it."

This short sermon from Mr. Ludwell brought us to several related topics, and I recall a heated exchange between the Randolphs:

"The wealthy can achieve a glimmer of immortality because they can leave something behind," pronounced Mrs. Randolph. "We Randolphs without any money will simply vanish when our livers fail." She always flapped her incredibly large hands when she spoke. Clay thought they resembled pre-historic bird wings.

She had upset her husband with this statement, however, and he pleaded: "What about family history? We've got it, the Ludwells have it; we're part of a long line! Randolphs aren't forgotten; it's a lineage people study. We are connected to something eternal."

"Randolphs are not forgotten *only* by other Randolphs…if they're lucky, and that's about all!" she exclaimed. "*Money* gets us into the club and gives us our identities in this country."

Looking at me, the outsider, she said: "Mr. Randolph considers himself to be a custodian of the national heritage by divine right. He thinks he's inherited a unique wisdom that qualifies him as guardian of the nation's history and therefore its identity."

We didn't walk the Randolphs to their car until well past midnight. We watched their taillights flicker through the long white fences, and I then asked Clay to join me on a walk to the river. He turned me down, so I wished the Ludwells a good night and wandered under starry skies alone down the back drive through the tall and spooky woods.

I sat on a fallen tree at the water's edge. The knowing moon, sparkling off a thousand ripples, cast a ghostly pallor over the Virginia shore opposite. Just beyond that far shore sat Stratford, ancestral home of the Lees. From that manor sprang two signers of the Declaration of Independence and a generation later the South's greatest hero and general, Robert E. Lee. I shivered, not from the cool river air, but from the majesty of nature and the grandeur of history that echoed across this land.

The following morning, much to my disappointment, I was forced to leave Posey Hall. I dressed in the dark to get to Philadelphia in time to see my sister

Binney off to Europe. From there I would be continuing on to Maine for the summer.

Under a crimson haze I sadly bid farewell to Clay, the only family member up, and drove the foggy driveway on tires munching and spitting out the red gravel. I have no recall of the long drive north—I remained absorbed in fantasies of Posey Hall, a special world. It had taken hold of me like a narcotic. I mentally wandered its corridors, catching glimpses of Posey in her flowing white gown. I sat at the ancient dining table amid piles of elegant silver, gazing down the Potomac River Valley, hearing the pop of the tennis ball blowing through the house on the steady summer breeze.

*   *   *   *

By mid-August the sunny days of sailing on Penobscot Bay had come to an end for me. I was expected to arrive back at college early to help paint the fraternity house and planned to stop at Posey Hall on my way south to pick up Clay.

Thoughts of Clay's sister had faded over the summer but re-emerged as I descended the East Coast into the high heat and humidity of the Middle Atlantic.

Posey Hall was still a furnace when I arrived close to midnight. As usual the door was wide open, but fortunately the panting dogs with wagging tails were not around to bark my arrival and wake the entire house. Suspicious eyes from the many family portraits followed me through the dark front hall and up the sweeping stairs. But when I got to Clay's bedroom, he was not there. I was excited to be back but disappointed with Clay's nonappearance.

Outside, the insects were making an enormous racket, and I sat briefly slapping mosquitoes by the front door. Soon, headlights flickered through the trees from the direction of the river, and the grind of an engine in low gear grew louder. I turned on the outside light and shortly Clay skidded his Willys Jeep to a stop beside me. Next to him was his sister. She was wet from the river and tan from a long summer outdoors.

"Tom, welcome back to Posey Hall! You remember my sister Posey?"

I thought I detected an expression of interest in her pretty face. Certainly she must have caught one in mine. Were we *both* momentarily captivated by what we saw, or was it just I? Clay probably didn't sense my feelings, or hers if they were indeed there. He ended what was for me a moment of awkwardness with the pronouncement that we raid the kitchen before bed.

Clay and I drove down the Shenandoah Valley the following day. I was not as anxious and excited to return to college as was he. Clay was popular in the house.

Smart, modest, and athletic, he could tell a good story as he had traveled extensively—hunting in Alaska, safaris in Kenya. He drank whiskey at a rate the rest of us couldn't match.

He was my roommate for three years. His agreeing to be my roommate was a surprise to most of the fraternity and certainly to me. Perhaps it was because I was better read than just about anyone in the house, and Clay liked to read.

The members of our fraternity were an anti-intellectual, brawling lot and too snobby to be involved in university affairs. The house members were generally from wealthy backgrounds, most from private schools around the South, who enjoyed snobbishly condemning the rest of the student body. Clay, the son of a man whose source of energy was community leadership, was irritated by this behavior.

Though I spent many hours with books, and was on top of many subjects that most of the house was only vaguely familiar with, I didn't get good grades. I wasn't motivated to study what the university required. Clay respected my intellectual side and didn't seem to care that my social naïveté often made me the laughing stock.

My being the laughing stock amused him more than it embarrassed him. I enjoyed encouraging the laughter by intentionally playing the fool—it was my primary means of attention.

An annual event in the house was the Hairy Buffalo Party. In the kitchen various alcohols, ice cream, and fruit juice were assembled on a dolly. Along with a large plastic trash can bought especially for the event, and to the beat of a drum and the clanging of a cowbell, the dolly was pushed periodically to the middle of the dance floor throughout the evening. The social chairman was then announced by the sergeant-at-arms, and the crowd parted as he came through in a white lab coat to "mix the buffalo chips" in the empty trash can.

It was on the night of one of these occasions that I earned as much fame as I would ever have on campus. Someone vomited into the punch, and I pushed through the crowd with empty cup, scooped up what I could of the vomit, and drank it! I became an instant legend.

The more I played the fool, the more it was expected, and I was therefore frequently a target of pranks. I could have avoided this role in most instances, but it gave me the rare chance to be on stage. At least once in the fall and once in the spring a bucket of water was dumped on me from the upstairs balcony as I walked in or out the front door, and it was clear to all that I had no intention of learning the lesson.

I was actually an isolated, quiet individual with thoughts on an intellectual plane different from my fraternity brothers. Though a respectable athlete myself, I didn't communicate well with them on professional sports and had no tales of women or adventure except those of which I had read. A ridge of books extended down the middle of Clay's and my bedroom.

My speech and etiquette were formal. I was sensitive and exhibited remnants of the seriousness still gripping the urban North in those post-Vietnam days. My contemplative moods contrasted with the exuberant spontaneity of these rough-neck southern boys who simply liked to party. The world was on my shoulders, and my eloquent manners and refined articulation set me apart and provided ample material for mockery and carefree fraternity fun.

My future brother-in-law, Danny Paulucci, recognized my vulnerability early in our acquaintance: "a Northern aristocrat in a Southern, redneck fraternity—you must have been a lightning rod for abuse!"

An enlarged picture of me as a twelve-year-old rests in a monogrammed silver frame on a secretary in my parents' library. I am a blond, blue-eyed pretty-boy standing in a tidal pool on the rocky Maine coast in over-sized madras swim trunks pulled up well above my belly button. Standing next to me on the rocks, wearing white hospital shoes, white uniform, and cardigan sweater buttoned to the chin in the summer heat, is the ubiquitous English nanny.

We were never without one. This particular lady, Nanny Hawkins, was a husky survivor of the Battle of Britain who spent fifteen years with us. When she went back to Warwick, she left my older brother, sister and me with a subtle English accent that would dog me later. "It's too refined and effeminate for America," Danny Paulucci used to say. We were ashamed of having a nanny, yet Nanny Hawkins was affectionate; she loved us, and we loved her. My brother, sister and I sent money to her church when she died. We even visited her in England—she was someone who understood us deeply, and each of us felt a strong need to thank her. But had she remained in her khaki uniform from the London blitz and occasionally subjected us to a similar, more rigorous ordeal, I might have been a little better off in later years.

*   *   *   *

I continued to wonder why even Clay, my best friend and an independent thinker, had been less than anxious to introduce me to his sister that first week-end in Maryland. Why, as time progressed, did he never encourage the two of us?

When I visited his farm, there was always a full agenda, but Posey was never included. She and I often passed but with little more than an awkward "hello."

As the seasons came and went, and I was in my fifth or sixth visit to Posey Hall, I finally confirmed that Clay was not purposely keeping us apart; he was just not making the effort to get us together. More importantly, I began to understand the role Clay's mother played in her daughter's life. Mrs. Ludwell left the boys to her husband and kept them at arm's length from her daughter.

Slowly I awoke to the difference between Mrs. Ludwell and the men in her house. While Clay, his father and brother talked about their duck blinds, the crops, local history, and their lives as country gentry, Mrs. Ludwell's conversation was superficial talk of people in high places—society names from Georgetown, Park Avenue, Swickley, or Lake Forest. What knowledge she had on any subject was only as comprehensive as the short articles in Pan Am, Delta and other airline magazines, or travel books of the sort that cover all of London in four pages.

She, Clay and I drove to Washington D.C. for a cocktail reception at which the Austrian Ambassador was the honored guest of the evening. When he appeared, Mrs. Ludwell pounced on him with raving compliments of his country. He stopped, looked at her cynically, and when she finally slowed down suggested: "You must have seen the *Sound of Music!*" He and I exchanged a discreet wink, and she, now furious and red-faced, grabbed the nearest available arm and forced a conversation.

Mrs. Ludwell was an aggressive talker, often argumentative. She always had an opinion, and her inability to master the facts didn't dampen her enthusiasm.

Many men her age were, however, charmed by her attempt to be knowledgeable in economics, politics and history. Her inability to get the facts straight and yet insist on her correctness provided an amusing game. They challenged her like a father would a daughter, and were rewarded with unconventional, often laughable ideas. Many men adored her because she *was* highly unrealistic, hated details, and was a careless manager of her own affairs.

Unfortunately, her female contemporaries considered her childish, and younger women with university degrees considered her a joke. As she grew older and watched her children and their friends become adults, she became ever more sensitive to what others of her gender thought and steadily lost her self-esteem.

Mrs. Ludwell betrayed her class by knowing little of the family history, and she neglected duties expected of the wife of a country squire. She was over-dressed and restless at Posey Hall. She was apt to go off for a month at a time, leaving her husband behind, the latter having no desire to leave the land of his ancestors.

Her maiden name created a challenge. It is a famous name in American industry. The history of her family is available in any public library, and Clay finally confirmed her ancestry to me when the initials on the towels, silver, engraved shotguns, and various heirlooms would not let him avoid my questions any longer.

In the Civil War Mrs. Ludwell's great-great grandfather, Charles, met Andrew Carnegie through Thomas Scott of the Pennsylvania Railroad. When Carnegie was looking for investors in the last half of the century, he looked up this Charles, and the latter ultimately moved to Pittsburgh. Four generations later Charles had perhaps fifty descendants, the combined trusts of whom place the family safely within the category of very wealthiest families in America. Tobacco was, therefore, only a quaint explanation for the lavish glory of Posey Hall.

So, Mrs. Ludwell knew who *she* was, and her greatest fear was that the wrong man would also find out and would aggressively pursue her daughter, but not for love. In my college days Mrs. Ludwell knew little about my family or me.

When I visited Posey Hall one spring, Mrs. Ludwell's parents were in town from New York City. They were introduced to me as "Gram" and "Gran," as if a deliberate attempt was being made to prevent me from learning the famous last name. They were an amusing couple, but two people who had obviously been well protected and spared the stress of worldly battles by a massive inheritance.

"They've been infantilized by their money—either made into infants again or never grew up," it was suggested to me years later by Coddie Codington, my boarding school friend from New York City whose family knew them. "They are self-involved, not connected with the rest of the world."

*   *   *   *

In my senior year Posey got away from her mother and finally became available to me by enrolling at a woman's college forty-five minutes from my college in Lexington.

I arrived back on campus early that year and witnessed the final worn weeks of a dusty Virginia summer. The Shenandoah Valley was anxious to be cleansed and freshened by the cool autumn rain and wind.

It was the season of fraternity rush, and the first night of my second week back Clay informed his sister that cars would arrive in front of her dormitory to pick up as many freshmen as she could muster.

In the late evening our band began with "Under the Boardwalk," and the first big party of the year was on. I spotted Posey from across the room soon after her arrival. I froze with excitement, however, and my conversation was, unfortunately, all stutters and nonsense. I suffered paralysis and managed only a few stiff words each time she and I passed. Most of the evening I spent in the comfortable shadow of my homely date. It seemed that wherever Posey walked, a small radius around her was the scene of heated competition.

When I awoke the following morning, my muddled mind clear and at ease, the paralysis gone, it was to sad and empty feelings. I hadn't thought it would happen so quickly: Posey had slipped through my fingers, already!

Jeff Pittman, a year behind me, was popular among the brothers and was certain of his prowess with women. Those women who knew him, at least from afar, worshipped him. A freshman like Posey was quickly at his mercy, and before I had had a chance to stake a claim, she was Pittman's girl.

Posey was back up the following afternoon for another rush party, and it was only a few weeks later that the two of them were locked for the night behind the elaborate brass bolt on Pittman's door.

The months passed and resignation, once firmly established, brought forth an end to my paralysis around Posey. I was not worthy of her, I would never have her, and there was no reason to freeze whenever she looked my way.

By Thanksgiving I was comfortable enough to ask her to dance. I was delighted to discover how much we both liked the jitterbug. And Posey didn't insist on getting her way on the dance floor: her slim body was malleable, I could lead in any direction, and she was quick to follow. We both knew some popular steps and learned more from Fred Astaire movies.

During those first evenings of dancing together there was never a word between us when the music stopped. Its abrupt finish left us to cope with an awkward, never-ending period of silence, both of us staring out at the crowd until the next song came on.

By the Christmas season we were dominating the dance floor, and other couples regularly stood in a circle watching our every step, wanting to learn. Often other girls asked me to dance, but I found it increasingly unsatisfying, as no one's ability compared with Posey's.

Pittman wasn't much on the floor, but he wasn't concerned—he didn't consider me a threat. After Christmas, however, and as the winter moved on and the various fraternities fought each other with snowballs, and we lit up the night sky burning fraternity furniture behind the house in anticipation of spring (and buying anew—it was an annual event!), Posey and I finally did begin to talk at length.

I was loosening up and my dry humor, appreciated by her brother Clay but by few others, played forth. Initially the prime target of my humor was Pittman. My comments were only between the two of us, and they closely resembled a snobby father warning his daughter what to watch out for in a wayward boyfriend.

Like Posey, I also hailed from a wealthy family. I could therefore anticipate her humorous though snobby comments about those around us who came from less fortunate backgrounds. I could paint amusing visions for her of how her mother assumed ladies were formally courted in Virginia. Being so well read, I was very knowledgeable in the history of her family, and it was evident and pleasing to her that I looked at her family's status in greater awe than did Pittman.

For the first time in her life, Posey Hall was not the backdrop for the stage she now walked. She was anxious to be recognized for her heritage; she was frustrated when someone didn't know it. I *had* been a visitor at Posey Hall, and because I understood her snobbish humor and her present frustration, sometime over the winter she must have begun finding me more appealing than Jeff Pittman.

I did not recognize this subtle change. As her feelings blossomed and grew ever more sure, impatience with Pittman became open. She was critical of his dress and his "hillbilly" accent. "Jeff Pittman is from a farm family," she complained, "but they're *not* country gentry. There *is* a gap between him and me." Though he shared many of her brother Clay's outdoor interests, Pittman lacked the sophistication Posey thought she deserved. The emotional and sexual rewards of the relationship kept her hanging on, however, as I was not forthcoming.

So, out of frustration, she got mean with Pittman. On more than one occasion when she was to be his date, she never showed. She disrupted his studies and made him, a boy on scholarship, pay all meal costs and tickets to weekend parties at her college.

These tactics were observed by Pittman's friends, and they stood by him. They could not, however, overtly mistreat Posey, as Clay was a well-respected member of the house. Nevertheless, there were sarcastic comments and an occasional prank in Clay's absence: Posey would come to dinner in the fraternity dining room to find a place for Pittman but not one for herself. One time the air was released from her tires.

Embittered by what she considered harsh treatment from the brothers and frustrated with Pittman, one night she turned to me.

It was a month and a half after spring break; my graduation was near. Virginia smelled of magnolia, and the rivers were full for tubing. The fraternity held an evening cookout to the live music of some West Virginia fiddlers. The party was in the yard at Rose Hill—a small brick house built in colonial times and rented as additional sleeping quarters by the fraternity. Hawaiian Punch mixed with grain alcohol colored our lips clown-red, and once again Posey and I were madly dancing, this time to Bluegrass.

Sometime in the middle of the frenzy Posey took my hand and pulled me inside. She led me to a bedroom door and opened it to darkness and the faint glow of white sheets. She turned to lead me across the threshold.

But how could it be, I thought, that Posey is reaching for me? How could I be the object of her desires? Posey is Pittman's girl! The right things, the correct things, are not so spontaneous; they are planned and calculated.

Such was my instinct, misplaced logic, and lack of belief in myself that I moved back, beyond her reach, not recognizing the reality of the opportunity. Sensing my confusion, she shrugged her delicate shoulders in frustration and led me back outside into the loud turmoil. I watched her vanish among the frenzied dancers with clown-red lips. Feeling confused, I moved over to a crowd of fellow seniors, and we left to strip off our clothes behind a hedge and take a swim in the adjacent, frigid pond.

So ended a chance to make Posey mine, of taking her from Pittman and ending my gnawing jealousy, of riding a streak of joy that would have so fulfilled my life. I wouldn't, however, see the incident as a missed opportunity, admit my mistake, and torture myself with painful regret until I had thought through its every detail over and over and over again in the lonely months that followed.

My college graduation was just a few weeks away, and for now geography would split us apart.

CHAPTER 2

▼

Aristocracy naturally leads the human mind to the contemplation of the past, and fixes it there. Democracy, on the contrary, gives men a sort of instinctive distaste for what is ancient.

—Alexis de Tocqueville

A man who boasts only of his ancestors confesses that he belongs to a family that is better dead than alive.

—Abraham Lincoln

The very rich in America are not dominantly an idle rich and never have been.

—C. Wright Mills

In my college days I enjoyed reading and was considered a reliable source of interesting but unusable information. I spent hours in the library, but not studying what the professors had assigned—I read mostly history and literature of my own choosing. My grades were often worse than mediocre, and graduate school was therefore out of the question. The consensus within my fraternity was that I should be a man of letters and live above a gentleman's club in the downtown of a major city.

There *were* moments of concern, though admittedly very few, when I awoke from a slumber on one of the red-leather library couches and, casting my eyes up through the tall Palladian windows to the blue sky, asked with a yawn: "Where will I be in thirty years?"

The majority of the time, however, I was not concerned with my future. I drifted along assuming that the world would pick me up and make something of me, that I would be *dealt* a grand and glorious career! I assumed that after college I would automatically go on to significant achievement—everyone else I was reading about in the history books seemed to have! And many of my ancestors had. Would I someday be an ambassador? Would I be in Congress? Would I eventually run one of America's largest corporations?

Unfortunately, I did not understand how large a place the world is, and that those famous people about whom I was reading in history books or in magazines were part of only a tiny minority, most of whom had managed to achieve fame only through hard work, by focusing, and by taking the initiative. At the time I had no comprehension of the intermediate steps required to get to the pinnacle, so couldn't argue myself into understanding that my lofty dreams were no more than simply that.

Needless to say, just assuming so strongly that something would happen to me, that I would be dealt a favorable hand and become someone of significance, left me unprepared upon graduation. One afternoon I discovered that several fraternity brothers were taking the Graduate Management Admissions Test. For once I was nervous and hiked out to the tennis courts in search of Clay.

"How come you're not taking them?" I asked.

"Because the old boy network is going to take care of me just like it's going to take care of you," he said confidently, his voice muffled by a wet towel.

*   *   *   *

The summer after graduation I had a job teaching sailing in Castine, Maine. My parents had owned a summer house in Castine for a decade. During my junior year we had moved up permanently from Philadelphia.

With earnings derived from sailing instruction, I took a solitary trip to Europe in the late summer and early fall.

To the older generations of my family, I was taking the "Grand Tour." My trip was, however, quite different from the ones they had taken decades earlier, complete with steamer trunks and passage on the *Queen Mary*, reservations at the Ritz in Paris and other exclusive hotels, and guides, chaperones and letters of introduction to some of the chief people. Mine was a late twentieth century version of the Grand Tour, complete with backpack, youth hostel card, and Eurail Pass.

There was no job that awaited me upon returning home. I was broke from my trip to Europe, my college allowance having been discontinued. I then discovered that, unlike myself, Clay had been given access to a considerable trust fund at age twenty-one.

I was desperate for cash and some independence. There were few if any career opportunities in Castine, so I made arrangements to stay with my grandparents outside Philadelphia while looking for a job.

In November I loaded a hundred books and what was left of my college wardrobe into my Vega station wagon and drove south to my father's parents' home on the Philadelphia Main Line. They lived in a thirty-four-room mansion set on 120 acres of prime suburban property within easy commute on the Paoli Local to downtown Philadelphia. The property was rolling, open horse country on which also sat extensive stables, a barn, and several tenant homes.

The property had been given the name "Leighsylvania" by a romantically inclined nineteenth century ancestor. Members of each generation to follow (including my own) had apparently thought the name pretentious, but it had nevertheless survived.

The lengthy gravel driveway was planted on either side with large sycamores. But there were gaps every thirty yards, as trees taken down by disease or storms had never been replaced. In this and other ways the estate gave the appearance of having *once* been formally planted. Some in the family complained that nature's leash had been let go. In the form of ivy and flowering shrubs, she was allowed to wrap herself around stone walls and fences such that they resembled hedges in the English countryside. A tenant house built in colonial times was all but hidden.

My grandmother defended what some of us called "nature's encroachment" by telling us her gardens were "English gardens, well planned but informally planted, not based on precise geometry that would demonstrate man's ability to control nature."

Apparently my grandfather was not always in agreement. "Reign of the haphazard. No Age of Reason here," he commented cynically.

The gardens, seeming to expand with their own sense of freedom, gave the house and grounds an intentionally decadent look by American standards, such that they resembled those ancient and beautiful country manors I had seen in the Cotswalds earlier that fall. I often found my grandmother sitting among her roses holding the well-soiled remains of a volume by Gertrude Jekyll.

I followed the winding drive to the main house and parked by the big front door. Across a broad lawn in front of the house sat the small ruin of a fieldstone farm building.

Glowing red in the setting sun, it was now indeed the last ember of the Quaker farmer who had settled the land in 1701. Baldwyn Leigh had braved the North Atlantic with William Penn aboard the ship *Canterbury* on the latter's second voyage to America in 1699.

In the summer baskets of flowering plants hung from the hollow window arches, and the ruin was smothered by brightly flowering shrubs and well-groomed boxwoods, all surrounded by a finely manicured lawn. It was such a pleasant site to behold that I once overheard a visitor inquiring if my grandmother had had the ruin specially built as a prop for her garden.

She had not, of course. She had inherited it along with the land and, partly at my grandfather's insistence, had preserved and beautified this ruin as a monument to her heritage and, more specifically, her early Quaker ancestor, Baldwyn Leigh.

My grandparents' three-story mansion was white stucco with freshly painted forest-green shutters. I went to the front door because I did not want to intrude on the help by entering through the back. I pounded the knocker and wondered who would receive me. With my grandparents both in their eighties, the door was too heavy for either of them: it measured four feet wide, eight feet tall and five inches thick. In recent years a younger member of the household staff had been doing the greeting.

This cold clear evening was no exception: a young lady, nineteen years of age, pulled the door open with great effort and expended just as much to keep it from crashing into the adjacent wall. Her name was Ole (both vowels pronounced as long vowels). She was of medium height and slender; she was pretty and outspoken, considering herself the equal to any member of the Lightfoot family. She was, however, the granddaughter of the cook.

"Good evening Master Thomas Williamson Lightfoot," she exclaimed in a mocking tone. She then exhibited her usual sarcastic playfulness by offering to take my bag, which was clearly too heavy for her, and then acting out the role of formal Victorian servant from an English stately home by asking such silly questions as: "Was the Master's trip comfortable aboard the four-in-hand?"

Indeed, she wasn't the least shy of her employer's family. She was not the humble servant, and her quick wit seemed to find a ready opening and strike an especially wincing blow when members of my generation came for a visit. There was one symbolic feature that immediately told all, however, that seemed to separate her indelibly from the Lightfoots: the formal maid's uniform that my grand-father insisted she wear. "We want the help to dress with dignity," he told me when I complained. "They take pride in a uniform."

Ole lived and worked at the estate on weekends and spent weekdays and nights at Bryn Mawr College where my grandmother paid her tuition, room and board. My grandmother had wanted her to attend Bryn Mawr because of its Quaker heritage and because it was her own alma mater.

After our brief conversation, in which I confirmed that cocktails would be at the usual six-thirty sharp and dinner at seven and "not a minute later," I wandered the house. Although it had been built as recently as 1926, it was nevertheless permeated by a dusty aroma of history. I had nicknamed it the "The British Museum," and the name had stuck among my siblings and first cousins. Many of its curious contents were hundreds of years old and from distant lands: Europe, the Orient, Africa. They had been collected over nine generations and each had a story.

My grandfather was only too happy to tell these stories many times over. In the process he lost the attention of the majority of his bored and unappreciative family. Most family members do not know their own history, and some are embarrassed by it, if not ashamed.

My mother and I are two who were prepared to listen, learn and discuss, however, and as a result my perspective on the world is, I like to think, broader and deeper. Perhaps it was because of my grandfather's influence that in my school days and as a young man, to everyone's consternation and frustration, I would regularly put forth long-winded and overly elaborate explanations of the daily happenings of my life and the world around me, explanations that were based less on events occurring in the past month or year than on events of previous eras and long past decades or even centuries.

My mother and I learned that the family had been active in colonial wars, been prominent in colonial politics, and counted the Byrds of Westover and Lees of Stratford as ancestors, not to mention the long line of prominent Philadelphians. A half-dozen ancestors had been officers in Washington's army, and my grandfather was active in the Society of the Cincinnati.

The physical by-product of our family history was the immense collection of memorabilia that had come down through the generations—treasures of a long and colorful past.

Family legend embraced my grandparents' house, its contents and the land. For some of us the estate was our source of pride: it showed us who we were and pointed to the direction we should take. We were assured of never losing the knowledge of ourselves as long as the estate survived. And, because of its exist-ence, we feared our mortality less because we sensed a spirit greater than our-selves—a family tradition never to be dislodged—that would be left behind to carry on.

I dressed for dinner and met up with my grandparents at the appointed time in what the original architect had apparently labeled the "Great Room." Like lord of the manor, my tall distinguished grandfather stood next to the mantle at the far end under a hammerbeam ceiling. At his elbow, in a chair whose arms, seat and back were covered in needlepoint, sat my elegant grandmother. She was calmly completing another great swath of needlework for a house already covered in it.

A pantry maid in black evening uniform (they wore light blue during the day) with white apron and white cap arrived with the bottle of Scotch on a silver plat-ter. It was from the small distillery owned by a Scottish peer whom my grandfa-ther had befriended in the Twenties: "I met him at the Royal and Ancient. Before the war I used to be over there on business, and I played a lot of golf. I was a fre-quent guest at his family seat."

After a half-hour discussion on my trip to Europe, the pantry maid returned to announce dinner. We gathered our things and followed my grandfather. He paraded forth like a duke to his state dining room—retinue in tow with the rega-lia: on this evening only hors d'oeuvres and whiskey!

We sat at the massive cherry table that had often comfortably seated sixteen or more guests. We called it the "Civil War" table because it had survived the siege of Richmond.

My grandfather's grandfather had been a medical officer for the Confederacy during the siege. He had owned a house in the city, and it was there that he brought the Confederate General Euell back to health. Euell, known as "Old Baldy," ate his meals at the table as did many another Confederate notable.

One was Judah Benjamin, the only Jew ever to enter the family history told by my grandfather. Benjamin was the brilliant lawyer and one-time planter who served the Confederacy in more cabinet posts than anyone: first as attorney gen-eral, then secretary of war and finally secretary of state.

"The Jewish population was small at the time," Grandad instructed me, as if he felt compelled to explain why a Jew had been a friend of the family and had sat at this table. "Jews had not begun arriving in large numbers from Central and Eastern Europe, and there were only about ten thousand who fought for the South. The anti-Semitism that has afflicted later generations in America was at the time mild to non-existent."

It was through Judah Benjamin that my grandfather's grandfather had come to know so well Varina Davis, wife of Jefferson Davis. She came to the house regularly during the war and had sat at this table for meals. She would apparently leave with the latest update for her husband on the conditions of the hospitals in and around Richmond during the siege.

Now, four massive silver candlesticks, perhaps two feet tall, paraded like torches down this cherry table. They flickered against numerous family portraits hanging from the off-white plaster walls.

In the 19th century Thomas Sully painted twenty-nine Biddles, twenty-three Wetherills, ten Ingersols, and eight Leighs. Grandmother Leigh had inherited three of the eight Sullys, two of which now gazed down upon us at dinner. Between them was a portrait of Isaac Leigh, Philadelphia Quaker and abolitionist, whose resemblance to me most of the family called "uncanny." It was painted by Robert Charles Leslie, an American who studied under Benjamin West in London. An artist himself, in his right hand Leigh held a portfolio of his sketches. And at each end of the room hung portraits that were unsigned: one of a Confederate naval officer, the other of his wife.

My grandparents' house was a world of golden antique light—of history, fine manners, and a place where even the most skeptical could become caught in the spell of "good breeding." Belief in "good breeding" made some of us confident and restful; to others it gave a mission; still to others, the very idea caused great inner turmoil.

This world had ended decades ago for many similar families on the Main Line. My grandparents, however, lived a life in the eighties not unlike the life they had lived in the twenties. Indeed, up until they passed away they employed five servants, and meals were served by various pantry maids from silver won at horse shows and from nineteenth-century Chinese export platters.

My grandmother had inherited the land from her grandfather when she was just two years old. By then her family had already farmed it for two hundred years. From the agreement between William Penn and the First Purchasers in 1681, we know that this one hundred and twenty acres was all that remained of an original five thousand belonging to our family founder in America, Baldwyn Leigh.

The Leighs of England descended from James de Lygh, a knight during the reign of Henry III, and from Otho, the Saxon tenant of Landsford at Domesday.

Early in his life Baldwyn Leigh had become a follower of the Quaker George Fox. Records show him identified with the Friends no later than 1657. It was not until 1699, however, that Baldwyn and his wife Hannah immigrated to America in search of religious toleration. They set sail on September 9 from Cowes, Isle of Wight, with William Penn in the *Canterbury*, sighting the new land eighty-one days later.

Their descendants were Quaker pacifists who refused participation in the American Revolution. For suspected loyalist sympathies, one was sent away during that war with the "Virginia Exiles," twenty of the most prominent Philadelphia Quakers of the day, including two Pembertons, Elijah Brown, Henry Drinker and Miers Fisher, all ancestors of boys with whom I had once attended private day school.

In the War of 1812, however, the then owner of the land, James Leigh, chose not to remain a Friend: he joined a volunteer musket company, which offered its services to the governor of Pennsylvania. Though himself disowned by the meeting, James's children were raised as Quakers, and it was not until 1900 hundred that the Leighs became Episcopalian, adopting "the church of J.P. Morgan, the church of wealth, culture, and aristocratic lineage"—my grandmother liked to describe it thus to tease Grandad.

Soon after the War of 1812, James Leigh built himself a handsome home over a spring on the land he now called *Leighsylvania*. The house stands today, and the spring still dribbles out the back. It is a wonderful house of early nineteenth-century charm and very livable for a small family. But to her regret, my grandmother never lived in "The James Cottage." When she was a child her guardian found tenants for the house and leased the land to the neighboring horse farm.

In the early twenties my grandparents, following hounds in pursuit of the fox, crossed the property often and recognized a building site atop a hill with a pretty view of the lush rolling farmland. Over a three-year period they built the present thirty-four-room mansion and nearby stables and barn.

Grandad was older and therefore must have had his way because in her later years my grandmother was embarrassed by the extravagance. "I would have preferred a more restrained elegance," she often said. With a strong tone of sarcasm she once added: "But, this big house, all this land, we're safe and well protected out here—what better answer to the ugly melting pot in the city?"

On many cool fall days of years gone by, members of the local hunt club would gather here for breakfast. Their horses were then brought to the courtyard out front, champagne was served to the riders atop their thoroughbreds, and the hunt would begin. In his early middle age my grandfather had his portrait painted on horseback—dressed for the hunt. The portrait is large, measuring at least five feet by four.

My grandparents were different from each other in their approach to the world. She was more lovable, humane, and egalitarian, while he was dogmatic, autocratic, and prejudiced. She was open and wanting to show emotion. He was a model of Victorian self-control. She was most interested in nature and in the arts such as painting and music. He was obsessed with civic duty and in the evenings read history.

"History and the literary classics were written by people who pay attention to their roots, region and community," he said. Clay Ludwell and he would have gotten on well.

My grandparents were both outspoken, and their conflicting opinions often lay at the root of family schisms that extended down to their children and grandchildren. Surprisingly, my grandfather liked to assume that he was the head of a strong, unified family at peace with itself. In actuality the family did not really come together until several years after both grandparents were dead. Until then it was generally my mother and grandfather at philosophical odds with my father and his mother. My older brother was in the same camp as the latter two, while my sister followed my mother and grandfather. The various cousins, uncles and aunts also took part, but in less obvious ways.

"Jack Kennedy and family are shanty Irish," I recall my grandfather proclaiming. My grandmother was quick to challenge him on such comments—"the Irish built Boston," she countered. "The Irish taught us that government has responsibility—that at times it must lend a helping hand. You're frustrated and jealous that you never ran for office."

Later, my grandmother whispered: "When Grandad was a young man he thought of getting into politics, but he was too much of a snob to campaign in the Irish slums. He wouldn't get his hands dirty...."

On the subject of the Kennedys my father, meanwhile, was not snobbish toward the Irish but, seeming to reflect his Quaker roots, was not impressed with the Kennedys' "obsessive need," as he put it, to run for office. My father is not the self-promoter my grandfather planned him to be. Perhaps Grandad secretly envisioned himself a kingmaker like Joe Kennedy, but his efforts certainly backfired with Dad.

Mother generally agreed with my grandfather on most issues, often putting her at odds with her own husband. *Her* parents had been my grandfather's best friends during his years at Harvard.

My older brother, Henry Leigh Lightfoot, was consistently at loggerheads with Grandad. "Grandad thinks democracy is the rule of the half-educated. He probably thinks people in government should come from some sort of landed, gentlemanly class. How does knowledge of fox hunting or the ability to murder a pheasant mean good government?"

Henry was at college in 1968, and in those days he was seldom positive about anything. I recall some typical comments his senior year: "The Kennedys are no better than the rest of the wealthy power-hungry: corrupt. Read the true story of the family—someday it will all come out about Old Joe."

"Your brother's college is where you go to learn anarchy," Grandad whispered behind Henry's back. "It's like Bryn Mawr where your grandmother went...Quaker school!"

Henry was indeed attending a college of Quaker heritage. It was very tough academically and had a national reputation.

A notorious pronouncement from Grandad that opened the family schism wider concerned the willingness of African-Americans to fight for the Confederacy in 1865. He produced a letter from an ancestor to Jefferson Davis about a poll taken of blacks in and around Richmond during the siege, and, according to this poll, "most" were willing to fight for the Southern cause. "The Old South was a paternal world," he insisted. "The Negro was willing to fight to preserve a world to which he had emotional attachment."

My grandmother, of course, heartily disagreed. "Your poll was flawed," she felt obligated to say without any investigation—her Quaker ancestors had been well represented in 1833 at the formation of the American Anti-Slavery Society.

My father and older brother were her staunch allies on this issue, while my mother suggested that we all take a visit to the library.

At a later date I recall my grandfather telling us: "Sacco and Vanzetti were convicted on the basis of valid evidence."

Fifty years after the 1927 execution of these two immigrants, my grandmother had a small fit, telling us emotionally: "Your grandfather is still convinced these people were a threat to the old-stock establishment. I say civil liberty was trampled!"

But though Grandad enjoyed expressing such controversial views among family in the library after dinner, I never witnessed him openly treat anyone from a different background with less than the greatest respect for that individual's sense of self-worth and dignity. "A true gentleman, a gentleman of the old school," was the way Mother always described him. Though in his letters from France as a twenty-six-year-old Doughboy he referred to African-Americans as "Niggers," today I try to defend the position that his often controversial views were less a reflection of any personal frustrations or failures than they were a reflection of his class and geographic background when he came of age.

For different reasons, therefore, my grandparents ran Leighsylvania as a sort of welfare state. She ran it as such because, politically, she leaned to the left, and in the thirties especially there were people in need. He ran it as such because his romantic vision of being country gentry included a strong sense of paternalism.

Leighsylvania employed more than twenty gardeners, groomsmen, and household servants through the Great Depression, many working there because they were simply down on their luck. My grandparents gave them room, board and a small wage. The estate offered security and a safe haven. Hard work was definitely not a pre-requisite; honesty and dedication to the family's values and its way of life were. Some employees stayed on the payroll well into their eighties: cutting flowers for vases in the house, walking the dogs, and helping the grandchildren catch goldfish in the garden ponds.

In my grandfather's oral histories of the family, wealth seemed to exist in every generation. Perhaps it was because he was the one telling the stories, and he had lots of money. My family can count civic leaders, politicians, and diplomats as ancestors, some of whom appear today in history books. Family stories seemed to imply that there was always plenty of money in the lives of these individuals.

What motivated our family's civic involvement, and to what extent would it have happened if the family hadn't been wealthy? This was an issue of controversy, and the sides were drawn along familiar lines.

My mother and grandfather insisted it was the family's traditional sense of duty—"noblesse oblige, it's in our blood"—that had propelled our ancestors to successful civic involvement.

My grandmother and father discounted any sense of noblesse. "Heritage or no heritage, money or no money, our ancestors simply saw people or a community in need, and their *conscience* told them they had to help," proclaimed my grandmother.

My brother-in-law, Danny Paulucci, was another outspoken family personality, and he revealed his "cynicism," as my parents referred to it, when he said: "If money hadn't first been in ready supply to support a comfortable lifestyle, your ancestors would not have gone beyond just trying to make it."

Even more cynical was brother Henry. He was ashamed of the Lightfoot wealth and considered money a source of evil: "Anyone in the family who got into politics probably did so just to increase his already substantial fortune."

Not until my senior year at college did it occur to me that my generation might be the first in many not to begin adulthood with a financial nest egg. There was no continuation of my allowance after graduation, or source of ready money as from a trust fund like Clay Ludwell was enjoying. Certainly Grandad had no interest in helping me financially. He had never been generous with my father; Dad's trust had come from the Leighs, and it was comparatively small. Nor had Grandad been generous with the other grandchildren when they had come of age. Perhaps various members of the family, among them brother Henry, were headed in the wrong direction and had set bad examples in Grandad's mind. It was not my place to ask.

I had, to be sure, confidence that far in the future my siblings and I would inherit at least something from the grandparents. The merciless chiding I received from friends when they visited the estate, about my supposed future inheritance, helped instill that confidence. "You should dig around for a copy of the will—I'm sure you're in it big time," more than one guest advised, embarrassing me in the process. Through the years I learned the hard way to be particularly selective about who would accompany me to Leighsylvania.

But if an inheritance lay in the future, my grandparents never discussed that future. The topic at dinner that first night at the Civil War table was, therefore, my plan to find a job and become "self-sufficient." Both grandparents took a sincere interest, but even on this first evening it was evident that Grandad was impatient that I didn't already have a well-laid plan.

"Are there not plenty of role models in the family? Isn't this why we study family history?" he asked. "If our ancestors have done good deeds, then it is justifiable to take their direction.... I am eighty-four years old and have now been out of the business world for almost twenty years. I have long since lost contact with people who have entry-level jobs available, at least ones that pay anything. You're not going to make much money working at the historical societies or philanthropic organizations where I spend my time at board meetings these days. There's no point in me trying to get you in there....They don't teach economics at boarding school, but you must have taken it at college. Have you considered business?"

"But there are family contacts, nevertheless, friends of my parents, Grandad," I said stubbornly. "I'm going to be calling them."

"There is the law. Have you considered graduate school?"

"Yes, I have, but for the moment I am interested in getting some work experience to better understand what kind of work I'm best at and enjoy the most." I certainly wasn't going to mention my mediocre undergraduate record and the slim chance of my being accepted at law or business school.

"If you haven't got a clue by now, after four years in college, then you had better just plunge in. Don't hesitate; by hesitating you'll just delay getting those questions answered. Get on the world and ride with it!"

Thus at that first dinner did my grandfather begin his unrelenting campaign to have me take immediate action. As a result I would ultimately feel pressured to accept the very first job offer I got. Through the rest of the meal and after dinner I was made to hear dramatic tales of how various members of the family had gotten *their* start.

*   *   *   *

Late in the evening, when my grandparents had gone up to bed, I was sitting in the library reading Fitzgerald's *This Side of Paradise* when I heard the sudden sharp roar of a cold engine. I discerned it coming from the back end of the house near the four-car garage that housed an antique Jaguar and large new Mercedes.

Was one of the cars being stolen? The help had retired to their rooms on the third floor; who could be leaving at this hour?

With pounding heart I moved quickly to a second floor bedroom overlooking the garage courtyard. The floodlights from the house glared down over a rusty Chevrolet station wagon that I hadn't seen before. A few seconds later a trim feminine figure in a tired parka walked out the door under my window and over to the car.

It was Ole. Her pretty black hair in a ponytail glistened in the floodlight. Turning to open the car door, she saw me in the window. She was as startled as I was by her spotting me. After a moment I threw an embarrassed wave. Her pretty face—white without a blemish under the bright light, like an over-exposed photograph—revealed a bemused smile, which soon disappeared in an expression of suspicion.

She drove off, back to Bryn Mawr College for the week, during which time that pretty face lingered on in my fantasies.

*   *   *   *

"We are rapidly approaching the day in which there will be few remaining occupational preserves for people like ourselves.... In fact, one could argue, that day has already arrived. Your own family has witnessed how someone of Italian descent graduates from college today and hasn't any fear whatsoever of having to break new ground in an occupation that only a generation ago would have been considered off limits to all except people like ourselves."

So spoke Benjamin Rawle Price in his office on Walnut Street in Philadelphia. Handsome and in excellent shape from two hours each day in the squash court, he was sitting beneath a Thomas Birch oil of a ship caught between waves taller than its masts. His beautiful wife, in jodhpurs and holding a riding crop, was featured in a monogrammed silver frame on the windowsill. When the telephone interrupted, I read the engraving on a silver plate that seemed to act as a sort of in-basket on the corner of his massive desk:

Sugartown Horse Show,
Working Hunters
Won By Leighsylvania,
Bond Street
Ridden By
Mrs. Benjamin Rawle Price
1940

"Is that your wife on the platter?" I asked when he'd hung up the phone.

"No, mother...Hope Hopkinson Price; my wife was only ten years old in 1940. Your grandfather had that champion horse, Bond Street was the name, and my mother was the only one who could manage to ride him."

"Yes, and my grandparents' house is full of silver won by that horse."

Ben Price was an old friend of my father's from their days in the First City Troop, a unit of army reserves. Founded as The Philadelphia Troop of Light Horse in 1774, "The Troop" is older than any regiment in the United States. A number of its original volunteers were also members of Philadelphia's first hunt club, so since its founding it has been as much an exclusive but rowdy men's club as a detachment of army reserves.

"This city is changing—it's considerably more competitive out there than when I was your age," Ben Price rambled on, not responding to any specific question. He mumbled and hummed some verses from *Pinafore*:

When I was a lad I served a term
As office boy to an attorney's firm—

I cleaned the windows and I swept the floor,
And I polished up the handle of the big front door—

I polished up that handle so carefullee
That now I am the ruler of the Queen's Navee!

"I certainly was in my share of Gilbert and Sullivans!" I proclaimed with a big comfortable smile.

Ben had made me feel very at home when his good cheer unexpectedly and abruptly disappeared, and he looked at me meanly and squarely across the desk for a long minute of silence. Perhaps he was recognizing that I was indeed too comfortable and that he had therefore not delivered the message he had planned on delivering. In a scolding voice he exclaimed: "You see it's not like it was in the old days! That's what I'm trying to say!"

Irritated, and with a tone of sarcasm, I asked: "Oh? It's not as easy today as it was for Sir Joseph Porter? Then why do they sing G-and-S at the prep schools you and I attended?"

I hadn't directly asked him for a job, yet he was now aggressively trying to explain the reason he couldn't get me one.

"No one is going to hire you just because you went to some prestigious prep school. The old-school-tie nonsense is now just that; the right prep-school used to be a ticket. It's the end of the seventies. It works the other way these days: if an employer finds out you've gone to a prestigious boarding school, he's not going to hire you because he'll think you're not going to fit in. Companies want people who are going to fit in with the diverse work force of today and tomorrow. Ethnic exclusivity is over—you're not just competing with fellow WASP boarding school grads. The people running the show in this country these days don't have names like Hopkinson and Biddle…it's names like Iacocca or Shapiro. Until 1970 the patrician DuPont Company had never been headed by anyone outside the family, much less a Jew. Meanwhile, Robert Abboud of Lebanese ancestry heads up one of the ten largest banks in the United States…. You're a fellow Episcopalian. We account for less than three percent of the population. Did you know that in the fifties about a third of the Fortune 500 chief executive officers were Episcopalian? That's no longer. Things are changing ever faster. Other groups have been making inroads and today a young Italian American of your age is not afraid to apply to firms that were previously WASP preserves. For him the ground has already been broken…."

He then abruptly fell silent, perhaps feeling a little guilty for being so harsh. When he spoke again he wasn't looking at me in the eye. Slowly the excitement in his voice diminished to a soft apologetic tone. I sat in silence while he rambled on to the wall or the window. He knew he couldn't help me the same way he had been helped twenty-five years before.

Ben was another from the list of what Clay called my family's "old boy network" around Philadelphia that I could supposedly rely on to get a start. Nothing came of these meetings. I usually met with such contacts downtown at the Rittenhouse Squash Club. I wondered if some of them didn't actually possess an office but, rather, came in from the Main Line or Chestnut Hill just for squash or court tennis, then a large lunch followed by a trip to the broker or money manager.

My appointment with Ben Price ended with some final disheartening comments: "Our day is over, Tom. We are now a class infested with self-doubt. There was a time when we were looked up to because we had arrived first and knew how things should be done before others had even stepped foot into this country. And when those other people came, they were envious enough of us to want to work hard and follow our lead. But today people see a connection with the past as an entanglement; they want everything to be a matter of choice. They don't want to emulate our *type*. The white Anglo-Saxon male has now been deemed an oppressor."

*   *   *   *

Each morning I was served breakfast with my grandparents at the Civil War table. During this time my grandfather would drill me about my plans for the day. I learned quickly to have a ready answer, one implying extensive activity.

After the table was cleared and my grandparents had retreated to their library to read the newspaper, I would drive to the nearest convenience store to purchase my own copy of the paper and review the employment section.

On a yellow legal pad I would compile lists of companies holding interviews. The only openings advertised seemed to be for candidates considerably more qualified than myself. Nevertheless, the following morning at breakfast I would recite to my grandfather the names from this list to give him assurance that an effort was being made. In the meantime I made countless phone calls but only managed to set up interviews with business "consultants." only.

The employment section was full of ads placed by these "consultants" advertising what seemed to be incredible salaries. One read:

THE ONLY THING THAT'S MISSING IS U!!
We are looking for individuals who are:
Clean-cut, hard working,
Overflowing with enthusiasm,
and want $25,000 a year!
Call Larry Ferg Business Consultants

Consulting sounded glamorous, but I soon discovered that in this instance "business consultants" did not describe a firm that did the work of a McKinsey & Company. Rather, it was a pack of headhunters.

Larry Ferg and his assistants were aggressive, fast-talking salesmen—selling recent college graduates to anyone who would buy. Their trick was to convince recent grads like myself that we weren't worth much to anyone, and that we should be happy with whatever job Larry Ferg Consultants could get us.

The hazing started in the waiting room. It was a room devoid of reading material because Larry and his team didn't respect us enough to make it available. They generally kept us waiting more than an hour beyond the time of our appointment, during which it was assumed we would be content to play with the assortment of puzzles and games piled across a coffee table, appropriate for children twelve and under.

When my turn came, I was told that Larry "himself" would "take the time" to meet with me. As I entered his office he was reading my resume and didn't say a word of greeting or even look up. Framed on the wall behind him were two outlandishly ornate diplomas from a university that I hadn't heard of and that I have yet to find in any college directory. Next to them was a small plaque that read:

NOUVEAU RICHE
IS BETTER THAN
NO RICHE
AT ALL

Larry wore a Van Dyke beard. I would have welcomed it in a seventeenth century portrait of Charles I and his court. The sight of it on Larry, however, did not put me at ease.

After a lengthy silence his opening comment was: "You majored in history and you don't have an MBA." I had no response, so he continued, "You are part of the largest generation of young people America has ever produced. Why did you think you could become a productive member of society with just a history degree? Are you aware of the incredibly fierce competition out there among the large number of people your age?"

With little conviction I said I was. He went on: "Most important, are you aware that this economy is in a recession and there is nothing available for you?"

I quivered another quiet "yes" as the thought of confronting my grandfather empty-handed crossed my mind. Eventually Larry Ferg did end the reprimand, and, with just a few minutes remaining in the appointment, asked me what sort of work I might like.

He didn't write down my youthful dreams, but did say I was an "attractive" individual and might make a good salesman. With that very small piece of encouragement, he stood and showed me to the door. As we shook hands he said, "You really look like you live on the Main Line. You're wearing a club tie. What's that print on your tie, a family crest?"

"No."

"Have you no family friends who can get you a job at a bank?"

"I wish it were that easy. I'm exploring every angle. Even family friends don't hire you these days if you haven't proven yourself elsewhere."

"Doesn't your family *own* a bank and, if it doesn't, why doesn't it buy one?"

Regretfully, I gave him a straight answer, which he didn't deserve. With the politeness and reserve of a Main Line WASP and the naïveté of a recent college graduate, I proclaimed: "No, we do not own a bank. The big banks in town are publicly held these days, and I don't think any of the old families are in control any more."

"O.K.!" He slapped me mercilessly hard on the back, and I left.

To my surprise I heard from Larry Ferg the next day: there would be openings at Burger King after the first of the year in the store-management training program. He would be in touch after the holidays.

For the rest of the week I continued to try landing appointments at various corporations around town, but only found success when answering ads placed by other headhunters. At these appointments I would generally be received in the same condescending manner that I had been by Larry Ferg, and I was soon reconciled to the fact that I would begin my working life at the very bottom.

In the evenings I was forced to face my grandfather, and he was anxious to know what progress I had made. As long as I could point to a string of appointments for the following day or for later that week or the next week, he remained somewhat relaxed. I didn't mention that these appointments were not actual job interviews.

*   *   *   *

When the first Friday evening of my stay at Leighsylvania arrived, my grandparents went with friends to their golf club. I ate a solitary dinner at the massive Civil War table. The lights were out and the candles had been lit when I sat down. Olga the cook, Ole's grandmother, brought out the soup. It was a ludicrous scene, and I told her that I would come into the kitchen to fetch the main course and dessert. I then became irritated, blew out the candles, and switched on the lights.

After dinner I browsed in my grandparents' library. There were many leather-bound sets of classic works, some volumes two hundred years old. Kipling was well represented. My brother Henry claimed Grandad recited *The White Man's Burden* every night before bed. I selected a crumbly book entitled "A Short Account of the Malignant Fever Lately Prevalent in Philadelphia" written in 1794 by my direct ancestor, Mathew Carey, who had witnessed the massive yellow fever epidemic of the previous year. I then settled into some dusty, feather-filled needlepoint in the Great Room and put my feet up.

My grandparents' house was shaped like a lowercase "h." Looking out the window from the short leg of the "h," I could see across the terrace to the windows of the other leg. The story of yellow fever was interesting, but the eighteenth-century writing style and typeface made Carey's work slow going. I soon turned off my reading lamp and from my darkened room could now see through the windows across the terrace.

Ole had returned from her week at Bryn Mawr College and was standing at a counter in the kitchen. As her grandmother talked, she wrote. Perhaps it was a grocery list or the weekend menu. She was slim and pretty but as usual very pale.

She must never be away from the books. Does she never get out in the sun? When does she ever party if she's here every weekend? Certainly *I* partied in college.

She took off an apron revealing more of the formal uniform my grandfather had her wear. On her feet were white nursing shoes. I could hear the faint mumble of her grandmother—the Hungarian accent.

Olga had come to America from the Austro-Hungarian Empire as a girl of nine. She told me she had often seen the Emperor Francis Joseph on parade. After landing at Ellis Island, Olga and her mother apparently spent some terrifying days alone in New York City until her father arrived from Philadelphia. He had arrived in America the previous year and worked as a stableman.

Ultimately, Olga would be employed by my grandparents for more than sixty-five years. A remnant of her Hungarian past, other than her accent, was the large quantity of paprika that she used in her cooking. Olga was overweight, jolly, and loved her employer's grandchildren. We couldn't make a visit to Leighsylvania without first going to see Olga in the help's dining room. When we were children she hugged us and with every squeeze garbled loving though unintelligible words in her strong Hungarian accent.

Olga had been married but had lost her husband in a farm accident. Her hard-working son had been employed in the steel mills of Bethlehem, Pennsylvania, until dying of an early heart attack. His wife, Ole's mother, still taught in the Bethlehem public schools.

Ole's real name was Olga, also, but when visiting her grandmother went by "Ole" to eliminate confusion.

Olga finished dictating the list to her granddaughter and retired to her room on the third floor. Her granddaughter folded the paper and disappeared. I sat quietly in the dark room, thinking of going to bed myself, when I heard Ole's footsteps. She entered the Great Room without turning on a light and gracefully walked through to the library. Her eyes had not grown accustomed to the dark, and she passed by unaware of my presence.

In the library she briefly switched on a light to gather up my grandmother's sweater and needlework. On passing me the second time, she was trailed by a mild perfume, the smell of which settled over me like a rejuvenating vapor of hope. A narcotic that smothered my depression, it launched me into fantasies of her, Posey, and other women I found physically attractive.

A moment later I was watching her again in the kitchen, through the windows from across the terrace. But she hadn't just picked up my grandmother's things; she had also picked up the tweed jacket I had worn at dinner. She put her arms through the sleeves, pulled it over her shoulders, and buttoned the front! She then opened a closet door to view herself in a mirror and, finally, took out my wallet and for several minutes studied my driver's license.

When she had left, and the lights all over the house were out, I entered the pantry, picked up the jacket, and sniffed through the lining for traces of her perfume.

*   *   *   *

I was awake at dawn the following morning. Mist puffed from the white surface of the pond below my window, and a honking "V" formation of Canadian geese blew by, circled back, and settled into the rising vapor. The day became a cloudless cool Saturday, and at breakfast my grandfather was impatient to know how I planned to spend it.

"I plan to spend the morning reading."

"What on?" he snapped.

"*This Side of Paradise* by F. Scott Fitzgerald."

"Oh? Great! Now you'll finally know who you are: another Amory Blaine, a kid lacking all sense of purpose who doesn't know where he's going in life…. Make something of yourself, boy!"

My embarrassed grandmother, resenting his confrontational mood, cut him off with aggressive conversation of her own until the end of breakfast, at which time he went to the library with the paper and she to her studio.

My grandmother was well regarded as a painter of oil landscapes. Her studio was a small appendage from the house with floor-to-ceiling windows on three sides overlooking a horse pasture. Skylights opened up the ceiling, and two faded Orientals were a splash of peach over the oak floor.

I spent several contemplative minutes at the table as the realization that I could not remain here for the day sank in. I got up and found the housekeeper, Clara, to tell her that I would not need lunch or dinner. I then stepped into my grandmother's studio.

This room was very much her personal space, and hanging inside was an original *Peaceable Kingdom*, one of many painted by the nineteenth-century Quaker artist Edward Hicks. The words from Isaiah were framed below: "The wolf shall dwell with the lamb, and the leopard will lie down with the kid; and the calf and the young lion and the fatling together; and a little child shall lead them." I told Grandmother that I planned to look up a friend from boarding school and would not be returning until late in the evening. I then lingered momentarily to enjoy the sweet smell of her oils.

I did not have, however, a friend from boarding school whom I felt confident enough to look up, given my jobless state, so I drove into Philadelphia to visit historic sites. This I did and exhausted myself standing before Charles Wilson Peale portraits of financier Robert Morris and other early Philadelphians, and engravings of eighteenth-century street scenes and landmarks by William Birch.

Tired from being on my feet all day, and cold from walking the length of Walnut and Pine Streets more than once, I arrived back at Leighsylvania long after dark. It occurred to me that I might get a look at Ole again like I had the previous evening. My grandparents had retired to their bedroom, and I informed Clara that I would be doing the same. Instead, I went to the library, dropped my tweed jacket on a chair, and collapsed in the Great Room on the same sofa as the previous evening.

Shortly thereafter Ole came through to tidy up. Once more I was rejuvenated by her perfume, and once more she collected my jacket along with my grandmother's things while I went unnoticed. I wanted to watch her through the windows across the terrace, but this time she switched out the lights.

The following day, Sunday, again I felt uncomfortable around the house and left at mid-morning. I returned to the cold city, this time to Laurel Hill Cemetery above the Schuylkill, to find the tomb of one of my ancestors and the memorial sculpted over it by Alexander Stirling Calder.

Alone under the empty trees of November and an overcast sky, I searched among the crowded nineteenth century Gothic monuments, tombstones, and oversized mausoleums, up and down the ghostly streets of that city of the dead. I became hopelessly lost and slowed my pace. My hands went into the pockets of my tweed jacket in search of warmth, and I felt some unexpected, heavy paper.

It was a dirty white envelope that I pulled out, one that I certainly did not recognize. It wasn't in there yesterday, I thought; someone had mysteriously placed it in my jacket! Was it a note from Ole? The envelope was not sealed, and I nervously sat on a cold sarcophagus and pulled out a crumbly letter, brown and soft with age.

ON ACTIVE SERVICE
with the
AMERICAN EXPEDITIONARY FORCE

September 21, 1918

Dear Granpop,

Well, I have had some thrills since I wrote you my last letter and I have so much to write you that I will never have time to do it in detail. Some time I am going to write all about the fight and when I finish it, I will send it on to you. It was some fight and I reckon you will read all about it in the papers, while I only saw a small part of it.

I wrote you that we had been hiking all night in the rain and hiding all day, didn't I? We hiked for five straight nights and it rained all the time and in the last night's hike we landed in the trenches at 4:15 a.m. and lord but it was raining. The last hike we passed thru much of our artillery, it was as thick in the woods as weeds and it surely did our hearts good to see it. When you are to go over the top, it gives you a fine feeling to think of the artillery backing you up. An artilleryman would whisper "give'm hell infantry! We're right with you!" And one of our men would whisper back: "then for Pete's sake, shoot fast and straight!" I thought we would never reach our place in the front line trench that we were to get set in but we finally landed there and by our compasses found the direction we were to attack. For a good while before this, our artillery had been giving the Huns and it was great to listen to.

At a couple of minutes before 5 a.m. everything opened up and it was an exciting time for us all right. The men dropped all their packs except their hard-tack and weapons and every one crouched down waiting for the hour. It was very dark and raining hard but when there was a flash in front of us, you could see the men's faces (Lord, but they looked mean) and the bayonets stuck out the top of the trench like a hedge. At 5 a.m. on Sept 12, 1918, Companies I, K, and M (with L in support) went over the top, to make a hole and start the ball rolling for the rest of the 11th infantry and regiments to follow. You can't imagine how it felt to climb out of that trench and get up on top, but once up I felt much better. The noise was so great it was just one steady sound and was hardly noticed. It began to get light right away which helped us a lot, although we could plainly see the flashes from those darn machine guns the Hun is so crazy about. They made good targets to shoot back at and I was glad I had a rifle. I got in several shots from the first wave before we reached their front line trench. There was an awful lot of barbed wire and it was nowhere near broken down by our artillery, so we did what I have heard our men have done before, that is tore through it with our hands. There was not a live Hun in the first trench (the ones who had not been killed had run) so we started for the second line. Same thing as before, mud a foot deep and barbed wire so thick that it was matted together. By this time my clothes were in tatters and sopping with mud, as I had fallen down a couple of times, and I had left both my leggins in the wire, so with my socks hanging down over my shoes and my bare legs covered with mud, I was a fine looking soldier.

The second line of trenches was just about the same as the first, only we ran upon more machine guns. One Hun machine gunner kept on shooting his darn gun and wouldn't stop. We closed in all around him, all of us shooting at him but still he kept squirting his gun. Finally his strip of bullets gave out but his hand was still clutching the gun. We dragged him off and he had been killed while shooting his gun and when he died his hand still squeezed the trigger. He was a brave man. The worst one I saw was just a few minutes after this one was killed. As we came up, a Hun stood up with his hands over his head yelling "Kamarad!" He would not have been touched if one of our soldiers standing right behind him had not noticed a cord tied to his foot and rigged up so he could shoot a machine gun from a few yards off. The next thing that happened was a howl from our soldier and the point of his bayonet came out of the Hun's chest. It was a dirty Hun trick and the bayonet is the only fit punishment for such stuff. I was all steeled up to meet a Hun hand to hand with just he and I to settle it.

Our objective was about a mile behind the Hun first line trenches and it consisted of a long deep trench running through some woods. There was plenty of noise from them when we were off a little distance but it quieted down when we got up on them. We found it full of Huns, all with their hands up, some crying, some praying, and some down on their knees begging like dogs. Some of our soldiers did try a little fancy killing, but taking it all in all, the Huns got off mighty light and were treated very well.

We stopped here and the rest of the regiment came up and went on thru us and the ball kept on rolling. The first thing I did was find me a dead Hun who had a pack on his back. I opened his pack and found a pair of new wool socks. These I put on, and also his spiral putters which are just like ours only gray in color. He had a nice overcoat which I put on and felt much better after this change of clothes. He had a canteen full of cold coffee, also a loaf of bread and a little pot of butter, also of jam and, as I had not eaten since noon the day before, it surely was a good meal. I don't care much for their bread, as it is dark and sour. The Huns seemed to have plenty of food and our soldiers had a pretty good time eating it. We found lots of cigars and cigarettes and they were very good too. For a while we were pretty comfortable as all of us got dry socks off dead or captured Huns who had their packs on their backs. Our kitchens could not get to us as the artillery was using all the roads, so we ate Hun bread for a couple of days.

There was no counterattack by the Huns that night but along about dark their artillery opened up on us and we had a rough night of it. I never imagined anything like it and their darn shells popped over and on us the whole night. We were in shallow trenches we had dug right on the edge of the woods and the Huns had the range to a T. Trees and tree limbs fell on us all night, to say nothing of iron ware and gas shells and I was glad to see morning come as they let up on us then. Our major went nuts during the night and had to be relieved by another major. It was a mean night.

The next day the Huns were sprinkling machine gun bullets up and down our line and I swear they fell like rain. They had Lord knows how many machine guns in a clump of trees on our right and, as our artillery was still trying to get to us thru the mud and shell holes, the Hun played an uninterrupted tune on us. My platoon was dug in on the right and for two continuous days and nights we hung in there by the skin of our teeth without food or water. Some of our artillery soon came up and knocked the spots out of that machine gun nest but we didn't have peace for long as the Hun artillery started in on us and made the ground around us dance. Every now and then they would drop a gas shell on us but that wasn't so bad because the rain had stopped and there was a stiff breeze to blow the gas away. After 48 hours of this a fresh regiment came up from behind and we pulled out. And believe me we did like the rear and never stopped until we were out of range.

We were finally collected in some safe woods and had our first meal in five days, also our first sleep. We stayed in these woods for three days and it was fine to be able to rest. The mail came and I received 16 letters! Several from you and one or more from the farm hands at Shirley and also several letters from Aunt Julie, Aunt Bessie, and several from Philadelphia. It was fine to get them and they all seemed to say "good work and congratulations and welcome back." They could not have come at a nicer time and I was very happy.

This is about all Granpop, and since I started this letter I have written on and off for three days. I came out of the fuss all OK, except for both my hands cut in many places by the barbed wire. A little iodine fixed them and they are now all right.

Well Granpop, lots of love. About my birthday, just wish me many happy returns of the day. We will make up for it when I get home. Love to you and the aunts. I will write you soon.

Your devoted boy,

Tom

1st Lieutenant Thomas Williamson Lightfoot
11th Infantry, "I" Co.,
American Expeditionary Force, France

My grandfather must have seen my jacket where Ole had left it hanging in the pantry, and then slipped this letter into its pocket! I stood up and staggered through the silent city of mausoleums, no longer interested in the whereabouts of my ancestor's tomb and monument.

How much more blatantly could Grandad tell me that I was letting him down? The letter had abruptly pushed him and me even further apart. My mind worked anxiously over my life and the long history of our relationship.

Grandad had survived a tough struggle and deserved to be proud. He was unaware, however, that I harbored a secret envy, one, certainly, that I would never be able to convince him of. Through his war experience he had earned a level of respect from other men that I knew I would never achieve. I would be denied the chance of being a hero. War is the topic of so much writing and reading, and, unlike myself, Grandad had firsthand knowledge.

In my college days anyone who had signed on with ROTC was the subject of ridicule. Over 200,000 of my generation had been accused of draft offenses. My class at boarding school had missed Vietnam by a year, and the remnant of anti-military feeling from the Vietnam era had conditioned us such that military service was never even a consideration. "Annapolis and West Point now and forever will be schools for just poor kids with brains," my cousin Appleton Crawford advised me when I was applying to college.

As I wandered from the cemetery, I recalled some comments from my father: "Your Grandad has never ceased to regard World War I as the great experience of his life. You know he opens a special bottle of French wine to observe the anniversary of the start of each offensive in which he participated? If I happen to talk to him on one of those days, he'll interrupt me to mention: 'Argonne, sixty years today'."

Military service and participation in war had apparently further validated my grandfather's claim to aristocratic membership. Dad had an elaborate dissertation on the subject that he had delivered to us verbally and in writing on more than one occasion:

"The Ivy League and the New England boarding schools liked World War I. Chivalry, glory, gallantry, courage: these were words still used in those days before America sent over her boys. It was a romantic view that no longer applied because trench warfare had changed all that. Before trench warfare you were a gentleman first and an officer second. But after 1914 war had become a dreary science of mathematical calculation.

"Across the Atlantic the British aristocracy had needed a war to prove itself. The House of Lords had been losing out over the previous decades to the House of Commons. The Lords were under attack socially and politically because they were not deserving of all their power, their inherited place in Parliament, their monopoly of the land. More than just the radicals saw them as an anachronism, as parasites in an industrial, entrepreneurial age.

"Going back through the centuries the aristocrats were a warrior class. They liked guns and horses. They made the best officers because they were used to managing the men who worked their big estates—just like your grandfather and his father before had grown comfortable managing teams of men. So the British aristocrats rushed off to prove themselves as the defenders of the national honor, and about twenty percent of them never came back.

"Meanwhile, here in America, as usual our upper class seemed to take its cue from the British. There was the desire to be like a European aristocracy and join the officer corps. Visions of knightly crusaders and chivalric heroes seemed to motivate boys your age to join outfits like the glamorous Lafayette Escadrille—they probably flew in white tie and tails!

"So, in those days your grandfather's heritage imposed certain obligations. Our family had been friendly with Sir Cecil Spring Rice—Teddy Roosevelt's best man, Britain's ambassador to the U.S., and a powerful force in converting Americans to Anglophilia. 'We are in receivership of the British Empire,' your Grandfather often said. 'It's a *special relationship*.'

"Nevertheless, there *was* a lot of disillusionment when our troops came home—how had America benefited with one hundred thousand of its youngsters dead in France? Entangling alliances: never again! America had been played for a sucker.

"But your grandfather never went through a period of questioning when he returned. It was the aristocratic and military tradition of his family that he had wanted to live up to—they had all been in the Civil War. It was his vision of the class he thought he belonged to. It took him a long time to question Vietnam, and sometimes I wonder whether he really did. He wouldn't believe stories circulating about atrocities committed by our troops over there. In *his* war atrocities were committed by enemy soldiers, only."

I left the cemetery recalling Dad's dissertation and later wandered the alleys of Philadelphia's historic district. In the early dusk, interior lights were on, and I found myself peering through the cloudy pains of two-hundred-year-old homes off Washington Square.

Now, even more certain of the low esteem in which my grandfather held me, my thoughts were of finding a place of my own. Those private, unthreatening, colonial interiors held overwhelming appeal on that particular evening.

I walked down small streets of eighteenth-century brick row houses and through and around ancient landmarks. The latter were, however, devastated with graffiti, and the benches around them served as quiet preserves for the homeless. When my contemplation was shattered by the mischief of a drug dealer, I returned to my car disappointed and depressed.

My mind continued to dwell on Grandad's letter as I drove back out to the Main Line in the late evening. I accidentally gunned the accelerator at a stoplight while an elderly man was crossing the road. He stopped and swore at me. Which war had *he* served in? I had never learned to swear; I wished I knew how.

I made fresh tracks in the gentle snow covering my grandparents' long driveway. Anxious to avoid them if they were still awake, I parked in the garage courtyard and used the servants' entrance. I pulled in next to Ole's car—why was she still here on a Sunday night? I kicked the snow from my feet and entered the servants' dining room.

Ole, alone in the expansive room, jumped up with fright. Her white uniform was hidden by a long and ragged thrift-shop sweater.

"Hi! Sorry to scare you! Are you not going back to Bryn Mawr tonight?" I was glad to have some company at this lonely hour.

"That's all right. I guess I should have remembered you hadn't come back yet…. Tomorrow. My classes aren't early, and I figure the snow will be gone by then. How was your day?"

She was curious about me. I took off my coat and stood still until she asked if I was hungry—I hadn't eaten all day. We both went to the refrigerator, and I filled a plate with leftovers. We sat across from each other at the servants' dining table and discussed Bryn Mawr College.

She had not applied to Bryn Mawr until my grandparents had come forward with an offer to pay tuition, room and board. Grandad had been discouraged by what he thought was the less-than-mediocre college performance of his own grandchildren. So when Olga had proudly mentioned that her granddaughter was scheduling campus interviews, he was quick to spot an opportunity: he would make a show of paying Ole's tuition, room, and board because he knew that she, coming from such a modest background, would appreciate the gift of higher education like his own grandchildren had apparently not.

Ole's life at Bryn Mawr was sober, responsible, and scholarly compared with the ever-present carnival of my fraternity days. She was younger than I by four years but in many ways more mature. She was content with a simple scholarly life on slender means, whereas I was depressed if not in prosperous surroundings. Political science was her major, and she hoped to continue on to law school and someday be active in government. While my career dreams were grounded by clouds, she saw only blue sky.

Then I moved us off the subject of college and asked: "Well, what do you think about being here in this house, and what do you think of my grandparents and their life?"

"Oh, it's not like I haven't ever been here before. But, yes, I haven't ever spent as much time here as I am right now. Now I'm here a lot of weekends."

"Do you like being here?"

"Oh, you know your grandparents are being very generous to me, and I'm thrilled to be here; I adore your grandparents!"

"What is your opinion of their lifestyle?"

At first she refused to be judgmental, and the conversation floated in new directions until, eventually, she relaxed. Then words came out that may not have earlier: "Your grandfather is obsessed with quality."

"You *are* perceptive. Yes, it is an obsession, I agree…. And it tells us something else about his beliefs. It's been written that in a democracy everything eventually becomes mediocre and people are content with that."

"So…are you saying he doesn't like democracy?"

"He doesn't like at least one of the directions it can take us."

"When something must be bought for the farm, he spends months hunting down the best possible quality—like he's collecting for a museum."

"Yes, anything he puts money into he wants to treat as a long term investment. He doesn't ever *spend* money, he *invests* it," I explained.

"Your grandparents are very aware of their history. They seem to like the archaic. They dwell on the past—I don't mean last week. I mean one hundred years ago…. Another thing, their lives conform to unwritten rules of…ceremony. There is only *one* way to act; they know exactly how things should be done as if they've read a rule book. There's a sense of order—it's very important. For example, there's always a formal cocktail hour and dinner is never before seven. And it lasts forever! In my family we eat as soon as, or whenever, everyone gets home from work or school, and the meal takes all of about ten minutes. Of course no one gets changed for dinner! But I don't *mind* the way your grandparents live at all; don't get me wrong! I'm not being critical. It's just that it's all new to me. It's certainly not offensive to me in any way, shape, or form. I think you're probably all that way, and I see it in you, too. You've read the rule book."

"Well, of *course* we only like certain things!" I was irritated but had no right to be; I had asked her opinion in the first place. "You have a culture; we have a culture. But I'm surprised you didn't jump in with the usual adjectives: stuffy and pompous."

"There's certainly that dimension, at least in your Grandad. But, don't get me wrong; like I said, I like your grandparents…. But, yes, there are lots of little things that I find kind of different, if not weird. For example, there's the Social Register—I've heard your grandfather and some of their friends call it the 'Stud Book.' Don't you think you're all in a world of the imagination to believe in a book like that? Also, you all have a very educated, refined way of speaking, a slight sort of English accent. It's like the prissy sound of FDR in the recordings I hear in history class. Your grandfather likes using the word vigor, but he pronounces it *vigah*. Why do your grandparents and you and the rest of your family say tomato the way the English do?" She pronounced it like my grandparents, with a short "a."

"Because," I responded, "it's been popular over the years to have English nannies on the Main Line. If you had an English nanny you also might have grown up pronouncing certain words like the English do. Some people pronounce certain words certain ways to identify themselves to other members of the tribe. There are lots of little signals we send out to find others like ourselves, to tell others we're part of the same…class, I suppose.…. Class is a bad word in America—snobbery, stratification, the hereditary principle—all are forbidden thoughts."

"You all suffer from Anglophilia. That's what it is that's so noticeable! Closet Brits! Anything from England has class to the Lightfoots. Maybe because the English were the first ones here? We Slavs and Magyars are such recent arrivals! You look to England for identity; what's the matter with things American? The English have a monopoly on polish and civility? Your grandfather's horses, I notice, aren't named after streets in Budapest. You need a map of London out there to get through the stable!"

I chuckled. "I know, and the two big champions that won all the shows back in the thirties: Hyde Park was the first one and then there was Bond Street."

"And who's out there now? Saville Row and St. James. How about the dogs: Winston, Marlborough, Horatio!"

"Grandad has a dry sense of humor."

"I think he's being funny, but I think he's also being serious. He wouldn't consult a map of Warsaw for pet names! I overhear the women in your family talking about *the* royal family. Prince Charles can't do any wrong around here. If he ever has to abdicate, his next kingdom could be the Philadelphia Main Line!"

I let out a chuckle. "Let me point out, though, that it's the stuffy England of the *past* that is more the object of our desire. But, tell me more; what else do you notice?"

"You like to imply country living in your dress. I don't mean the overalls they probably wear on an Iowa pig farm, or the T-shirts they wear on rundown Vermont dairy farms. I mean the tweed jackets and polished leather boots that imply horse farms, fox hunting, or cattle breeding where you trace the bloodlines back…. It's all very different where I come from in Bethlehem…."

Our discussion continued for another hour. She mentioned that she would not be coming out from Bryn Mawr the next weekend and the weekend after that would be Thanksgiving. I said I was planning to leave for Maine the Wednesday before the holiday.

"Why not go through Bethlehem on your way north and have Thanksgiving with me and my Mom?"

What an incredibly bold move! Ole wasn't for waiting around. After a moment of stunned silence, I agreed to arrive Thanksgiving evening and spend the night.

She had no reservations about asking me home. I cannot say I would have extended her a similar invitation. She was pretty, graceful and slim, but that white uniform under that thrift-shop sweater and those white nurse's shoes were in the way.

CHAPTER 3

▼

Amongst aristocratic nations, birth and fortune frequently make two such different beings of man and woman, that they can never be united to each other. Their passions draw them together, but the condition of society, and the notions suggested by it, prevent them from contracting a permanent and ostensible tie.

—Alexis de Tocqueville

What...is this American system? Is it not the abolition of all artificial distinctions founded at birth or any other accident, and leaving every man to stand on his own two feet, for precisely what God and nature have made him?...What else is it that we are constantly throwing in the face of the Old World?

—Orestes Brownson

The steel works ran endlessly along the river through Bethlehem. With difficulty I found Ole's plain brick row house, and I was late.

The front steps were covered with green outdoor carpeting. This carpeting depressed me. Why was I spending Thanksgiving dinner here? Ole let me in, wearing tight jeans and high heels.

The interior was worse than I had expected. Overshadowing all else in the living room was not, needless to say, an elegant Newport highboy, but a large television set. Grouped around the television and through the rest of the house was factory-made furniture, probably picked up at some discount furniture "mart." I was sure there wasn't a dovetail or tongue-and-groove in the entire house. The wall-to-wall carpeting was stained, as were the frayed curtains. In the next room an old man wearing a Coca Cola T-shirt lay in the dingy yellow light. Watermarks ran across the flaking plaster ceilings. From the back rooms came mumblings in an Eastern European accent.

Such surroundings snuffed out my enthusiasm. Just short of what I considered poverty, they were surroundings in which I hoped I would never have to live. It was clear that this family was never going to get *me* anywhere. I had made a mistake and was depressed about spending Thanksgiving dinner with such low class people. Why wasn't I at a fancy restaurant or exclusive club in Philadelphia or New York? Why was I not with sexy, well bred women who spoke with the same affected accent as I—through the teeth with a stiff jaw, pronouncing every syllable deep in the throat, missing *r's* like the English? I should be eating off Chinese export plates with antique silver knives and forks inlaid with family crests and ornate, worn initials. What conversation could Ole's family and I possibly have that would be of interest? What could possibly be exciting about these people's lives?

"Tom, how was the drive?" asked an enthusiastic Ole. "Oh! I'd like you to meet my mother!"

Her mother was coming toward us in a pink jump suit. I was wearing a blue blazer with gold monogrammed buttons and a silk tie.

"Nice to meet you, Mrs. Vasedi," I said with a coldness that shook away her smile.

She swallowed hard and replied nervously: "I am glad to meet you, and aren't you generous to visit us over the holiday." Her accent was actually very slight, so I was surprised when she called down the hall to *her* mother in Hungarian. The nervousness was contagious: now Ole caught it, and Mrs. Vasedi's neckless mother, calm when she entered the room, caught it the moment she was introduced.

I did not catch it. None of my dreams would ever be dependent on these Dacron people!

In a panic Mrs. Vasedi moved over to a small bar set up for the occasion. "Can I make you a Bourbon'n Ginger or Brandy Alexander?" she asked in a kind but shaky voice.

"I can't stomach drinks that sweet," I muttered down my nose and brutally stepped up to the bar. I threw some ice cubes in a glass and filled it full with bourbon—there was no Scotch—while the three women stood watching in a quiet semi-circle. When I was done, Ole and her mother motioned me to a chair.

Desperately hoping to save the evening with an exquisite meal, Mrs. Vasedi broke the silence by announcing that she must return to the kitchen. Ole sat down nearby, speechless and discouraged, clearly panicked that she had made a major mistake. Her face had gone pale and with it her playful wit. Her overweight grandmother, the Neckless Wonder, mixed a sweet but potent concoction at the bar.

"You see Mr. Lightfoot, we are still learning how to celebrate the American Thanksgiving in this family," she said as she turned from the bar and sank deeply into a sofa. Her statement was delivered apologetically and, as such, gave me pause. They clearly knew I had expected more than I found. Perhaps my nonchalance *had* gone far enough.

"We did not celebrate this American Thanksgiving where I grew up in Europe, and so we haven't really celebrated it here." She gulped down her drink and went to fix another. It steadily became clear that my wool blazer, silk tie, and gray flannel pants were not going to kill her pride. She was building her courage enough to let me know that *her* family had a story as well.

In those days I had the habit of obnoxiously probing the social credentials of strangers, and I survived lengthy interactions with people I didn't want to be with by using them as a means to learn social history. What sort of Americans were they economically and socially? How long had their families been in this country and why were they here? What cataclysmic event of history had driven them from their native lands? I would riddle my victims with questions and affix them in their socio-economic and historical context. Perhaps it was closer to entomology than social research. It was obnoxious and exploitive, but a way to get interested in people who were not my kind.

So, as the minutes passed and then the hours, my curiosity went to full throttle, and I did find Ole's family to be interesting in its own way, as all families are, of course. Its members had withstood hardships certainly greater than my present, confused ordeal. It was a family that had lived well in Budapest at the turn of the century, but unemployment after World War I had pushed the Vasedi grandparents and great uncles and aunts to leave for America. They ultimately found employment and stability in and around the steel mills of Bethlehem.

Ole's uncle, eighty-five years old and asleep on the bed when I first arrived, had worked at Bethlehem Steel for more than forty years. I treated him, even more than the others, as a rare insect: he was the first blue-collar worker and union member with whom I had ever eaten dinner. Did Karl Marx have *him* in mind? I spent until midnight learning the mindset of the working-class world.

My initial involvement with this family was thus like an anthropologist visiting members of a primitive tribe. But despite my overbearing self-assurance among these three women and one man, they eventually conquered their nerves and seemed to view me not as a threat to their pride, but as someone anxious to learn. Others would have been insulted by the exploitive nature of my interrogation, but this humble family seemed flattered by my curiosity. They were proud of their Hungarian heritage, and they liked nothing more than to talk about it.

After midnight I was led upstairs to what I guessed was the largest bedroom in the house. Finally, I *was* touched: as I undressed I pulled open a few bureau drawers and saw what appeared to be Ole's mother's clothes. She had vacated her room for me! I would later learn that her mother had spent the night on the living room couch.

The following morning we awoke to snow flurries. I ate a large breakfast, during which I revived the discussion from the previous evening on organized labor. Then I gathered my possessions and thanked Ole's family. She walked me to my car.

"I'll be looking forward to seeing you when I'm back at college," she murmured. She was uptight again—possibly because she hoped my thoughts were the same intimate thoughts as hers. I made no response—afraid of her embarrassing herself—so I pretended I hadn't heard. Instead, a little rudely, I simply thanked her for dinner the previous night.

But as I drove back along the river by the steel mills and turned north, loneliness, gone since the previous evening, seeped in once again, like the cold.

*   *   *   *

I had planned to stay in Castine for no more than a week but instead remained until early January.

It was a frigid winter, and in some places ice extended well into Penobscot Bay. I wandered the rocks along the shore on windy days. Wind stirring the trees, water, and snow was drama, and there was no drama in the quiet home of my parents.

My father, William Williamson Lightfoot, had been a trust officer at a Philadelphia bank. He was continuing to manage portfolios now, but in the quiet of coastal Maine. He spent several weeks each year traveling the country investigating companies, and a day or two a month down in Boston, New York, or Philadelphia talking with clients.

In his free time Dad painted oil landscapes like his mother. He also had a secret interest in arranging flowers. At one time he had tried hard to conceal this interest from my older brother and myself but was unsuccessful.

The consensus was that Dad had moved from Philadelphia to put more distance between himself and his father. "He's too introverted and separate from the world for Grandad's liking," my brother Henry pointed out. Our brother-in-law, Danny Paulucci, called Dad "the Exile," a comment that offended me. But when my grandparents were finally dead, I realized that perhaps my brother-in-law's description had come the closest. By definition an exile wants to return.

Dad was, however, very close to his mother. As a boy, and at her insistence, he had attended Westtown, a Quaker boarding school founded by our ancestor Owen Biddle. He had not gone to one of the prestigious Episcopal boarding schools of New England or Virginia, schools Grandad believed would have given him the son he wanted.

Dad then went on to another institution of Quaker origin, the same college later attended by my brother Henry. My grandmother had won this battle also, leaving my grandfather even more embittered: his only son had not followed him to the Ivy League. Signing on with a unit of army reserves, the First City Troop, was a meager effort to please Grandad, but it had come too late. Dad had no passion for it, anyway, as it ran contrary to his Quaker education.

My father is a quiet man and not one for community involvement; he does not like self-promotion. He used to quote William Penn: "meddle not with government; never speak of it, let others say and do as they please." In contrast, my grandfather got himself on every board and committee that had an open seat. "He likes being on stage," Dad once snickered. Grandad came close several times to running for Congress.

Unlike my father, my mother did spend her time in community and state affairs. Literacy and public libraries were the causes over which she was most passionate. In this sense she was like my grandfather, and they got along famously—so well, I suspect, that the move to Castine had become necessary to save my parents' marriage.

My mother is a Boston Claflin and descendent of William Claflin, a post-Civil War governor of Massachusetts. Governor Claflin's father, a successful boot and shoe manufacturer, had been a financial founder of Boston University. He and his son established a long family tradition of civic involvement. My mother's father, dead before I was born, had attended Harvard University in the same class with my grandfather Lightfoot.

One common interest that kept my parents together through the years was wooden boats, and they spent considerable time encouraging local boat builders. They owned a fleet themselves, all crafted on the Maine Coast.

Life with my parents was easy as there was no sense of urgency, no challenges to prepare for. But with each passing day I awoke with an empty feeling that grew ever stronger: I needed a focus; I longed for the proud feeling of accomplishment. I also needed a girl. I spent my days gazing out to sea, fantasizing that either Posey or Ole were walking the rocky shoreline beside me or were in my arms by the late afternoon fire.

Finally, in early January, Larry Ferg returned my calls. He had lined up some interviews for mid-month. I packed and drove south.

*   *   *   *

I entered my grandparents' house after midnight on a weekday evening. The house was dark and quiet as I came in through the back, walking slowly enough to make no sound.

But the quiet and calm were more like the anticipatory hiss from speakers before the tape begins to play: when I pushed through the swinging pantry door into the dark dining room, I was startled to an abrupt halt and gasped loudly.

Gazing like a ghost down the Civil War table from the far end of the room, glowing golden under a spotlight from the ceiling, was the first William Williamson Lightfoot. His spooky eyes followed me as I slowly crept round the table. I shivered as I pulled up a chair before him. Was he not beckoning me to sit down as his guest?

William Williamson Lightfoot, born in 1813, wearing a black jacket with high collar almost to his ears, was a handsome, romantic figure at age twenty-five when this portrait was painted. His brown hair windblown, his brows heavy and his eyes tense, I imagined him pacing the deck of one of the fleet of seven ships that accompanied Commodore Matthew Perry to Japan in the 1850's.

"It was an expedition that marked the beginning of America's interest beyond its borders," I recalled my grandfather telling me.

"Then was William Williamson Lightfoot an imperialist?" I had asked.

"I don't know to what extent he was a believer in American expansionism, but I am sure that at the end of his long life he understood the potential worth and purpose of American power. A country that has power like the United States, with such a large share of the world's wealth, has a disproportionate responsibility. This country must play the leader because it's the only one that can."

William Williamson Lightfoot, my ancestor five generations back, had been born into a family that could trace its roots to Jamestown and counted Pocahontas and the Lees of Stratford as ancestors.

In 1861 Lightfoot was an admiral in the US navy. He did not believe in secession, but like others of his native commonwealth, he considered himself more Virginian than American. So, when the Virginia legislature voted secession, he resigned his commission and became one of a handful of Confederate naval officers.

My grandfather had once written me at boarding school about Admiral Lightfoot: "Like many others who joined the South in arms, he did not foresee the crisis turning into the total war that it did. He had thought the South would be allowed to go in peace. Even when it became clear that Lincoln and Seward planned to raise an army, Lightfoot felt the South would still be allowed to go before any real fighting began—the population of the North would simply not go along with its war crazed leaders."

History proved him wrong, of course, and William Williamson Lightfoot saw plenty of war as a Confederate. Among other accomplishments he played a key role in building the South's first ironclad, the *Virginia*.

"This man was your grandfather's primary hero," my father often told me. "Your grandfather called him the Lightfoot family's very own Robert E. Lee. Lee's biographer wrote that for Lee the Civil War was a 'drama of ill-fortune nobly borne,' and in that way a 'triumph of character over catastrophe.' When I was growing up your grandfather would borrow those words when he spoke about the man in this portrait."

Penelope, wife of William Williamson Lightfoot, hung on the opposite wall. She was dressed in a formal silver gown that left her delicate shoulders exposed. Her hair was pulled back in a bun. Her face was sweet and attractive though round. Her eyes were not tense like her husband's, and her mouth exhibited a subtle smile that may have been a permanent fixture.

I arose from the chair, switched out the ceiling spotlight, and went up to bed.

*   *   *   *

My first interview, courtesy of Larry Ferg, was for the position of assistant manager at one of a chain of little-known fast food restaurants. Burger King had canceled its hiring plans.

In preparation I spent a day visiting several of the company's restaurants in Philadelphia and surrounding suburbs. I ordered fries or a soft drink at each and sat to observe their operating procedures and the behavior of their customers.

The following day I found the Larry Ferg waiting room to be, as usual, without any reading material—just puzzles and games like those found in the waiting room of a pediatrician. I had bought a copy of the *New York Times* at the railroad station, but soon found I was more curious about my competitors for this job than the headlines on Miss Lillian and her son Jimmy Carter.

Directly across the room sat a recent college graduate in a polyester three-piece suit. ("We Lightfoots are a pre-synthetic family," my cousin Appleton Crawford often proudly instructed me.) A silver chain extended from a buttonhole in his vest to a small pocket below that appeared flat and empty without a watch. The chain was composed of peculiar square links that did not imply the wisdom or dignity such an accessory is intended to imply. He was overweight and fascinated by a plastic box through which colored balls were rolling. He jumped up when "DeCarlo" was called and disappeared into the conference room.

I was one of the last to be interviewed, and it was only for fifteen minutes. The interviewer, the neckless Larry Barfus, was depressingly overweight—too many shakes and fries? A clip-on tie rested stiffly over an exploding Dacron shirt. What cousin Apple called a "nerd pack" hung from his breast pocket. Larry's visor cap—with open space in the back with a strap for self-adjustment—sat on the corner of the desk. It read: "UP YOURS!"

Despite the hat, Barfus was warm, jolly and very talkative. His accent was heavy Philadelphia, emphasizing the "r's". I'm sure he wondered about mine. He spent five minutes enthusiastically outlining the duties of a fast food assistant manager while his great stomach bounced along like gelatin. He loved fast food, his job and his corporation!

"Now, give me a sketch of ya-self."

Instead of answering directly, I made the mistake of presenting a socio-economic analysis of his chain's customers and their motivations for eating fast food of the deep-fried variety for which the chain was known. Larry sat speechless, his eyes looking ever more puzzled. He didn't care who his customers were; that was someone else's job! His was operations, only. I was trying to impress him with my insight, but as Larry Ferg made clear later, Barfus was not interviewing for a marketing manager.

A knock on the door alerted us that my fifteen minutes was up. On the way out, he asked what I was doing in my spare time between job interviews.

"I've just begun reading Tacitus!" An enthusiastic smile lit up my pretty-boy face. "His detailed account of the events from the death of Augustus to the year 69."

Barfus didn't answer, just walked me to the door. "Ancient Rome," I muttered, disappointedly.

*   *   *   *

I called Larry Ferg the next morning to confirm that I was not wanted for a second interview.

"When did the visor cap go on?" he asked. I told him it went on about a minute after I was asked to talk about myself. "That's probably a record, then. Barfus said he puts on the visor cap as soon as he's decided *not* to hire someone. The lead candidate was DeCarlo. I think you met him. He was in the waiting room when you were. Don't feel bad! DeCarlo had several years in the food and beverage business already."

Larry then humored me, and when I hung up the phone, I was feeling better about myself and able to laugh at yesterday's experience. He said that more interviews with companies in different industries were very possible and that I should stay in town.

I was suddenly, and momentarily, very hopeful when our conversation ended, and I thanked him sincerely. I sat in my grandparents' library, in my grandfather's comfortable armchair with my feet on his ottoman, thinking: I love Larry Ferg! There just may be someone who wants me! If I can keep getting interviews, sooner or later someone will take me! I leaned my head back against the leather to gaze up through the tall windows at the blue sky. I was feeling hopeful that sooner or later I *would* get on in the world, and that it would finally rotate with me aboard.

A mantel clock struck ten chimes, and the house was quiet. I had no plans for the day except to call some new headhunters. I thought of Ole and her slim figure. Would she come out here this weekend? If only she didn't wear those white nurse's stockings and shoes!

I was preoccupied and didn't hear the squeaking echo of approaching footsteps down the recently waxed wooden floor of the hall—my mind lingered in a fantasy of Ole—and my grandfather was at the doorway before I'd had a chance to even take my feet from his ottoman.

His cheeks were still red from his walk in the cold, and he stood tall and straight for an old man. His eyes, glaring at me, asked: What are you doing in here? Why aren't you out making something of yourself? Why aren't you a banker or in a profession worthy of this family? You're not upholding family tradition; you're a sponge in this house! You're lazy!

When I saw those eyes, I was quickly on my feet groping for words. "I'm just making a few phone calls, trying to set things up," I said in an apologizing tone and moved away from his chair.

"Sit down boy," he said firmly. We both sat, he on the chair I had just vacated. An uncomfortable silence followed as he gathered his thoughts.

"So, if you get a job, then you'll expect Olga to have breakfast for you every morning at 6:30? Is this a hotel? When I was your age I was experiencing ordeals that shape character.... If you didn't have this house, what would you do?...Don't think you're going to *find yourself* by just sitting here in my library thinking philosophical thoughts about the world. You've got to dive in like you dive into a swimming pool.... The trouble is you're timid and what kind of man is timid? I thought your timidity would have been beaten out of you at boarding school. Didn't you learn that in this country we don't tolerate a man who suffers from a sensitive disposition!"

"I...I am lucky to have this house to come to and thank you for letting me stay here." I made every effort to sound appreciative through the lengthy, firm lecture that followed but couldn't change his mood. I finally gave up trying to defend myself and at times stopped even listening to that deep scratchy voice in which a trace of southern accent still lingered from his years growing up in Virginia.

My grandfather wanted me out of his house!

I felt empty and wondered: Wasn't Grandad betraying his heritage by betraying me? Wasn't our class supposed to be preoccupied with self-perpetuation? Was it not the principle duty of he and every other family member to insure the continuing prominence of the Lightfoots? Had I been mislead into believing in the permanence of this family? It had existed successfully over so many generations, but maybe in America we cannot assume the permanent status of *any* family.

My mother and her relatives considered themselves Boston Brahmins and born a Brahmin, always a Brahmin. In India castes are hereditary: no matter what your circumstances in life have become, you remain a member of the caste you were born into until death. The father of Justice Oliver Wendell Holmes coined *Boston Brahmin* to describe a "harmless, inoffensive, untitled aristocracy."

From my grandfather's bushy gray brows, my eyes briefly wandered around the room and settled on a small pencil sketch of Pocahontas. Grandad claimed to have descended from Pocahontas. I had challenged him on this years before while on a weekend visit from boarding school. At the time I was taking an American history course and considered myself an authority. About a week after presenting my evidence in person, I received a letter back detailing every member of the family, when each was born and died, in direct line between myself and the Indian Princess almost four hundred years before.

When I was a dreamy young teenager I had viewed Pocahontas as the Lightfoot family's Aeneas. To help legitimize the imperial family's power, Virgil had traced the genealogy of Augustus Caesar back to the legend of Aeneas, son of Aphrodite and founder of the colony from which the ancient Romans traced their ancestry. Pocahontas was *our* Aeneas in the sense that this connection with the first European settlement to survive in the New World was evidence of our right to a permanently superior status.

Grandad's lecture came to an abrupt end with a final command that I would hear so many times again: "Make something of yourself, boy!" He then settled back in his armchair and lifted his khaki pants and navy-blue sneakers atop the ottoman. I left the room downcast, took my coat from the hall closet, and went to my car. My back was wet with sweat, my hands were shaky, and I drove the lengthy driveway with my mind adrift—bobbing alone in an expansive sea, beyond the sight of land.

I drove to Christ Church in Philadelphia to explore its cemetery. Along with Benjamin Franklin, several of my ancestors were buried there, ship owners who had prospered around 1800. Their sons had grown fabulously wealthy from the China trade in partnership with the Delanos, Franklin Roosevelt's ancestors, and had made a second fortune in opium. The latter money was considered tainted, and, when it reached my grandmother, she had apparently given her share away.

Near the church was a pay phone, and I called Larry Ferg again. He was encouraging about the handful of future interviews, and, sensing my down mood, humored me once more. I went back to the cemetery feeling better.

Later I walked up to a small historic park and read the markers until the presence of street bums made me uneasy. Down the street I stopped by an eighteenth-century government building, now a museum. The sign read: "Closed Until Further Notice."

I drove back to my grandparents' through freezing rain. As usual cocktails were formally served by a roaring fire in the Great Room, during which my grandfather was in a friendlier mood than in the morning. He was relaxed at dinner, and the three of us had an enjoyable evening discussing the arrival of my grandmother's family with William Penn aboard the ship *Canterbury*.

Late through the night I wandered searchingly through the dark upstairs of the mansion. The long ghostly halls were covered with eighteenth-century English prints of fox hunting, and in the dim light I rubbed the dust from photographs of my grandparents with their hounds and horses.

Hanging among these English prints and yellowed equine photographs were various family documents. I pulled down one that announced an ancestor's admission to nation's first learned society:

The American Philosophical Society held at Philadelphia for promoting useful Knowledge, desirous of advancing the Interest of the Society by Associating to themselves Men of distinguished Eminence, and conferring Marks of their Esteem upon Persons of literary Merit, have elected Matthew Carey of Philadelphia.

The year was 1821. The same society had elected Washington, Adams, Jefferson, Hamilton, and Madison.

Another document, this one on sheepskin, announced the "Marriage of Mary Armitt Brown and Joseph Askew, merchant son of Parker Askew," also in 1821. Someone's commission in the United States Navy, signed by James Madison, was overshadowed by an authentic land grant affixed with the seal of William Penn.

But of greatest interest were the bookshelves. Five feet high and stained a dark mahogany, they clung to the hallway walls full of old volumes, some two or three hundred years old. I opened a few of the oldest and sniffed the warm, dusty aroma. When I catch the scent of an old book, even today, it brings my grandparents' house strongly to mind.

Most of these volumes were not collected by my grandparents. They had been collected over the previous three hundred years primarily by the Lightfoots. The Lightfoots had amassed large libraries on their Virginia estates. They were a scholarly group and their remaining letters show extensive communication with several of the Founding Fathers. Among the books in the collection was George Washington's copy of Jefferson's *Notes on Virginia*, now in the Morgan Library.

For much of Saturday and most of Sunday I quietly browsed these halls avoiding my grandfather.

Ole *had* come out that weekend, and I saw her pretty face early Saturday morning. She was wearing that hideous daytime uniform; it spoke so blatantly of her position as servant, and it embarrassed me.

"How was your Christmas?" we both asked simultaneously.

"Uneventful. How about yours? In Bethlehem?"

"No, here."

"Here?"

"Yes, I stayed with your grandparents through Christmas, and helped Olga cook up the big turkey dinner, and helped the rest of the crew wait on the table. I also put out the presents for everyone."

And on we went for several more minutes, talking about Christmas and *my* family. I wasn't interested in hers. Her relatives were a depressing group, and I kept recalling the wrinkled body of her uncle on that metal bed under the water-stained plaster ceilings of that hot little house.

Soon Clara came by and collected Ole for a chore in the basement. I wandered back upstairs to one of those hallways full of books. My grandfather had been driven downtown to the Philadelphia Club and my grandmother was in her studio.

Pliny the Younger caught my eye—his collected letters. For a few minutes I sat on a needlepoint chair with my feet up. But I couldn't concentrate on Caius Plinius Secundas, A.D. 23-79, and his contemporary, the emperor Trajan. My thoughts were on Ole. Through the morning I caught fragments of her soft voice drifting up the stairwell. On the way to lunch with my grandmother I did my best to avoid her, fearful of revealing my attraction with an uptight voice or foolish comment.

After eating, and with Grandad gone, I felt comfortable reading the paper in the library. Through the window I watched Ole's car pass between the high stone walls on its way down the driveway. I got up and climbed the stairs to the third floor. For a minute I stood quietly gazing down the deep stairwell.

The only sound echoing up the three stories came from clocks. There was no carpet on the stairs, and there was considerable bare oak flooring between the colorful Orientals strewn across the floors below, so a symphony of clicking was quick to claim the air when no one was about.

I moved down the third floor hall cautiously, to the room I suspected was Ole's, and pushed open the door. In the back of my mind I was operating under the pretense that this was *my* family's house and that I was therefore not trespassing—Ole was merely a visitor.

The room contained a few simple pieces of furniture provided by my grandmother. The walls were bare, but photographs of Ole's mother and other family members stood in frames on the bureau and chest.

I opened the closet to look at her clothes. They were drab: black, white, and various shades of gray and brown. They looked inexpensive, probably bought at some discount chain in a mall.

In the bathroom I dug through a canvas pouch, and, among evidence that she was in her monthly, found her perfume. I passed the bottle under my nose.

On top of a desk were books she was reading for her courses at Bryn Mawr. I pulled the first stack apart—all political science and psychology—but made little effort to put it back together as I had found it. The subject of a messy pile of loose papers and books nearby was Hungary and Hungarian-Americans. The bureau drawers were full of more drab, inexpensive clothing of synthetic blends.

I shut the last dresser drawer, the one nearest the floor, stood up and turned to leave the room, my curiosity satisfied and my boredom relieved for the moment.

I was reminded of vacations home from boarding school. My classmates and I all dispersed from school to distant points on the map, and I would find myself at home with just my parents and not knowing anyone in the neighborhood. My parents hadn't moved to Castine yet, and I spent lonely, bored days wandering their large home on the Main Line.

To escape the boredom I would dial random telephone numbers and ask personal questions like: "how old are you?" "Are you divorced?" "Did you go to prep-school?" "Do you descend from anyone who signed the Declaration of Independence?" "When did your ancestors first come to America?" "Are you in the Social Register?"

I quietly closed Ole's door and turned down the hall. But as I did a hot wave of embarrassment crashed over me: Ole was standing in the hallway and had been observing the last few moments of my search through her possessions. The pretty eyes under her dark brows had a puzzled look, while her mouth was fixed in a cynical smile.

"I'm sorry.... I was just looking for something."

"Looking for something? Were you enjoying yourself, Lord Thomas Williamson Lightfoot, future Count of Leighsylvania?"

"I'm sorry. I guess I was doing something that...yes, a lord of the manor might do." I tried to smile. "Obnoxious!"

"Yes! Are you going to go around the neighborhood demanding certain favors from your peasant women next? You know this place shouldn't be called *Leighsylvania*. It should be called *Transylvania*! When I tell your grandfather about what you've done, do you think he'll agree to change the name? Maybe he'll build a castle...."

Her dry humor released some of the tension, but it was not forgiving and didn't end my embarrassment. "Well, yes.... I...I think he should change the name." I tried to laugh. "I guess I'm...bored silly around here.... Will you come out to dinner with me tonight?"

There was a long silence and surprise, of course, in her face. Finally, she looked me sternly in the eye and said: "if Olga doesn't need me, and if you decide to mind your own business, Count Dracula!"

I apologized again and told her I would be back at the house at six. I then left her in the hall and, still embarrassed, went downstairs and outside to my car.

I spent the afternoon wandering through Valley Forge Park. I encountered "Mad" Anthony Wayne silhouetted there against bleak winter skies. He gazed in bronze from his horse across icy fields in the direction of Waynesborough. I found my ancestor's oration, delivered on the 100th anniversary of Washington's encampment, engraved on a memorial arch.

At the chapel nearby, built to honor the Continental Army and those who gave their lives for the cause, I found more traces of the family. On a tablet was mention of my ancestor Richard Henry Lee of Virginia, signer of the Declaration of Independence and president of the Continental Congress. Richard Henry seemed to be remembered most in family legend for the mysterious black-silk mitten he wore over a hand disfigured in a hunting accident. But what I found most worthy of remembrance were the words inscribed on his tomb by those he left behind: "We cannot do without you."

I read the long list of old Philadelphia family names who had contributed funds to build the chapel in 1891. It was a banding together of first families to confirm their identity, and I was envious of the strong sense of belonging that must have been their reward from this project.

*   *   *   *

At around six I was waiting in my car by the pantry door for Ole. Her attractive slim figure flickered through my headlights, and we were off to a small restaurant on the Main Line.

"I'm sorry again."

"That's all right, Count." Underneath a veneer of resentment it appeared that Ole was actually pleased with the attention I was paying her. My invasion of her privacy may have boosted her spirits. She was more relaxed because she now really had something on me, and spoke candidly as we drove down Lancaster Pike.

"You are so formal it makes us all laugh. And we, I mean my Mom and my two grandmothers, think your pompousness is surface only. Below it your ego is drowning! I might as well tell you that we spent the weekend imitating you after you left us in Bethlehem. We had each other in hysterics."

"I deserved it," I moaned. "And I guess I deserve anything you want to say about me now, and anything any one else like your mother or grandmother wants to say about me."

We arrived at the restaurant and were being shown to a table when I was surprised by my name being called. It was Sam Cohen, a classmate from boarding school. He came over, and I introduced him to Ole. I insisted that he sit down and have a drink while we ordered.

Sam had lived directly across from me during my junior year and in the same hall during two other of the five years I was there. We had known each other well and had gotten along.

In those years Sam amused me by calling every Jew or ex-Jew of importance, whether dead or alive, his "relative." Benjamin Disraeli was his "great-great uncle." Meyer Guggenheim was his "great grandfather's, first wife's, sister's husband." August Belmont was his "aunt's cousin, twice removed."

Sam was knowledgeable on all Jewish issues. He knew daily happenings in Israel and read stacks of books on Jewish history. His passion, above all, was for verbal discussion of Jewish questions. I used to see him in the school dining room long after dinner was over, when the boys with table duty were laying down the heavy white plates with the blue school crest for breakfast. He was vigorously debating Jewish history or current Jewish affairs with one or more masters and a handful of students. Often they would continue the discussion in the adjacent living room, under portraits of previous headmasters and famous WASP alumni, long dead, until well past the start of study hall.

I was envious of Sam because he had something to be so passionate about. Later he spent a year on an Israeli kibbutz. Eventually he went to Wall Street from where word of his brilliance and success in international finance has often reached me. "He's determined to be Bernard Baruch reincarnated," was the word I got from our class secretary years later. When I stumbled into him that night with Ole, he was working toward an MBA at Wharton.

"It sounds like you've really got your act together, Sam," I said wistfully.

"Well you know…I guess I knew where I was going back in prep school. You know what it means when you're Jewish." He then clarified his statement in Hebrew, as if the English language didn't have the words. In school Sam did this so often that within a month of his arrival we all stopped asking what these phrases meant. He went on: "If I hadn't gotten into graduate school, I wouldn't have shown my face (more Hebrew). But tell me about *you*. What are you up to, Tom?"

"I don't have anything to report at this time. I'm trying to get things going." Sam was kind enough not to pursue the issue. In prep school he didn't put others down, and he hadn't changed now. He had been well respected in school and could have been a leader had he chosen. He certainly wasn't a follower and didn't mind if someone caught him studying in the library during a football game. He spent equal time with the popular and the unpopular. Dormitory politics were trivial in the face of the much larger game of the future for which he was hard at work preparing himself.

Ole and I ordered dinner, and Sam and I exchanged phone numbers.

"You must come by my grandparents' for dinner some night."

"Give me a call." He waved and went toward the door.

Ole and I talked through a range of subjects over dinner. One was my manners. My unending formality and good manners often drove to exhaustion those who tried to reciprocate in kind. Unfortunately, I had now tarnished the substance of those manners by being caught in her room. My actions had made it clear that the Lightfoot lineage was no guarantee of good behavior and thus did not compel unqualified respect.

Tonight Ole was, understandably, in a sarcastic mood. Whenever I exhibited what she referred to as "idiosyncratic Lightfoot behavior," she issued a caustic, though often humorous, comment. And coming from a considerably less formal background, she seemed to consider most things I did "idiosyncratic."

When I had finished my main course, out of habit I placed my knife and fork tightly together at four o'clock on my plate.

"Whenever I clear plates at Transylvania, you've all got your silverware in that position. Is it some kind of religious sign? Are your knives and forks pointing to the East? Perhaps to England, your Paradise Lost…Is it a kind of pagan signal to us ethnics that WASPS are superior?"

I looked down at her plate and smiled as she placed not only her own knife and fork at four o'clock, but now began piling spoons, knives and forks from neighboring place settings on her plate in this same position.

"The Gods are going to finally notice me!" she giggled. "You know, the longer I'm at Transylvania the more trifling WASP rituals I recognize that separate me from your family. I used to think that class was only a question of money. Now I see that it's got more to do with style. I didn't see these differences in style right off—probably because I didn't expect them. They surprised me. Now I see how you all go through so many rituals; it's like you practice some kind of religion out there at Transylvania. When we eat in my family, it's free and easy. We have fun. But there's a sequence of events that must be followed when your family eats—

my God you're all so uptight! Do you get irritable bowel syndrome if the last utensil, last crumb isn't cleared away before desert comes in? There seems to be a deeply ingrained tradition that inhibits you from doing anything spontaneous.... You all speak with a certain stiff, almost English sort of accent, and wear only natural fibers. Polyester is probably my family's favorite material. *You* would never wear a white, Dacron, short-sleeved shirt! You're always in the same uniform: a Shetland crewneck sweater with the collar of an Oxford cloth shirt visible by about half an inch.... You like to ask people where they went to school, and are constantly uptight and self-conscious with a pinch of condescension thrown in. You're all trying to abide by some code—form over function. But it's not a code that's really taking you somewhere like Sam Cohen is going somewhere.... Can I say it?"

"What? Sure, what haven't you said?"

"Your code is like a wall you use to separate yourselves from the unwashed masses. We ethnics aren't allowed—'No Chinamen or Dogs'—wasn't that a sign on the gate to the American compound in Peking?"

"I don't know," I murmured. "...Actually, despite what you say about style, money *is* what starts the separation process between *us* and what you term the 'unwashed masses'. When the money runs out and the well is dry, just having this *style*, or certain code of conduct you're talking about, doesn't do us any good. In fact it hurts us, and we're fish out of water. It's not a code of conduct you can get rid of, either, because it's become a permanent dimension of your personality by the time you realize you may have to change course.

"We were all sent away to good boarding schools in this family. We've been led to believe that our good breeding and excellent educations qualify us to be racehorses. Unfortunately, the real world doesn't need too many racehorses; I'm finding it needs toilers. So, when one of us ends up toiling, doing something with little or no glamour or excitement, it can be very difficult to accept. I was—"

"Let's take the issue of college," she interrupted. "Since that's where I spend my time. You've told me what went on where you went. You were concerned with a certain status down there that I'm not concerned with at Bryn Mawr. I think I'm having a very different college experience than you."

"I know. And you're probably going to be all set when you get out, and you'll end up like Sam Cohen with a destination in mind and attend some top notch graduate school." My voice was testy.

"I guess I'm giving you a hard time."

"If you've grown up your entire life a member of a privileged family, and then the rug gets pulled out from under your feet, and you have to compete at the bottom rung, it's not easy. It's a downer, and you're not prepared. You've been given high expectations but no wherewithal."

After a long silence, she changed the subject. I consumed a considerable amount of wine until the bartender yelled last call, and then I paid the bill.

We walked outside into the cold. "The north wind doth blow, and we shall have snow," I mumbled in my drunkenness, recalling a rhyme from Nanny Hawkins. Ole had to drive us back to Leighsylvania.

We entered the pantry without switching on the lights, then suffered through an awkward separation. In the shadows we played a silent game of darting eyes. Through the window a tree limb wagged across the midnight moon—a chaperon's finger admonishing me. I didn't dare meet her pretty eyes with mine, reminded of her comment at dinner: "You WASPS have such strict standards of sexual morality!"

My voice was jittery with repressed desire. But we parted: she up the backstairs and I to the front.

In the dining room my grandfather had once again left on the spotlight above the portrait of William Williamson Lightfoot. I stood momentarily contemplating his wavy reflection down the polished cherry table. He, like other Virginians of his day, had referred to the Old Dominion as his "native country."

What could I find to be so loyal to? What cause, larger than myself, could I embrace?

*   *   *   *

Monday morning I was out of the house before breakfast to search out a restaurant or hotel lobby with plenty of phones to use as my new headquarters. I was not comfortable calling anyone with my grandfather pacing round the house on the threshold of loosing his patience with me again.

I got several recruiters on the phone, or left messages, before putting in a call to Larry Ferg. Once again he was encouraging and said I stood a good chance of landing a job with a finance company he had just been talking to. An interview was scheduled for Friday afternoon.

I was excited, which made Friday a long time in coming. I spent the days prior living a street existence in Center City Philadelphia—walking from one hotel lobby to the next in search of the most available and private bank of telephones. Occasionally I found a chair to pull up and in comfort go through the long list of numbers I had compiled from help-wanted ads and the yellow pages. Lunch and often dinner were at cheap restaurants where there wasn't a chance of me being recognized by family acquaintances or cousins. When I'd had enough of the phones, I wandered through old Philadelphia graveyards.

But at last Friday did arrive, and at three o'clock I was once again in Larry's waiting room. To work for a *finance* company sounded lofty and prestigious! I was floating in a fantasy of myself as a Nathan Rothschild leaning against my pillar at the London Stock exchange, or as the mustachioed J.P. Morgan in the Edward Steichen portrait.

When my turn came, I was introduced to a tough middle-aged man who had spent his life on the street collecting delinquent loans. He was heavy-set and his face round and pockmarked. His nose was a potato and his bottom teeth looked diseased—horribly yellow and crooked. He now managed fifteen branches for Eastern States Financial Services, a consumer finance company.

I sat quietly as he read me the lengthy job description. He was incapable of pronouncing "the," replacing it each time with "da." After the reading he asked if I was still interested. I was; in a few months it would be a year since college graduation, and I still did not have a job. We conversed for a few extra minutes about Philadelphia politics, after which he asked me to meet with the regional manager in Chester the following Monday morning.

I stopped in Larry Ferg's office on the way to the elevator and told him excitedly that I'd been invited back for a second interview.

"This one's for you! You're going to fit right in there. It's your kind of place!"

I took a euphoric train ride back out to the Main Line and arrived at Leighsylvania in time for cocktails. When I reported the results of the day, my grandfather was enthusiastic that progress was being made and that a job offer might be forthcoming.

After dinner I announced that the following morning I would be driving to New York City to visit Binney, my older sister. She had invited me to join her and her husband, Danny Paulucci, at a dinner to be held at the Metropolitan Museum of Art.

"Did you bring your formal attire with you from Maine, dear?" asked my grandmother.

"Will it be black or white tie?" asked my grandfather.

"I didn't bring anything with me, as I plan to rent it when I get to New York."

"Why don't you take my tails," volunteered my grandfather excitedly. "I don't think they'll fit anyone else in the family but you. I bought the coat in 1909, and it's in excellent shape. At my age there are few parties that I can get to anymore."

*   *   *   *

Instead of driving I took the train to Manhattan and a cab to my sister's building on the Upper East Side. Seven years older than myself and still without children, Binney lived in a spacious, four-bedroom apartment crammed with American antiques. Her husband, Danny Paulucci, was an investment banker on Wall Street and made considerable money.

Binney was alone in the apartment when I arrived. Though a Saturday, I was not surprised that Danny was not around, as he frequently put in long hours on weekends. Besides, it seemed Danny was never around when I was to arrive.

I had grown used to it over time. He was three years older than my sister and very well established in his career. To him I was a joke; I wasn't to be taken seriously and would not amount to anything. Whenever I was under the same roof with Binney and Danny, especially on vacation in Castine, they generally avoided me and seldom extended an invitation to join them sailing or picnicking.

It was thus not subtle avoidance, and if by accident our destinations were the same, Danny's discovery of my presence generally caused his nose to twitch up, as if he had caught a foul smell. When his nose relaxed, his expression would take on the dispirited look of someone taken ill, though his pallor stopped short of actually turning green.

Daniel Victor Paulucci was the son of Italian immigrants. He had grown up in Rhode Island and had been offered a full scholarship by several universities. My grandfather referred to him as "the scholarship boy."

"Harvard took him and completed his metamorphism into a WASP," my brother Henry put it. "Danny has proved the new rule: if you behave like a WASP, you'll be treated by others as a WASP, and you are therefore a de facto WASP. Ancestry has gone by the wayside: WASPdom can be achieved, and the boundaries of the American upper class are ever expanding."

Wall Street was Danny's choice after Harvard. By the early eighties he was well on his way to amassing the substantial fortune with which he would end the decade.

The more successful he became, the less patience he had for Binney's family. I respected my sister enough, however, never to complain about the condescending nature of her husband.

Binney and I caught up with each other through most of that afternoon in her New York apartment. Danny came in around five from an all day squash tournament; he hadn't been at the office. Initially he was courteous, probably because he had played very well—there were rumors that he was a bad sport. He brought me a beer and one for himself and flopped onto the leather sofa directly in front of me. He tilted his head back and took an endless quaff. Finally his eyes settled down from the ceiling and were affixed squarely at me. I sat up, nervously preparing for the coming interrogation.

"So, did you arrive in New York through the Port Authority Bus Terminal?" he asked with a snicker. I smiled and didn't bother to answer. "But tell me, I hear you've had some job interviews? What have you come up with?"

"I've got a second interview with a consumer finance company on Monday, and I think I've got a pretty good shot."

"Consumer finance company?…Great, have fun all day collecting delinquent loans in ghetto neighborhoods!" He chuckled and took another long swig. My fantasies of becoming another J.P. Morgan or living the life of a Rothschild ended abruptly. Maybe I didn't really understand what this job was about. I avoided being embarrassed further by aggressively moving the conversation in new directions. Danny tried to bring us back but was unsuccessful, and my sister finally saved me by announcing that it was time to get dressed for the evening.

As we parted he reminded me: "Don't think that you'll get a decent job by knowing someone's family or school friend. Lightfoots think that still works."

An hour later I was dressed in white tie and my grandfather's ancient tails. My sister appeared in a sparkling blue gown, her shoulders exposed. She had managed to keep some of that deep tan from Christmas in the British Virgin Islands.

A half hour later we were climbing out of a limousine at the Metropolitan Museum of Art. We walked up the steps and soon saw that most of the other men were carrying or wearing white gloves. Danny was very irritated at this discovery and began venting his frustration on Binney: she hadn't told him to request gloves with the rented tails. He took such trivial matters so seriously! Why would someone who engineers multi-million dollar deals be so uptight about white gloves?

"He's new money," cousin Appleton Crawford remarked when I recounted the story later. "He's not self-assured and casual about such things like the rest of us because, after all, he's not a true member of the tribe."

Danny seemed determined to embrace our WASP rituals to the fullest and show the Lightfoots how things should be done. We had apparently lapsed in our ways and didn't appreciate what we had.

He and I stood in the receiving line barehanded, observing other men pulling on their white gloves. He held his hands upright, less than six inches from Binney's face, and pretended to pull on gloves like a surgeon before an operation.

Then he took one last look at me and shrugged his shoulders before bowing his way down the receiving line.

When he got through he looked back, and I detected a cold surprise in his face: I *was* wearing gloves! My grandfather's coat contained a hidden pocket in the crotch of the tails, and inside he kept a wonderfully smooth and soft pair of kidskin gloves. Once white, they had aged nicely to a pale yellow, authenticating their many decades in high society.

Danny and Binney were soon engulfed by friends, so I wandered to the bar. With Scotch in hand I drifted through the crowd. I passed a small group and heard mention of Lawrenceville and several New England boarding schools. From another I heard names of Ivy League universities.

A familiar pretty face popped up in front of me and disappeared. I moved quickly in its direction and recognized the elegant bare shoulders and slim waist of Lea Creswell. I had known her several years back in Philadelphia and had attended her debutante party. She was enthusiastic and smiling when I caught her eye.

"A familiar face…Tom Lightfoot! What are you doing here?"

"My sister lives in town."

"Well, when was the last time we saw each other?" We moved to an empty table to catch up. Lea was working at a New York bank. After boarding school in Maryland she had gone on to college in the Rockies. There, she had apparently spent most of her time in search of the best powder.

"And tell me about yourself. Are you working?"

"Not yet. I spent last fall in Europe and have been just shaking the trees, so to speak, in the last few months."

"And has anything fallen out and knocked you on the head, Sir Isaac Newton?"

"I may have a job in finance. I'll find out on Monday." Her escort for the evening was her brother, so we were able to continue uninterrupted for at least another half hour. Eventually, we saw plates of prime rib, and I felt a tap on my shoulder.

"Are you going to join us for dinner?" asked Binney.

"Will you join us for dinner, Lea?" I asked.

Ten minutes later the four of us were together at a small table. The two women were immediately in conversation about mutual friends in Philadelphia. Danny and I sat quietly listening. Danny had already downed several drinks and now ordered another. Riding on alcohol and bored when not receiving attention, he finally interrupted Lea in mid-sentence: "Did you know Tom is hoping to get a job collecting bad loans? He'll find out Monday."

"We all start somewhere," said Binney trying to rescue me, but with a traitorous smile that encouraged the cynical side of Danny's humor. Her subsequent impish chuckle did not help my cause.

"If you don't pay your bills I'll be after you," I said to Lea with a forced smile. No one laughed, and Lea looked completely puzzled.

Eventually, Binney did step in and change the subject, and the better side of Danny's charm and humor was unleashed. When its torrent wasn't in my direction, even I started to like him. He had us all in stitches through the rest of dinner.

Lea and I spent much of the evening together. Her black gown and slim figure held my attention. After midnight I took down her phone number and accompanied her and her brother to their limousine. I waved as they drove off and for several minutes stood quietly on the curb feeling happy under the stars.

*   *   *   *

Fantasies of Lea kept me occupied on the train to Philadelphia Sunday evening and kept me awake until well after midnight. Nevertheless, Monday morning I was up early to put on my suit and be the first at breakfast.

Soon my grandmother sat down across the table but, after a polite "good morning, Grandmother," I was back to visions of Lea on pink coral sands. When my grandfather finally appeared, I knew I had to be talkative.

"I saw Lea Creswell in New York."

"Oh! How wonderful," exclaimed my grandmother.

"We know her family. Thomas Creswell was a wealthy Quaker in colonial times," mumbled Grandad with a full mouth.

An hour later I was in my car headed for Chester to meet the regional manager of Eastern States Financial Services.

Dom Regula, I soon found, was in his late fifties. His success at growing a mustache was no better, however, than an adolescent boy's. His socks were not long enough to extend much above his ankles, and the hairless, waxy skin of his legs was visible whenever he sat. Polyester was by far the dominant blend in his shirt, tie, and baby-blue suit.

From the moment I entered his office it was obvious that I had a job.

"We start at eight sharp. Forty-five minutes for lunch. We're out by five. You'll sit up front where the customers come in to pay up. You'll get a feel for who we serve this way...." And on he went. He was sincere, hard-driving, all business. He had little or no interest in my background or education level. He just needed a body with a college degree.

"We can have you start a week from now at a three-day orientation seminar to be held a couple of hours west of here."

CHAPTER 4

▼

In the midst of the continual movement which agitates a democratic community, the tie which unites one generation to another is relaxed or broken; every man there readily loses all trace of the ideas of his forefathers, or takes no care about them. Men living in this state of society cannot derive their belief from the opinions of the class to which they belong; for, so to speak, there are no longer any classes.

—*Alexis de Tocqueville*

The tempo of the whole capitalist development made it impossible for an inherited nobility to develop and endure in America.

—*C. Wright Mills*

I returned to Castine to wait out the week. I read more Tacitus and once again took solitary walks along the icy shoreline rocks. The ocean was a metallic blue in the low sun of mid-winter. In the crisp cold I smothered anxious thoughts of beginning an unknown job with fantasies of the women in my life, past and present. When would I be allowed to wrap my limbs around the delicate frame of Lea Creswell and share her warmth behind frosty winter windows? I was afraid to assume that such coziness lay anywhere in my future. Would I be forever denied such contentment?

After five days in the quiet of my parents' home I was wanting to ride the world again. I drove south on a Saturday and spent the night with Binney in New

York before continuing on to Philadelphia. I ate breakfast with my grandparents Monday morning and an hour later was on the road again—for a Ramada Inn near Harrisburg.

I arrived after mid-day. A reception was not supposed to begin until five, so I spent the hours attempting to read in my room. I had grabbed one of the four volumes of Douglas Southall Freeman's *Robert E. Lee* from my grandparents' library on the way out the door.

I sat with my feet up, gazing through the window at the black asphalt and beyond to the endless strip of car dealerships, fast food restaurants, and service stations along the interstate. My book was open but face down on my lap. My mind was running in all directions in nervous anticipation of the five o'clock cocktail hour. Despite what Danny Paulucci had said about this job, my vision of the crowd at the upcoming reception was one of expensive suits and sophisticated talk about the economy and current events. Would I measure up?

I picked up Freeman for another fruitless attempt but after less than a paragraph drifted to an incident from my past.

I was alone in my fraternity house one day in April. Why was I alone? Was it my own lack of initiative, or had I been purposely left out? I remembered the empty feeling compounded by the silence of the house: everyone else was out and involved, and I wasn't. Somehow I hadn't gotten the word.

I was sitting on the front wall of the fraternity, gazing at the pale green of early spring, when my eyes caught a well-polished black Jaguar. I hopped down, crossed the street and walked up the hill to where it was parked. My instincts were correct: the license plates were Pennsylvania and a discreet sticker on the back window was a familiar country club insignia. This was my grandfather's Jag!

I walked across the warm lawn to the adjacent university chapel, to the front brick patio built by the United Daughters of the Confederacy. I opened the chapel's big white door to a gust of cool air, a refreshing last remnant of winter.

At the far end hung my favorite portrait of George Washington; painted in 1772 by Charles Wilson Peale, it is the earliest known portrait of the man. For his proud pose in the glossy oil, Washington had selected his red uniform from the French and Indian War.

To the right of this portrait, under battle flags of the Confederacy, was the marble statue by Edward Valentine of a recumbent Robert E. Lee in full uniform. Lee had been president of the college in the years after the Civil War. He had built this chapel and was buried in the crypt below.

My grandfather stood with both hands on an arm of this beautifully detailed, recumbent Lee. He was dressed in a suit and stood silently in contemplation…perhaps in prayer? I moved hesitantly up the aisle, unsure what to make of his surprise visit and this mysterious vigil. Certainly it confirmed the belief of family members that my grandfather had an obsession with Lee.

"Grandad!"

"Hello Tom!" We shook hands. I had startled him. "I'm sorry I didn't call. I'd hoped to get in and out of town without disturbing your studies." It was the one time he ever looked sincerely embarrassed in front of me.

We sat in a pew and shared family news. He was on the board of several Virginia institutions, including a military academy and a college. A meeting at one of them was apparently the reason for his coming down.

"I have to be in Charlottesville by dinnertime so I can't stay. But I couldn't pass by here without paying my respects to this gentleman." His gaze was on the recumbent Lee. "He didn't want the country to split up, you know. And Winfield Scott wanted him second in command of the Union Army in 1861, which really meant he would have been in total command because Scott, general in chief, was too old."

"I know that, but he couldn't side against Virginia if Virginia was violently attacked."

"Yes, you see here was a man whose roots and family were, after God, the uppermost in his life. You know the history of the Lees: statesmen, soldiers, planters. You're a descendent of one of the Signers. They were a dynasty that played a significant part in the settling and founding of this country. So this Lee knew where to turn for direction: his heritage.…"

I listened politely to Grandad's short history lesson, the sort of lesson that most members of the family complained of having to suffer through too often, and once again to Grandad's contention, shared by Douglas Southall Freeman, that for Lee the Civil War was a "drama of ill-fortune nobly borne," and in that way a "triumph of character over catastrophe."

We then walked to Grandad's elegant Jaguar in which now sat his driver, and I waved them off.

*   *   *   *

I heard the rumble of men's voices at an open bar and entered the small reception room in a charcoal-gray, Brooks Brother's suit. I was painfully aware that my entrance aroused curiosity. It was a shirtsleeves crowd, and the shirts were not starched cotton. I was the only one wearing a tie, much less a suit; again I hadn't gotten the word.

I asked for a beer at the bar and nervously stood by myself, looking for another loner. Those in the crowd reminded me of younger versions of Dom Regula. I scanned the nametags and detected no one with a Northern European last name. The overwhelming subject of discussion was professional sports.

"Mr. Polansky, I'm Rudy Russo." A solidly built man of dark complexion, perhaps twenty-five, reached out to shake my hand. I took his but told him I was not Mr. Polansky.

"I'm Tom Lightfoot."

"Oh! I do apologize. I thought that maybe you had to be him. But you *are* from the home office, right?"

"No, no. I'm here for the three-day orientation and training session. Who is this Mr. Polansky?"

"Oh! Polansky is the vice president in charge of branch operations. I thought he might be here tonight. But maybe not. The guy I do know will be here is DeMille, you know, the trainer?"

"Yes, I read about him in the material we received."

"So, where you from, Tom?"

"I'm living outside Philadelphia but will be working in the Chester office. How about yourself?"

"I'm living in South Philly but commuting out to the Main Line. There is an office out there in Bryn Mawr."

"That's not far from where I'm living."

"I should have guessed! But we don't get Main Liners into our office. We get people who go there to work but live in places like I live."

"Why not Main Liners?"

"Are you kidding? Main Liners don't need us; bankers get on their knees when a real Main Liner walks in. They get all the credit they want at much lower interest rates at the banks out there. We get the blue collars coming in for the day. Your grease monkeys at the local service stations or the women who mop the floors at the big castles up and down the Main Line."

Rudy Russo had recently completed a two-year degree at community college. He had been with Eastern States Financial Services two months and already seemed to know the business.

About a half-hour later our group of fifteen moved spontaneously to the dining room and to the large table set up just for us. Rudy sat on my left and two women, both in their early twenties and the only women in the group, were on my right.

"Mr. DeMille, I'm Terry Dagavarian and this is Ella Collobi."

"I'm not Mr. DeMille. I'm Tom Lightfoot. It's nice to meet you."

"You *are* from the home office, right?"

"No. No, I'm working out of the Chester office."

"So am I!" exclaimed Terry. "I'm the credit checker. You're the new hire Dom was telling me about!" She was single and during the entire three-day session would pay me undue attention. She was short, with dark hair and dark complexion, and living in a large apartment complex near the Philadelphia airport.

Terry's friend, Ella, worked in the North Philadelphia office. She had moved in from Pittsburgh to be close to her boyfriend.

We all sat down, and Rudy Russo and I resumed our discussion about how daily business at Eastern States was conducted. Occasionally I overheard the two women talking on my right. Ella wanted to know more about the Philadelphia area and was drilling Terry. I caught a few words: "The Main Line is where Rudy, over there, works."

"What's the Main Line?" asked Ella.

"WASP blue bloods," replied Terry loudly—she didn't feel the need to be discrete. I was reminded of a comment years before from my boarding school friend Coddie Codington: "Take the movies. When a story has to pick on a particular group in this country without creating controversy, the screen writer knows that he can always play it safe by picking on WASPS. When has anyone gotten into trouble by publicly slandering or being indiscreet toward WASPS?"

We were into dessert when the mysterious Mr. DeMille finally stood up to introduce himself and welcome us. Ronnie DeMille, the training manager, worked in Northern New Jersey. He was just less than six feet, unathletic and heavy. His black hair was slicked back stylishly like a model in a men's fashion magazine. His glasses were preppy tortoiseshell. His clothes were better fitting than what the rest of the group was wearing, and their blend of fibers weighed strongly in favor of the natural. Ronnie, about thirty years old, spoke with enthusiasm, and his voice and selection of words greatly excited this group of idealistic young people.

As he spoke his eyes kept coming back to me. The third or fourth time they did so I began avoiding contact. Even his body language revealed his curiosity about me: his chest always faced me even as his head swiveled hard to the right or left. What kind of spectacle was I?

After dinner I introduced myself. For the moment he held his obvious curiosity in check and was considerate enough to respect my privacy in front of the group by not asking any personal questions. Nevertheless, through the remainder of the evening I would catch him looking at me from a distance, and when we were standing near each other, I could feel his eyes examining my clothing. Was he calculating what my suit must have cost?

For the first group meeting the following morning, I was dressed casually in khaki pants and polo shirt under a crew neck sweater. Nevertheless, I was still more formally dressed than the others. Most of them wore sweatshirts with the names of high schools, state universities, or NFL teams across the front.

A confident DeMille began that first morning session by asking each of us to introduce ourselves to the group with some background on our education, previous jobs, and outside interests.

I recalled Clay Ludwell's warning: "There are people who consider anyone, with even the least bit of inherited money or position, an asshole. They want you to be ashamed." Some advice from my mother came to mind: "use self-deprecation to charm away envy. Use some humor to mock yourself, and you'll win almost everyone over."

When my turn came I commanded undue attention. Was it my physical appearance, or was it because I spoke with what Ole called the "pseudo-English" accent of the Main Line—through the teeth and with a notoriously stiff jaw—rather than with the better-recognized Philadelphia accent that heavily emphasizes the "r"?

DeMille's glaring curiosity and the group's sudden concentration on me instantly stifled the "self-deprecating humor" Mother had prescribed. Nothing came to mind that would take the edge off! My voice sounded too educated, my grammar too precise and formal, and my vocabulary too extensive. My back was sweaty from the group's undivided attention, and when I was done the room remained uncomfortably silent. DeMille finally broke it with the question I dreaded most: "What high school did you go to?"

Most of the group grew up and was educated in and around Philadelphia. Those who had introduced themselves before me named their high schools by simply stating the name of the football team, the school mascot, or even just the school colors, and as such invariably received cheers or fun loving boos and hisses. When I answered DeMille, again the response was silence until he finally asked, "It's a prep school, a boarding school, right?"

He had now confirmed everyone's suspicion that I was indeed an oddity. Whatever questions remained in anyone's mind about my identity had now been answered. My shirt was stuck to my back, and I was caught in the bright spotlight of DeMille's inquisition, "Didn't Paul Newman send his sons there?"

"I don't think so."

"But it is the type of place someone like Paul Newman would send his kids?" he persisted.

"I don't think so."

"What are the school colors? Did I see them once playing Conestoga High?"

"You may have, I'm really not *sure!*" I exclaimed coldly and then buried my face in the papers and notebooks before me. DeMille moved on to Terry Dagavarian.

No, the school *never* played public high schools in sports activities. The school colors were blue and gray. I sat back and thought about the colors blue and gray. Why blue and gray? I was now oblivious to the responses from Terry and the rest of the group; DeMille's questions had cut the ropes holding my attention, and my consciousness sank below the surface to be swept along by deeper currents of self-reflection.

I had learned the origin of the school colors in the headmaster's study the evening before graduation. Immersed in the comfortable smell of his pipe, insulated from the world by books from floor to ceiling, the tall and frail William Frothingham, our scholarly headmaster, had gotten into his favorite lecture on the purpose of the school. "Why blue and gray?" I interrupted.

"During the Civil War," replied Frothingham, delighted by the question, "as many boys fought for the North as fought for the South. Charles Bulfinch of Boston, the then headmaster, believed that his purpose after 1865 was to create a class of young men who would mend the nation. Thus he changed the school colors to blue and gray.

"Lincoln was assassinated and then came the corrupt administrations of Ulysses S. Grant and the era of carpetbaggers and robber barons. Bulfinch continued as headmaster until 1895. With each passing year he became ever more passionate about creating a national class of men who were morally and ethically honorable.

"Bulfinch believed in a ruling class. His vision was not, however, of an abusive feudal aristocracy. Rather, his vision was one of people obligated by their upbringing to serve their communities and the nation: unpretentious, intellectual and, above all, not insecure in their social status by being without money. Bulfinch wrote that, if a class of people can be made to feel money is not the only prerequisite for status, if a class can be socially self-assured without feeling money must be the first priority, then there will be men with enough time and desire to get involved and lead their communities and the nation. His vision was modeled on the better qualities of the English class system."

William Frothingham was himself a published historian and a leader in secondary education. Originally from Boston like Bulfinch, Frothingham's particular interest was the Adams family of his native city—"*The* first family of American history."

"We don't want a headless, rootless society," he used to instruct us in chapel at least once a semester.

I pulled away from the deeper currents of past reflection and rose to the surface. Expression in my face was resuscitated by laughter from the person next to me, and my eyes focused once again on DeMille. He seemed to have his audience's attention better than Frothingham ever had the attention of his boys. The group laughed at DeMille's every joke, no matter how pathetically weak.

He gave me a nickname before the session was over: "Mr. Harvard." At drinks after dinner I overheard him loudly telling someone that he had attended "Public Elementary School 31." I didn't have to turn to know his eyes were on me.

A small group was still at the bar around midnight. DeMille had disappeared, and I finally relaxed. Somehow, perhaps because my presence inspired it, the conversation turned to family status. Those with whom I was conversing all made mention that their families had moved "from working class to middle class" in just the last generation. I remained silent and listened to examples of the American Dream come true, too embarrassed, of course, to mention the Lightfoot family's long lineage. One young man my age told the small group: "My mother grew up in the Great Depression. She and her sisters would wait by a bump in the road coming from an apple orchard…for a truck to roll by, and they hoped that some apples would spill. And if some apples didn't spill, Mom would chase the truck until some did because this would be all she'd get to eat for dinner."

I became very tense during this interchange—my shirt again stuck to my back. *My* mother was chasing hounds and foxes during the Great Depression.

During the second day DeMille was all business and, to my relief, never got personal with me. The material therefore received my full attention. I was actually quite comfortable as the day turned to afternoon and then to evening. I enjoyed dinner and remained again at the bar until very late.

It was just Rudy Russo and myself after midnight. Rudy was brimming with enthusiasm over what he saw as the "fantastic opportunities" offered by Eastern States Financial Services, and we spent most of an hour talking about Rudy's dreams.

Just before we parted for our respective rooms, however, he changed the subject, interrupting me in mid-sentence with what appeared to have been on his mind for some time: "Why did your parents choose to send you away to a private boarding school? I guess that's what they do in the upper classes…. But isn't it un-American *not* to support local public education?"

I was a bit jolted by Rudy's questions about what I considered a very private matter. His use of the term "upper classes" made me very uncomfortable. *Class* is a word my father has never been able to use in speaking. "New Money can use the word *class* and feel comfortable. Old families in America have problems saying the word *class*," my brother Henry once mused. "It makes us uneasy, maybe embarrassed or even ashamed. We feel guilty and try to deny its existence. But without success, I think."

I responded to Rudy after a moment of thought. "That's quite a question. It's understandable that you ask it because this country doesn't want an upper class. And, by the way, I cringe whenever I use that term, *upper class*, because I don't want to imply that I'm in any way superior to you or anyone else in this group. And please, whatever we're saying here, please keep it between you and me because if I want to get anywhere in this company, I can't be an oddity. DeMille seems to have already picked up on what I'm all about."

"Okay, sure. Hey, don't take things too seriously. I'm sorry; it's *not* my business."

"No, no, don't worry. Private boarding school. Yes, well, there is kind of a contradiction going on. Perhaps there does exist an upper class in America, and maybe it is running away from its responsibility toward public education. One could argue that America's upper class—and, again, I hate using that term—is betraying this country. I will say, however, that there are a lot of people who have come from schools like mine who have devoted their lives to successfully leading America. There's Oliver Wendell Holmes, Franklin Roosevelt, JFK. How about George Bush?

"…You see, the handful of boarding schools that exist in this country were founded on traditions coming from Great Britain, where, you might be aware, there are lots of boarding schools. These schools were, and I think still are, supposed to give their students a sense of civic responsibility, and as a student you're supposed to learn the duties of inherited privilege."

Rudy nodded an understanding, though I'm certain from his blank look that my explanation had lost him. Of course I didn't mention brother Henry's theory on why private boarding schools came to America: "The boarding school phenomenon caught on when the waves of immigrants from Eastern Europe and other undesirable places came crashing down on our shores. J.P. Morgan and the Roosevelts and the old money families had to get their sons and daughters away from the great unwashed."

We paid the tab and went our separate ways. Rudy and I were to maintain only a cordial relationship at best during those years at Eastern States Financial. I was never certain how far I could trust him and to what extent he and DeMille were conspiring. Rudy was status conscious and remained curious about my background. In the future I would find him always wanting to know what I was up to, not because he wanted to cheer my success, but because he was set on keeping me behind him in the race. I was suspicious of his ever-present curiosity and forever fearful of him waiting in ambush.

*   *   *   *

During my first two weeks on the job I spent a day working alongside each member of the Chester office staff. At the end of those weeks I was given a stack of several hundred account cards and charged with updating them when payments came in. I was to telephone or visit my customers when payments were late. I was also charged with encouraging each customer to borrow to his or her maximum.

We were lending money at exorbitant interest rates for cars, home appliances, medical bills, and for whatever other purposes the poor need cash. Indeed, our customers *were* the poor; the middle class went to banks where interest rates were considerably lower. Our customers were *not* white Caucasian; they had minimum education and often spoke English as a second language, if at all.

I had been with Eastern States Financial about four weeks when Dom Regula handed me an account card that had come to his attention. "Tom, we haven't heard from this woman in three months. No payments either. None of our telephone calls have gotten through to her. Tomorrow on your way in, why don't you stop by and knock on her door."

So, the following morning I slept beyond my usual 6:30 wake-up, as the office wasn't expecting me until noon. I did get up, however, in time to eat breakfast with my grandparents. They joined me after the pantry maid had delivered my scrambled eggs on the usual Cantonese plate. I stood up when they entered the room and enthusiastically wished them "Good morning!" I did not, however, get a similarly enthusiastic response from them. My grandfather was glaring in a way that made me uneasy, and I quickly braced for another lecture.

"How is breakfast at the Leighsylvania Coffee Shop this morning? Tom, do you expect to treat our house as your hotel for the rest of your life?"

He delivered this surprise broadside before he had even pulled out his chair! I was too stunned and hurt to respond, and we all sat in awkward silence.

In hindsight I should have been ready for such a confrontation. The same message had been delivered in countless other ways as soon as I had been offered the job at Eastern States Financial. On several occasions, for example, I had returned from work to find a collection of unwanted items dumped in my room, as if someone had been cleaning out a closet or chest of drawers and considered my room a catchall. There were some vacant rooms in the house, and I would gather these unwanted clothes and odds and ends and stack them neatly in one of those countless empty rooms.

More blatantly, on other occasions I would arrive back at Leighsylvania in time for dinner, only to discover that no place had been set for me.

The silence at breakfast continued endlessly, the three of us buttering our toast and sipping our coffee. To avoid eye contact I contemplated the sterling silver vegetable dish in the center of the table. The edges were ornately flowing flowers. Along the sides of the dish and up over the lid were the engraved signatures of about twenty notable persons from the first part of the nineteenth century, including Nicholas Biddle and Henry Clay. The former, president of the Second Bank of the United States and ultimately sacked by Andrew Jackson, was my great uncle five generations back. Henry Clay of Kentucky and the other signatories had presented this beautiful piece of sterling silver to my direct ancestor Matthew Carey, book publisher and pamphleteer.

"The 1832 election of Andrew Jackson was the end of Anglo-American hegemony in this country," Grandad once proclaimed. "Nicholas Biddle was proper Philadelphia. Jackson was just Scotch-Irish frontiersman."

Brother Henry gave a heated but eloquent response: "Aren't we glad social revolution has been institutionalized in America? Thank God we allow for the continual inclusion of talented outsiders—this is our nation's strength."

In a follow-up letter to me at boarding school, Grandad quoted H.L Mencken. Mencken had written that since the days of Jackson, "Judicious men warned that giving the vote to incompetent, despairing and envious people would breed demagogues to rouse and rally them, and that the whole democratic process would be converted to organized pillage and rapine."

As the silence at breakfast continued, I determined that the best use of my lunch breaks in the upcoming week would be to look for an apartment or room for rent. Finally the morning paper arrived, and my grandparents divided it and burrowed in. I stuffed my mouth with what remained on the pretty blue plate before me and asked to be excused.

Minutes later, a road map across the wheel, I was driving south to Chester in search of Front Street and a Mrs. Ilene Jartran.

*   *   *   *

The sky was gray and the wind cold. The car heat was on high, as in my rush to leave I had neglected my lined raincoat. All I wore over my shirt and tie was a red, summer jacket bought for me years back for debutante parties and better worn dancing to Cole Porter love songs.

As I approached Mrs. Jartran's neighborhood, the roads had a greater frequency of potholes and the houses appeared increasingly dilapidated. Number 53 Front Street, a 1940s two-story row house, was sprayed with green and blue graffiti under the windows.

I parked my car and walked a little nervously up the path over ugly brown grass bursting like stuffing from cracks in the concrete. I pressed the doorbell and waited. I pressed it impatiently several more times without response. Then I pounded loudly on the metal door, still irritated by my grandfather's question at breakfast. Finally I heard a very faint woman's voice: "The door's open."

It *wasn't* locked, and I pushed it open to the foul smell of unemptied trash cans. A tiny woman stood in the hall, perhaps four feet tall, with an oversized head and long scraggly hair. Her worn bathrobe covered what appeared to be a very crippled, crooked body with one leg withered and much shorter than the other.

"I-I'm here from Eastern States, that's Eastern States Financial Services, and we are…ah…wondering if you are going to resume payments?" My earlier irritation had evaporated in seconds, and I didn't recognize the gentle, soft voice with which I now spoke. Could Dom Regula have sounded so sweetly? Maybe that was the reason he had sent me.

"Yes, yes," she whispered.

The only piece of furniture in an adjoining room was a large dirty couch with a bundle of scraggly wool blankets on top.

"Well, thank you very much," I whispered back. There was an awkward silence. "…You know where to send it?" She nodded her pathetically large head, and I backed out the door.

I was shaking when I unlocked my car. The site of this deformed woman! Scary—someone from a freak show—especially being by myself!

I was soaking in hot, overwhelming guilt and embarrassment by the time I pulled into the Eastern States parking lot. I could only shuffle papers at my desk for what remained of the day. When I looked at customer files, I felt I was nosing through someone's personal business, snooping through someone's private mail, and reading confidential histories I had no place reading.

After five I picked up the local paper and at Burger King for dinner looked up rooms to rent. I called several numbers and set up an appointment for after work the following day.

*   *   *   *

My new landlord was to be Steve Van Brugh. He was in his early thirties and very involved in the gay community. "Do you know what a *queen* is?" he once asked me. I had no idea. I hadn't even suspected he was gay; he had to tell me—weeks after I had moved in.

Steve's dress was non-descript. His hair was straight and long, just off his shoulders. His face was handsome, his features fine. He was thin and just under six feet.

His house was white clapboard, well painted and in good condition, though a very plain exterior without shutters—a working-class house built in the Twenties. It was furnished nicely with older furniture, not antiques, but solid pine bureaus, tables and beds in excellent shape. It was located at the extreme edge of the Main Line, south of Lancaster Pike in Paoli, pressed into a row of almost identical homes.

Steve lived on the third floor in a clutter of odd but interesting artifacts. He had a large collection of machetes from the Philippines hanging along the hall; their blades curved down the walls like creeping snakes. He had a score of hats and helmets from past ages that he had picked up from a defunct theater group. Steve had never finished college and was now working on an assembly line at a factory in Chester.

I moved in just two days after that mostly silent breakfast with my grandparents at which I had been accused of living in a "hotel." My room was on the second floor. Down the hall lived a girl who worked the cash register at a nearby convenience store. "She's a graduate of a special school for teenagers with severe emotional problems," warned Steve. Also on our floor were the common bathroom and kitchen that the three of us were to share. Both were clean and well kept but had not been remodeled for three or four decades. Only the refrigerator was new.

Becky, a divorcé, lived on the first floor in a self-contained apartment. She did not leave her rooms much and never threw out her newspapers. She had neat yellow columns of them standing in every room, and occasionally I'd see her with a decade-old Sunday paper.

My move out of my grandparent's house was so abrupt that they may have thought it vengeful. Steve's house was the first one I looked at. After visiting his available room, I gave him one month's rent and drove back to Leighsylvania where I encountered my grandparents on their way in from an early dinner at their golf club.

"I've found a room to rent and shall be moving over there tomorrow," I announced in the doorway to the sound of freezing rain. They didn't say anything that I can now recall. Perhaps they were stunned by my abruptness. I'll never know, but I actually wasn't trying to get back at them.

That evening I loaded up my car and bid farewell to Olga, Clara and the rest of the help. I planned to leave before breakfast so as to drop off my possessions at Steve's house.

Ole had stayed past the weekend to get a political science term paper written. The Kennedys were now her favorite topic, and she had recently read Arthur Schlesinger's biography of Bobby. I found her in the servants' dining room with papers and library books spread over the table.

"I guess we won't see you much around here," she sighed with a pretty but forced smile. We knew each other quite well by then. She *was* available to me physically. I probably could have pulled her to me on the deep library couch after one of our midnight chats, or maybe even slipped into her bedroom after Clyde, the seventy-year-old handyman, had made his midnight rounds turning out the lights and locking the doors. There had been times when I wanted to kiss her high cheeks and silky hair, and if I had done so perhaps my life would have begun again. But for now I couldn't get past that uniform my grandfather insisted she wear and the memory of that shabby little house in Bethlehem.

I am a Lightfoot. Somewhere down in the artesian depths of my soul, I had committed myself to marrying into the right family. There are few of we Light-foots left: my grandfather was an only child—my father has two sisters, so only my brother and I shall pass on the name.

"I'll be back," I said in an effort to cheer her up. She made a gallant but unsuccessful attempt at concealing her disappointment. "And we'll probably see each other on the Main Line." But I knew I wasn't going to make the effort. I wasn't a person who took advantage of a situation if my intentions were not fully sincere.

At midnight I stood and wished Ole a good night. She hopped up and caught my arm at the door. "Good luck," she whispered and kissed me. I smiled, thanked her awkwardly—as usual, uncomfortable showing emotion—and, with a stiff, self-consciousness walk, went to the front stairs.

CHAPTER 5

▼

Thus not only does democracy make every man forget his ancestors, but it hides his descendants and separates his contemporaries from him; it throws him back forever upon himself alone and threatens in the end to confine him entirely within the solitude of his own heart.

—*Alexis de Tocqueville*

The regicide so shocked the people that…all indeed was in doubt, all coherence gone, and a host of seekers began to populate the melancholy land of England, very much in the style of the lonely and lost souls of our own day who once gathered at Woodstock and are now joining the Jesus cults.

—*E. Digby Baltzell*

I generally worked late at Eastern States so as to arrive back at Steve Van Brugh's when he and the girl down the hall had finished in the kitchen. Several weeks passed, therefore, before he and I had a lengthy talk.

Usually Steve was downtown on Friday evenings, so he surprised me one Friday by staying home. When I came in, he was still sitting at the metal kitchen table, circa 1959, under the lifeless neon light and immediately offered to make me dinner. He cooked and I drank and we talked.

He seemed to have sensed my being the scion of some important early Phila-delphia family. It may explain why he so desperately wanted me to know exactly who *he* was.

His mother's father, so he claimed, was the fourth son of an English lord. Though his knowledge of this connection was scanty, what few stories he had never changed. It is my general belief that liars can't remember what they've told before, so their stories change. On this subject Steve's stories didn't. He often described with great delight the family seat in England as it was when he made his one visit there as a boy: a stately home of vast proportion, with sagging ceil-ings of dry rot and crumbling plaster, now very empty, most of the priceless fur-niture and art having been sold. He had found his cousins eating dinner from plastic chairs in a small kitchen—the grand dining room containing nothing save one last Gainsborough, destined soon for auction.

He so enjoyed describing the family's decadence; it made him feel his own lif-estyle was more acceptable.

Of greater interest to me was his father's lineage. Steve also claimed to be a *New York* Van Brugh, a family that had once amassed 100,000 acres along the upper Hudson River in the days of Peter Stuyvesant. The best-known member of this branch was Robert R. Van Brugh, a member of John Adams' cabinet and later a United States senator. He was also an early financier of steam travel on the Hudson.

Unfortunately, Steve had just a superficial awareness that the Van Brughs had once done great deeds, and, as such, I found his claim to be a New York Van Brugh highly suspect.

Steve had been carried away in the student movements of the late sixties and was proud of having been at a "siege" of the Pentagon in October 1967. He was also proud of having been accused of draft offenses and indicted.

"They were the days of incense and Nepalese hashish. Really exciting times that I wouldn't trade for anything," he told me. "This country had no conscience at the time. It had lost its soul; 'just a remnant of the democratic tradition was left, and it was a flag in tatters,' to quote Tom Hayden, my hero at the time, though those probably weren't his exact words.

"Atrocity stories about Vietnam were what we wanted to hear more of, and then the Cong handed it to us on a silver platter: Tet—the Vietnamese New Year....

"Every month we were being told that the U.S. was winning the war. Leaders like Humphrey were saying Vietnam was as important as Dunkirk and Valley Forge and Yorktown. Then all of a sudden you had Tet and no one from LBJ on down had any credibility whatsoever any more. Even Walter Cronkite was saying we should negotiate. What was the point of the slaughter?

"Johnson announced the big reason to party: 'I shall not seek, and will not accept, the nomination of my party for another year as your president.' And that's when I went big time on LSD.

"...my Dad and I had some real fights. We never really got it together as a family and that's why I live down here and they're still up in New York—it's a Park Avenue address. It was open season in those days for confrontation and disruption of the Protestant Establishment and all its institutions...."

"We had some of those conflicts in our family, too," I told him. "My older brother, Henry, went up to Columbia University and got involved with the occupation. 'Columbia owns slums and cooperates with the military,' he told me. The police came in and beat everyone up. Today his explanation of why the cops were so brutal is somewhat of a self-indictment: it was *class* war, the Ivy League students were spoiled rich kids and the working class cops resented them."

Steve wanted to know everything about Henry and his relationship with the family, so I obliged him through dinner.

"My brother had been on a family black list for some time and would remain on at least my grandfather's. I guess he's still there. He keeps himself there by making regular pronouncements like: 'the CIA can do nothing but commit atrocities.' He never mentions that the KGB may have an even darker record. Once he even announced: 'Washington is the real enemy in this Cold War, not Moscow.'

"My father came out against the war as early as '64. It took a long time for my grandfather to come around. Maybe he never really did.... Grayson Kirk was president of Columbia and my grandfather somehow knew him—they must have served together on a board. Anyway, Grayson came out with a statement that went something like 'the war is escalating civil disobedience to a virtue.' My grandfather began thinking that the anarchy had gone far enough, and he was sick to death of what he called the 'nihilism of the youth' and the 'nihilism' of my brother. 'This is a major assault on traditional authority that has to end,' he said. 'We all need a guiding light.'"

"Hell, I was your ultimate nihilist. Maybe I still am," responded Steve. "I went through a big drug stage about ten years ago, and then I got involved with an acting group. I was pretty good but never got a job that paid. I played every role imaginable from street bum to minister to an English lord—and I had fun. Then I met Anthony.... You know I'm gay?"

"No!" I said, startled. There was a long silence, awkward for me but not Steve. He gazed out the window at the street lamp for several minutes; his emotions had suddenly welled up, and he fought to compose himself. When he did begin talking again his voice was quiet and soft, sometimes a whisper.

"Well, I won't tell you Anthony's last name because it's a famous name here in Philadelphia." He was not uncomfortable, only sad, making what at the time I mistakenly considered a "confession." He was so totally unthreatening and pitiful that in a few minutes I was sympathetic and no longer uncomfortable, either.

"If you can believe it, Anthony is the youngest partner at probably the most prestigious law firm in Philadelphia." His eyes were now wide, and he wore a big admiring smile. "And I won't tell you the firm's name until we get to know each other a little better. He was in law school when I met him up in New York City, and I came down here to live with him in West Philadelphia.... His family never knew what he was up to. Occasionally he would have to put on a blazer and go meet them for Sunday dinner at one of the cricket clubs out in the western suburbs. Finally he finished school and got into his firm, and it didn't take too many years before he was partner. There's no question the guy's brilliant, but I think it was also family help that got him to be partner.... It was when he became partner that he drifted away. He started bringing friends to our apartment. Other gays. We'd all be in bed together. It was wild. But Anthony drifted away. It's been very hard for me.... I bought this house and moved out of West Philadelphia when I couldn't take it any longer. But Anthony occasionally comes over. I'll have him over to meet you some time."

"Okay," I whispered sympathetically. He had told his story so mournfully and gently that I couldn't turn him down. He then went on to explain a little of his gay life, about his first relationship with another male—it was in the tiny MG he had received from his parents as a sixteenth birthday present!

∗   ∗   ∗   ∗

Spring had arrived, and in the evenings and on weekends I felt the urge to make a more concerted effort to dig up friends from school days. There were not many; I was in boarding school by eighth grade, and all but a handful of classmates were from other parts of the country. I tracked down Sam Cohen, and we agreed to meet on a Saturday night at the *Paoli Local*, a bar and restaurant near the Bryn Mawr train station.

When I met him at the *Local*, he was with Philip Brooks, another classmate from boarding school. Originally from Boston, Brooks was now studying medicine in Philadelphia. Later he would go on to practice at university hospitals and teach at their adjoining medical schools.

Brooks had snubbed me back in boarding school days. He was now still wearing that DON'T TREAD ON ME scowl that had kept me at a distance in the rough-and-tumble dormitory world.

The three of us had several beers each before dinner and a few laughs talking about school days, especially about faculty members who were rumored to be gay.

"When I tell people that I attended an all-male boarding school for five years, one of their first questions concerns the homosexuality that they presume runs rampant at such a place. Do you ever get that question?" I asked.

"I've never been asked," replied Sam. Both he and Phil gave me a suspicious stare, and I regretted what I'd just said. I now knew I couldn't possibly mention Steve Van Brugh, and I suddenly realized that no one should be allowed to visit my new dwelling place. Ultimately, I never gave the address to more than my immediate family.

After several pitchers of beer our laughter grew a little too raucous and the maître d' came by to quiet us down. When dinner had been cleared, Brooks drank an entire pitcher by himself and his mood turned surly. I had seen this surliness back in school. He was an overachiever and scornful of anyone who didn't hit hard on the football field and get listed on the honor roll at least a few times each year.

"It must be nice living out at Leighsylvania," he chided.

"How do you know about Leighsylvania?" I nervously asked.

He put on an impish smile. "You know I'm the son of an Episcopal minister?…Well, your grandfather is a fund-raiser and on my way down here from Boston once Dad had me bring a package, and I delivered it to Leighsylvania…. It must be nice out there getting waited on hand and foot…. Remember Thorstein Veblen? The *leisure* class has four options: war, sports, government, or religion."

I was at fault, in Phil's mind, for being born into a wealthy family. I deserved some blame. Furthermore, inheritors are apparently condemned to lead purposeless, self-centered lives that end with alcoholism or some other drug addiction.

Money was a source of evil and little else, according to Phil. It could lead to nothing constructive. Even if one was self-made, his money was tainted because it must have been accumulated through exploitive means.

"Phil, we've had this discussion before. First, I'm not living at Leighsylvania any more. Yes, living with wealth is a challenge. But it's a challenge that can be won and there are plenty of good examples. Look at the various members of the Rockefeller family. How about the Kennedys where you're from? Inherited wealth is like anything else God-given. It's like any innate physical or intellectual ability—it can be squandered or used to its full potential to the good of the possessor and one's fellow man. We all remember Sandy Gates—apparently a genius. Whenever he gave just a little attention to a course, he aced it. So, he was never challenged. No one grabbed hold of him and pointed him in the right direction and helped him unleash his tremendous God-given talent. And, what's happened to him: in and out of jail on drug charges! You see, money isn't the only prerequisite for dereliction.... And by the way, you should know that your city of Boston seems to have historically done an excellent job of creating a wealthy class of people who know how to use their wealth constructively—look at those Brahmin names like Cabot, Lawrence, Adams, Saltonstall and lots of others."

Phil was silenced for the moment, but he had stereotyped me, and his perception would never ultimately change. I would apparently spend my life coasting and never do anything meaningful. I later caught him passing this image on to others, not directly, but through constant backhanded compliments like: "Tom must play a great game of golf; he's always had the time!"

Our conversation turned again to days at school, and we had a few more laughs. Then Phil came after me one last time: "You skipped daily chapel our entire senior year!"

"How did you know that?"

"A member of the faculty knew it. It was Mr. Peabody. By the time he found out, you had missed so many days that they probably would have had to expel you or done something else to make a point—which Peabody didn't want to have happen. So, he approached me to find out a way to get you to go. I suppose because I'm the son of an Episcopal minister. That's why I used to pull you into those debates about religion."

"Interesting...I never knew that. But I guess you weren't successful."

"No. Have you changed? Do you belong anywhere?"

"No," I said pensively. "You know, in this day and age everything is so rational that I can't seem to reconcile the Bible and the pulpit with daily life. I feel like such an alien when I'm in church. I say to myself: 'What are all these people doing on their knees? It's downright weird!'"

At this point Sam spoke up: "I agree with you in that we have learned to be so rational that it's hard to reconcile religion with what we've been taught, but there is nothing that can replace the feeling of community and sense of belonging that I get from being Jewish and going to the synagogue."

"And I have to admit that I'm very envious of that, Sam...." I was staring at the bar as I replied, and my words trailed off. Phil and Sam followed my eyes. Lea Creswell was sitting at the bar, and no one was near her.

*   *   *   *

My relationship with Lea took months to develop. She ate dessert with Sam, Phil, and myself that first evening. Sam dated her first, until his semester was through. He then left for an internship at S.G. Warburg in London. Phil stepped in briefly and unsuccessfully. Finally, at the end of June, I was given a chance.

I visited her up in New York and spent an afternoon and evening. I slept at Binney's. My visit was a success, and I asked if we could schedule a repeat performance. To my disappointment, however, I wasn't able to book a date until the end of August.

Lea led a busy life that summer—weekends in the Hamptons and three weeks straight on Nantucket. When I got on her calendar again, it was to help her with a charitable event supporting the arts that she was organizing in Manhattan. Unfortunately, the chores associated with that event were never ending, and on weekends I was used as a gopher. She had an office in a small decorative arts museum, and from there I was sent out on regular missions across the city. Our time for meaningful conversation was almost non-existent.

"How is your relationship with Lea going?" Binney asked in September.

"What relationship? There is *no* relationship."

"Would you like one?"

"Yes."

"Why don't you take her away from her charity work up to see the foliage in Vermont? You can stay with brother Henry in Manchester. Early October is the peak—it's the place to be at that time of year; there won't be anywhere else she'll want to be—unless there's an Ivy League football rivalry her friends are going to. Besides, she knows Henry through her sister Mary."

I checked out early on the second Friday of October from Eastern States Financial and drove through rush hour traffic into Manhattan. We left my car there, and Lea drove us north in her BMW. It had been hers less than two days, so she made it abundantly clear that I would not be doing any of the driving.

We arrived at Henry's just outside moonlit Manchester after midnight, and opened our doors to the sound of a stream roaring in the valley below. Wood smoke lingered over the house as contentedly as pipe tobacco. I saw him through the window: with his full unkempt beard he resembled Karl Marx. He opened his door to us not with a welcoming smile, however, but with a lonely wistful countenance. Depression was a lifelong foe.

Eight years older than myself, Henry had been divorced for three years and now lived alone. Before the divorce he and his wife had built this hilltop house of stained wood on the foundation of an old barn.

The south side of the first floor was primarily sliding glass doors framing an uplifting view of the valley below and Mount Equinox. Pasture sloped down from the house to the stream and then woods bordered by a rambling stone wall. The wall and the house foundation had been built before the Civil War when Vermont was clear of woods, and livestock roamed the rolling green hills.

Cut into the rocks deep in Henry's grove of sugar maples was a pool of clear mountain spring water, a popular spot on hot summer days for the collection of castaways deposited by the tide here when the sixties receded—urban expatriates and social crusaders whom Henry befriended. At the trail entrance, Henry's large sign read:

Absolutely NO Suits!!

My brother earned a small income from his sugar maples and the flock of sheep in the pasture. He was almost self-sufficient from the land: in the fall he canned and bottled produce from his massive garden and slaughtered a pig and some sheep. He also had a chicken house. Two stoves, for which he cut all his own wood, burned continuously through the winter.

For life's other needs he generally lived by his financial wits, supplementing whatever came in from the sheep and syrup with dollars earned from freelance jobs at magazines, a few of them national. He mostly wrote about social issues, but occasionally an article would appear on life in the country—sprinkled inevitably with quotes from Thoreau.

My father didn't endorse Henry's lifestyle but didn't try to talk him out of it, either. "Your brother hasn't lost his mooring as Grandad would have you think. But I'm not sure he's really thinking about his future, either. He lives for the moment, and in our society that can be dangerous."

Mother and Henry could not communicate. In those years she used one of a handful of refrains whenever she spoke of him: "He's got to reinvent himself," or "We all require the psychological support of some sort of authority to maintain our mental health."

Henry took pleasure in being earthy around Mother. He thought her too formal, and in his mind she was symbolic, along with Grandad, of the society that had led the country astray during the Vietnam era. With her in earshot, he would, for example, describe in vivid detail the delivery of a lamb in his barn. He couldn't resist talking about the rough underside of life in front of our mother, whose family had shielded her from it and perhaps denied its existence themselves. He peppered his language with local idioms and sometimes spoke with an adopted Vermont accent.

I recall Mother's rationalizing voice, addressed to no one in particular: "Every family I know seems to have lost at least one child to the Sixties."

My grandmother suggested that Henry was one of our "Quaker ancestors re-incarnated."

"Is it not possible," she asked, "that Henry inherited the same genes that gave our Quaker ancestors the propensity to choose plain living and simple virtues over pomp and prestige? They rejected the fashionable, as does he—he wears clothes until they're totally worn out, and he has no qualms about relying on thrift shops. He was a conscientious objector during the Vietnam war. There have been many like him in this family before, and in many respects their influence has made the country a better place."

Henry and my grandfather were, of course, virtual enemies. "It seems that your brother has a general mistrust of institutions," Grandad grumbled. "If an institution is old, it's probably bad, so he thinks. Shouldn't we wait until it's proven itself harmful before we abolish it? The passing gusts of popular passion...!

"Henry is someone who's never learned to accept authority. Tolerant irresponsibility is the doctrine he and his group preach, and excessive tolerance produces chaos; revelation replaces reason.... He's a believer in true democracy and therefore has little patience for hierarchies....

"Your generation illogically thinks that the rules our society has placed upon you are more demanding and more restricting than the less familiar ones of other cultures. You convert to an Eastern religion and, though you have to get down on your knees everyday and look to the East, or shave your head and wear a pink robe and hang out at airports collecting money, you think you're liberated....

"In your new world *freedom* must be all. I don't think you quite understand freedom.... The Founding Fathers fought for freedom, yes. But it was not alliance with anarchy. They fought because they felt the law had been broken....

"It was those years at college in the sixties that did it to Henry. You know there was a discipline problem on his campus in the sixties with all the Vietnam

War protesting? It's a college that was founded and built by Quakers, and the Quaker attitude toward authority makes them an impossible people to govern.

"That goes back to the time of William Penn. They stopped using 'Mr.' and other terms of respect. Penn took warped pleasure in wearing his hat at court, especially in the presence of King James II, whom he called, simply, 'James.'

"You know your grandmother doesn't like to hear me say it, but Penn couldn't attract any real leaders, and in fact there hasn't been much leadership coming out of Philadelphia ever since. Ben Franklin came from Boston. I have no patience with the sort of amiable anarchy that your grandmother and her Quaker friends want. Read a biography of Penn."

Henry loathed family history and considered anyone with such an interest "self-important." Family history "is good for snobs and snobs only," I recall him lecturing me the summer before his junior year. "If a society allows heredity to select its leaders, it will ultimately be governed by a class of silly, shallow, and ineffectual, if not downright incompetent, fools!"

He considered it his duty to lecture me often in my formative years. In his favorite pronouncements he rejected the legitimacy of an upper class however defined, its institutions, and all its more subtle manifestations. He warned me about Frothingham, having graduated from the same non-Quaker boarding school as I.

"Our headmaster, Frothingham, was right out of Boston's glacial age. He would have burned witches at the stake if he'd been around before 1700. It took a vote by the trustees to force him to let boys remove their ties and jackets on one hundred degree days, and I think it was a vote of Congress that finally allowed blacks into that school."

"Money in large quantities can only be bad," was another one of Henry's favorite advisements. He considered its making a zero sum game: anyone who makes a lot of it is making it at someone else's expense. Furthermore, there was no way to possess it without becoming "wasteful or degenerate." It was the primary cause of corruption, and he refused to recognize that at least some people have figured out how to spend it in ways that benefit the common good. "The problem with this country is that men are appointed or elected for plutocratic reasons rather than because they show qualities of good leadership."

*   *   *   *

The first day of Lea's and my visit to Vermont went well, as we wandered the woods, bright with the red and yellow of autumn's peak. "The hills and mountains are strawberry and lemon candy!" she exclaimed. The air was cool at night and warm by day and the sky an optimistic blue. On Sunday Lea announced that she would prepare lunch for us all, and that she and I would leave around three p.m.

Over soup and sandwiches it became apparent, however, that Henry was not going to let Lea depart without challenging her basic view of the world. A subtle friction had been building between them since the moment we arrived. I hadn't known every side of Lea at the beginning of the weekend, but by the end of lunch on the second day I was certainly making progress.

Perhaps Lea Creswell was selfish because she was the youngest in her family by a wide margin and hadn't had to compete with brothers and sisters of her age for parental affection. Surely the fact that she was so much younger than her sister Mary meant that she wasn't old enough to have been exposed to some of the altruistic winds of the Sixties. Or, perhaps her parents had made it a point to keep her at a safe distance from her questioning, radical, older sister who had been known up and down the Main Line for her involvement in anti-war activity and civil rights crusades. Mary's voice was not in the back of Lea's mind at every turn in the road as was my older brother Henry's in mine. His scratchy voice has always been one that emerges like a questioning echo at each major decision in my life.

At the core of Henry's character is a fear of vanity. Fear of vanity has been called the "core" of the Quaker ethic.

Our lunch conversation began with what I considered an unremarkable statement from Henry, one that I generally ignored because I had heard it so often before: "We are not just Europeans in this country, yet the history of the United States has been written in the interests of white Anglo-Saxon Protestants."

I was about to comment on the health of Henry's sugar maples, but Lea wouldn't let Henry's statement pass without a response, "Because this country has been shaped by British tradition and culture," she instructed.

"But, we *do* have our own destiny that's distinct from Europe's," I suggested to Lea. "You know, when American GI's went to Europe to fight in World War II, Italian Americans found they had more in common with their fellow Americans than with their Italian cousins. Irish Americans found the same thing. What I'm saying is that we have forged a unique culture that—"

"But one that includes not just the cultures of Europe," Henry interrupted. "It includes the cultures of many parts of the world. Our schools over-emphasize the European cultural heritage. They shouldn't be offering multiple European history courses when there is not a single offering in Afro-American. Furthermore, why should the Queen's English be the only one taught? African-Americans speak English a certain way; haven't they made a contribution to the language spoken in America? Did you know that there are over two thousand words used in English derived from various Native-American languages? Hispanic contributions should be recognized as well. Teaching English the way we do, and especially to children who speak another language at home, is a form of political oppression."

"Okay.... Let me tell you about one of my relatives," Lea responded. "Sara Creswell—very attractive family—she went to St. Paul's and Princeton just like her dad. Now she's married a Chinese-American. Her parents are sick about it. Her dad says: 'in the next generation our family identity will be no longer—our ethic and culture gone.' I think he's right. It's *our* ethic and culture that built this country. It's being diluted, lost, and its loss is America's loss."

"Nonsense! You don't know this country!" Henry blurted. Passions were now rising in both him and Lea. I also perceived Henry's irritation with me—I didn't seem to be joining his side.

Being so much older, Henry considered it his right to praise or scold me like a parent. A part of my superego is thus of his making, and I hear his admonitions to this day.

He had been particularly incensed by my joining a fraternity in college and continued to talk disparagingly of it for many years after graduation: "What have college fraternities contributed but snobbism and hell raising?"

The autumn I went to Europe we were both coincidentally in England at the same time. He tried to dissuade me, and visibly seethed when I wouldn't listen, from making Oxford, followed by Cambridge and then Canterbury, my primary destinations after London. England to him was not the seats of tradition and power; it was the countryside as seen from footpaths through hamlets and farmers' fields, barnyards, and cottages.

He spoke disparagingly of my entry into the business world: "First-rate minds don't go into business; the subject is too mundane. Only commonplace minds can get absorbed in commerce. The poets view it as lowly."

He was now admonishing Lea with a vigor that I considered rude and unnecessary. "There's going to be a day of reckoning for the robber barons where you work on Wall Street—sooner than later, and don't let yourself get carried down with it!"

In those days the terms Henry used to describe the world of business were more appropriate to a discussion of nineteenth-century American capitalism. "Moneylord," "money trust" and "monopoly" were frequently in his vocabulary.

The 1980s were another "Gilded Age." Grandad once sarcastically asked him if he had just read Upton Sinclair's *The Jungle*. "If you have, I hope you know how long ago it was written. I don't think the appalling conditions in the Chicago stockyards of 1906 are still the way of the food industry seventy years later. You're sounding a bit like a turn of the century Progressive."

Lea was a fighter and her voice had now become almost a shriek. "What are you talking about, Mr. Preacher? How could this country be what it is if it wasn't for Wall Street? How would this country have ever opened up the West? How would small companies have become big companies and developed products that have made life better for us all? How would the bridges, roads and schools have been built? You're not a builder! It's very easy to tear something down, much easier than creating it, than building it up in the first place. Institutions that took hundreds of years to create can be destroyed in a day. You've taken the easy way out—you've chosen the life of a critic! That's *so* easy!"

"You're a selfish little princess—go home to Daddy!" was a refrain I heard more than once from Henry over that lunch. "Get with it! Do you really think this country has a right to be treating people the way it does?"

"It takes a lot more passion to build something up than to tear it down," Lea reiterated. "Lazy people are attracted to causes that break things down; they don't have the staying power for the projects that have built this country."

"Greed's running the show now," countered Henry. "Maybe you'll learn that just having *more* is not all it's cracked up to be. Too much money undermines the good intentions that produce it. Unbridled capitalism! Plutocracy! Among your type, work is no longer good by itself—it has to achieve some personal, selfish end. Your God is yourself! I'm proud of being a heretic to what you and your friends think is the American Dream. Why don't you try *helping* some people? Do some good!"

He had become inexcusably harsh, and I attempted to calm him down but to no avail. At stake, however, I recognized a much larger issue, and one of which Lea was totally unaware: Henry's belief that he had been right and his ex-wife wrong.

Sarah and he had met in the late sixties at Columbia University where both attended summer school. Together they had worked against the Vietnam War and through much of the seventies remained nomadic. But as the decade came to a close, a streak of competitiveness surfaced in Sarah. What won peer support in the sixties and early seventies no longer counted, and she sensed the country crossing an "obvious threshold" when we entered the eighties.

Henry stopped using drugs and cut his hair, but it was too late. Sarah ultimately became romantically involved with a developer at a local ski resort. At the
time of my visit with Lea, she was apparently still in the area, betraying my
brother's values by driving a Porsche and practicing "rampant materialism," as
my father said. "My *God* the pendulum has certainly swung the other way! What
a woman of extremes!" he exclaimed. "She's totally forgotten the spiritual dimension, now. Perhaps when she's older and realizes how short life is, she'll remember again and understand it's the most important."

My brother-in-law, Danny Paulucci, sympathized with Sarah, of course,
describing the situation with a predictable comment: "Henry doesn't recognize
that marriage is economics. We don't call it the *marriage market* for nothing."

"Henry didn't change with the times," Sarah had said when the divorce was
finalized. "And besides, the modus operandi of the sixties was abnormal. It was an
artificial lifestyle created for the times—to achieve a purpose. Now that the purpose has been achieved, it's time to move on."

I had become quiet as the debate between Lea and Henry disintegrated into an
emotional brawl. Eventually, I went outside and loaded the car. When I returned,
a truce had been called, and the house was quiet.

An hour later, on the thruway south, I said to Lea: "You have to admit he's got
the greater good in mind."

"If the greater good is chaos. He's not a believer. How can you get anywhere
without being a believer?"

"What do you mean?"

"Henry's going nowhere. If we let people like him run things, we're going to
be in a mess. Sure, maybe it's all just a game, but what else is there? What else can
we believe in but *the system?*"

CHAPTER 6

▼

In America, the aristocratic element has always been feeble...and if at the present day it is not actually destroyed, it is at any rate so completely disabled, that we can scarcely assign to it any degree of influence on the course of affairs.

—*Alex de Tocqueville*

A civilization without history ceases to have identity. Without identity there is no purpose; without purpose civilization will wither.

—*Michael Kammen*

Perhaps the option of becoming a WASP is no longer as attractive as remaining a hyphenated Pole or Italian; a lot of third-generation Americans, moreover, are trying to reclaim the religious and ethnic affiliations which their fathers tried to disown a generation ago.

—*Peter Schrag*

The hallowed Philadelphia Assembly Ball is an institution founded in 1748 by fifty-nine of Philadelphia's first citizens. George Washington danced at several Assemblies, including one held specifically in his honor in 1793. The ball is not a charity event. Tickets are not costly, comparatively, because the money isn't going anywhere except to pay for the party. Those attending are prosperous, if not always wealthy. The shabby genteel are a minority. The right to attend is inherited or is won through marriage. Only a small percentage of new blood is accepted each year—generally Philadelphians of high achievement with the right contacts, or auslanders with glorious lineage, great wealth and intimacy with the right people.

It was a week before Christmas, and for once Lea and I had arrived at our plans by mutual agreement: we were off to the Assembly. Despite the weekend at Henry's that had ended disastrously, we had seen each other numerous times since, always in or around New York.

It was by now becoming painfully clear, however, that I was doing all the pursuing, yet she was making all the plans. I would generally call her in mid-week with what I thought was a great idea, and she would initially accept. A day later, to my disappointment, she would come up with something more "appropriate" that she would insist on, and we would spend the weekend being seen in the particular New York crowd of which Lea wanted so much to be a part. Maybe we would attend an exhibit opening at a museum, or a reception at a gallery, or a party in Greenwich or East Hampton.

Tonight this tug of war came to mind because for once there had been no friction, and as I put on my grandfather's white tie and tails out at Leighsylvania, I was not downhearted by the fragility of Lea's and my relationship. Besides, visions of the Bellevue-Stratford's grand ballroom decorated for this event and for Christmas, and of beautiful women—white gloves to their elbows—swaying to the uplifting magic of a Viennese waltz, quickened my pulse. I was excited to be attending and felt lucky.

*   *   *   *

Subscribers attend the Assembly, they will tell you, to have a grand time. But to a varying degree they also attend to confirm for another year that their blood is genuine. The ball is to be enjoyed, but it is also held to celebrate continuity and identity and the security such feelings provide.

"The Philadelphia Assembly is a target of criticism, even by some of those people who are members and go every year," I complained to my mother at eighteen, the first year I was eligible to attend. "Isn't it ironic that so many people who go every year are so quick to say that they don't take the Assembly *too* seriously? Do they feel guilty?"

It was the mid-seventies, and Mother had just presented me with a set of rented white tie and tails.

When Henry had become eligible eight years before, he had turned her down, and he still had yet to attend. Back then he had provoked Mother with the comment: "it's not reality." The remark did not make her happy. "It's another way you have of concealing reality," he accused her. "Your vision of the world is too sanitary; there's a rough underside you're denying. It's your Victorian heritage come back to haunt you. Here's some news for you: there's a war going on in Southeast Asia. Did you hear about it?"

The evening of my first Assembly I didn't want to make Mother unhappy again. Nevertheless, I now thoughtlessly reminded her of Henry's remarks eight years before by posing another difficult question: "Why do some of *us* suffer enough guilt to want to break down our own world?"

I hadn't meant to be challenging, but I now watched her quietly take a seat and gallantly fight back a gathering storm deep in her soul. I recall her replying calmly with a lengthy articulate lecture, one that had probably been delivered numerous times to Henry: "If some of *us* suffer guilt, then we need a broader view of this society and its history. The Assembly, Tom, is another institution on which we, who are born into it, must rely to help us determine who we are. Our families traveled across the Atlantic so long ago as immigrants that much of the Northern European tradition and ritual of our ancestors has long been forgotten, and we must now rely on what has been invented here, in America. These days people who descend from more recently arrived ethnic groups—Italian, Irish, Polish, Greek—and who have achieved middle class status, are allowed to exhibit open pride in their heritage without condemnation. But the collective memory of the cultures of *our* origin is buried by three hundred years of life in America. We aren't removed from our roots by just fifty years. Aren't *we* also entitled to celebrate a sense of self? There shouldn't be any criticism of our possessing a nostalgic appreciation of the lost traditions of *our* ancestors, either."

"And Mother, to go along with what you're saying, certain Mexican holidays are as well celebrated in Texas as they are south of the border."

"Yes. And everyone of Irish descent these days seems to celebrate their heritage whenever possible. Through such celebrations Mexican-Americans, Irish-Americans, all hyphenated Americans, reaffirm pride in their identities. Why can't white Anglo-Saxon Protestants celebrate their sense of self without criticism?"

"But is it a worthy self that we choose to celebrate?" I asked, expecting her to reassure me that it was. Certainly I was in need of reassurance after all the guilt-inspiring chapel sermons of William Frothingham. "Is it the case that we know when to wear white tie and tails but have forgotten our responsibilities?" I could have stood in for Frothingham at chapel with words like that.

"Our critics make us ask such questions," she impatiently answered, taken aback by my youthful seriousness but cognizant of the times through which the nation had just passed. "A disproportionate share of wealth and power *does* reside with us, and with that *do* come certain responsibilities. Yes, it's called noblesse oblige. We as a group have a long history of revering our wealth as an instrument with which to uphold and maintain virtue. And as such, we should be honored for our contributions, and such institutions as the Assembly should be respected. Democracy should not be predatory, and we should not be its victims. There *is* plenty of guilt in the old families. Too much."

I sorted through memories of this and similar conversations that night six years later in the early eighties as I dressed at Leighsylvania, putting on my grandfather's white tie and tailcoat. My grandfather had bought it in 1909 for his first Assembly. Standing in the mirror, I fantasized for a moment about the lavish parties at which it must have been present, and the elegant women who must have waltzed before it, placing a delicate gloved hand upon its shoulder.

I went to the closet for my overcoat. It wasn't gray herringbone or camel hair; it was just a cotton raincoat. I didn't have the money for something better, and, besides, walking into Eastern States Financial in camel hair would have had Terry Dagavarian on the phone immediately to Ella Callobi in the North Philadelphia office.

I peeked out the door of my room to confirm that all was quiet and no one around. Ole was out from Bryn Mawr for the weekend, but I was making every effort to avoid her. My grandparents had been driven down to the Philadelphia Club for an early dinner, telling me they felt too old for the Assembly.

I walked cautiously down the hall and gently but quickly down the front stairs. I got out to my car, however, and found I had forgotten my keys! When I went back to the house, the door swung open mysteriously before me. "Good evening Count!" I heard Ole say with a snicker. "Did you forget your blood?"

"I forgot my keys," I said sheepishly.

"Olga has your meal prepared in a silver chalice! Do you want your blood piping hot or the temperature of vichyssoise?"

"I think I left them in the bathroom." I moved passed her and ran quickly up the stairs. As I rummaged through my clothes, I felt my back wet with sweat but not from exertion; I had been caught and was embarrassed. I had selfishly done something that in good conscience I should not have done. I could have very easily picked up the tails in the middle of the week and not gotten dressed here.

I paused at the top of the stairs, searching for a humorous line to throw at Ole on my way out the door—"I like clots more than potatoes floating in my soup," I whispered aloud as I descended the stairs. But when I got to the door, she was not to be found. I jogged to my car, started it, and sped down the driveway.

*　　　*　　　*　　　*

I was to pick up Lea Creswell at her parents' house down the Main Line and continue into the city for dinner at an exclusive woman's club. My grandmother had once been this club's president, and I had often been her guest there. The Creswells had been founding members at the turn of the century.

Lea's parents lived in a 1908 Georgian manor house designed by Horace Trumbauer, architect of many Newport mansions. A maid, Ilene, greeted me at the door. The house smelled warm with turkey, but even turkey couldn't hide the ever-present smell of dogs. Ilene showed me into a small library to pay my respects to Lea's parents who had already begun their cocktails.

They were older than my own parents—he well into his seventies and she in her mid-sixties. She had given birth to Lea at age forty-two. The library was full of leather bound books to the ceiling. I turned down Ilene's offer to fetch me a whiskey.

"Tell us about your grandparents," requested Mrs. Creswell warmly. She was sitting beneath an engraving of her ancestor, the Presbyterian clergyman John Witherspoon. "Is your grandfather still involved with those southern charities?"

"Yes, he is involved with a bunch of things down in Virginia," I replied enthusiastically. "He's on two university boards and an assortment of historical and charitable institutions and spends a fair amount of time down there."

"Isn't it amazing that someone over eighty can do all that?"

"Well, he does have his driver."

"He's been involved with Mount Vernon. He's been involved with the Society of Lees of Virginia, and Stratford. He's a mover and a shaker at over eighty. He's always traveled so quickly; my husband could never keep up!"

Mr. Creswell, recently returned from a trip to Scotland and eccentrically dressed all in tweed—jacket, plus fours and cap—finally broke his contemplative silence: "Dear! Tom's grandfather and I have always gotten along well. What *are* you saying?"

"Well, I'm not demeaning you, dear, I'm just saying you are two different people. You savor the moment; he lives for future accomplishments. You're a poet of life and an artist. He isn't. But, Tom, your grand*mother* and Mr. Creswell are cut from the same cloth—you know they're both Old Philadelphia Quaker. My family, in contrast, came to Boston with the Winthrop fleet in sixteen—"

She cut herself off for another taste of Scotch and abruptly changed the subject: "Now tell us, Tom, about your older brother, Henry. I never heard about your weekend up there with Lea last October. Did you know your brother knew Lea's sister, Mary, long ago?"

"Yes, Mrs. Creswell, Mary was down at the University of Virginia and Henry got a graduate degree there."

"That's right, the University of Virginia. First Mary announced one Christmas vacation, back from boarding school, that she wanted to attend a land grant college—'free from the snobbish traditions of the East and not an outpost of the Old World—a place full-blooded American,' she told us. Then, when she came back for spring break, she wanted to attend the University of Virginia so as to become, I quote, a 'Jeffersonian.' Now, what do you think of all that for a sixteen year old? Nuts!"

A defensive Mr. Creswell came to Mary's rescue: "Yes, it was a bit idealistic, but you know at the time she was into toleration and equality and so on, nothing bad, in fact, lots of good."

"Tolerant but irresponsible! And she became a democrat down there," spoke Mrs. Creswell condescendingly from the lip of her glass. She munched on an ice cube.

"Well, democrats have a lot of heart," sighed Mr. Creswell.

"And no intellect!"

"Now come, come, let's not get into this again…. You don't need another drink, either. You asked Tom about his brother. Tom, where is he now?"

Ilene was presenting Mrs. Creswell with fresh drink off a small silver tray. I caught the inscription:

Devon Horse Show 1939
Working Hunters
Won by Leighsylvania
Charing Cross
Mrs. Cadwalader Creswell

"Did you ride a horse from my grandparents' stables?" I asked excitedly.

"Yes, Charing Cross. Read this platter. But while we're on it, what about your brother?"

"He's living in Vermont. A very contemporary house of stained wood. He's got a beautiful spot on a hill."

"Sounds ideal," said Mr. Creswell, gazing out the window in a dream.

"For we must consider that we shall be a city on a hill. The eyes of all people are upon us…." Mrs. Creswell cracked another ice cube in her teeth. "Yes, that does sound pleasant, but what *is* there to do up there, I mean professionally?"

"Well, my brother raises sheep, and he has a few causes that—"

"He and Mary are both crusaders," interrupted Mr. Creswell enthusiastically. "You know she works for the American Friends Service Committee these days. They won the Nobel Peace Prize in 1947. They've done good things all over the world."

"Mr. Creswell is a seventy-year old hippie. He would have made a great revolutionary. Why didn't you go to Moscow with John Reed in 1917, dear?" She then turned to me: "Mr. Creswell never liked authority; it's in his blood to avoid it."

"Mrs. Creswell is the daughter of a State Department official and college president, so she has a certain urge that I've never had," he responded.

"Mr. Creswell has an ancient lineage—Quaker. But they didn't do anything but mind their own business and follow their own inner light.... *the rector's sermons had first repelled her, and she had expressed a desire for a more inward light.*"

"We did have a novelist," he pleaded, and waved off Ilene whom he could see coming down the hall with a fresh Scotch for Mrs. Creswell.

"Yes, you did have a novelist—Charles Brockton Brown. America's first, so you say."

Lea came floating into the library in a red gown, strapless and becoming. I couldn't keep my eyes off her shoulders; she managed to maintain a slight tan even in winter.

"It was great talking to you Tom, and come by whenever Lea's in town," urged Mr. Creswell as he gave his daughter a kiss. We said goodnight to the Creswells and, leaving them in the library, walked out to the front coat closet.

"Where's your camel hair?" asked Lea.

"This is what I'm wearing tonight."

"Just a raincoat? Well, at least it's not a black polyester raincoat. *Then* you would be in serious trouble. Help me...it's mink."

"I can't afford a camel hair at this point in my life."

"I *can't* believe you would openly confess to that!...*Money pads the edges of things and God help those that have none....* Your car's in.... Let's take my car. You can handle my BMW? It's not too lively for you, is it?"

"It'll get me going," I said, trying to stay calm and not appear irritated. I opened the front door and followed her outside. We passed my car on the way to hers.

"When are you going to get rid of that little granny station wagon you drive? You know it's really not doing anything for your image."

"What should my image be?"

"You say you're in finance, although as I've told you before it's not the type of finance I know up on Wall Street. Anyway, if you're in finance you need a BMW. And get a loan from Eastern States Financial and buy yourself a camel hair coat. You don't want to be like the type of people I bet you work with who wear short sleeve Dacron shirts with nerd packs. *They* probably wear leather overcoats. Leather is for shoes and belts only. *You* need to look like you just left your yacht!"

I closed an ice-encrusted door and jerked the car out the driveway, trying to get used to the incredible pick-up. My Vega station wagon had more than 90,000 miles and wouldn't go over sixty.

"You know I do find your parents interesting," I said thoughtfully after a several minutes of silence.

"Argue, argue, argue. They've argued all my life but somehow have been together forty years. It's getting worse. The older Mom gets, the more alcoholic and outspoken she becomes."

"There's lots of history in your family."

"What's that, the twenty-fourth time you've reminded me? I admit I don't know it as well as I should. But I know we're special people because of it."

"What do you mean?"

"Well, why do you think? Why are the Creswells in all the right clubs, and why are we going to the Assembly tonight?"

"Why *don't* you know your family history?"

"Dad doesn't know it either, even though he's got lots of it. Mom knows it and uses it to preach to us—it's supposed to be where we look for our purpose in life. She's pushy that way, and so it's been a turn off. Besides, who cares? Why do I need to know it?"

"So you'll appreciate what you have and won't take it for granted. So you'll know how to live your life. If we forget our history, this country will be more susceptible to demagoguery—to passing gusts of popular passion. That can be dangerous. Without knowing our history we'll more readily tamper with what shouldn't be tampered with."

"Give me a break, Tom. Are you saying I should be a Pilgrim and go land on Plymouth Rock? I celebrate Thanksgiving, isn't that enough? Maybe I should dress up like the Quaker Oats Quaker. You and your history. What's with you? People know who the Creswells are, and I know what I want from life!"

We drove in silence for several long miles to the expressway, Lea impatient with me once again. The driving was slow because of ice, and the delay, along with Lea's mood, gave rise to irritation of my own.

We were soon in a tug of war, initiated by me, over Lea's remaining in New York during the previous weekend. She had stayed up there to attend another formal gala and hadn't invited me.

"It was about $200 a ticket," she argued defensively.

"Well, at least you might have asked," I sighed. I was not in a position to attend such events regularly but could afford one on occasion. Lea was earning on Wall Street probably four times my salary, and I now regretted that I had been so honest with her about my own finances.

As I was pleading my case about being included in New York, a rusty station wagon came up too fast from behind. Out of control, it smashed the left fender of the car in front of us and sent it to the shoulder. I frantically pumped my breaks, turned onto the shoulder, and pulled up behind the damaged car. Meanwhile, the reckless driver in the station wagon miraculously regained control but kept going.

My heart was pounding and my body weak. Lea was motionless and silent. I became nauseous. Nevertheless, after a minute I felt just strong enough to open the door and get out.

"Where are you going? We don't have time!" screamed Lea above the loud traffic coming in through my open door. Apparently *she* hadn't been unnerved.

"They may need some help up there!" Just then a police car pulled onto the shoulder down the highway and began backing up toward us.

"Look, the police are here. These Ukrainians don't need us, and I don't want to be accused of causing an accident! Let's get out of here!"

"You're trying to be funny at a time like this? You're crazy!" I walked to the damaged car. The officer was already leaning through the open rear door, and I heard a sad moan from a hurt passenger inside. I gave my name and telephone number and described what I had seen. Apparently the officer had been a witness as well, and the guilty party was being chased by police up ahead. I probably wouldn't be contacted.

Just then Lea's black BMW began maneuvering to get back on the road. "Let's go!" she yelled from behind the wheel.

I got in, exclaiming: "You are so selfish! Look, those people may have needed help!"

"I saw the police car sitting on the entrance ramp we passed just as the whole thing was happening."

"Maybe so, but look, you can't just keep going. You were trying to be funny by calling them *Ukrainians*? This isn't time for a joke!"

"We are so late!" she snapped firmly. We drove in silence all the way to the club and didn't speak again until I took her coat in the lobby. When I came back from checking it, she had disappeared, so I went to the bar. I asked for whiskey on the rocks and finally began settling down.

For a long time I stood against the wall at the end of the bar feeling depressed, hearing over and over that sorry moan from the victim in the car. I gazed at the crowd and saw a number of familiar faces, but lacked the energy to mingle.

Across the room, with drink and cigarette in hand, was my first cousin Appleton Crawford. Apple was about five and a half feet tall and overweight. He was proud that he had never done a mile in less than fifteen minutes. His hair was black and slicked straight back without a part. His skin was pale and his jaw unobtrusive, making his face resemble a rodent with a twitching nose. Nevertheless, women thought him handsome—they liked his eyes. Or perhaps it was his charm: when he confronted a pretty woman, he was more gentlemanly and witty than any potential competitor.

Robert Appleton Crawford had first been called "Apple" in second or third grade. The name had followed him to his New England boarding school where, sometime during his five years there, he simply stopped introducing himself as "Rob." These days he seemed to encourage "Apple." It may be that people protected by money and exclusive society, exposed only to people like themselves, can get away with what other segments of the population consider silly and demeaning nicknames. Street fighters, such people are not. Thus Apple encouraged the use of this nickname because it gave his image just a little more authenticity.

He was forever dressed in expensive clothing and drove well-polished cars of a foreign make. He now lived as a bachelor in a two-centuries-old, Society Hill, brick townhouse (though only his family knew that he was not the owner), and, at age twenty-nine, took most of his meals at the Rittenhouse Squash Club. He owned a seat on the Philadelphia Stock Exchange where he spent his days.

After a few drinks Apple was apt to make such comments as, "I'm overbearing, rude and inconsiderate of people who have vinyl floors in their living rooms. Alarm clocks and TV sets in living rooms are just as bad. I was born with the privilege of looking down on these lesser beings!"

When he made such comments his crowd of friends was entertained and wanted more. This perverse sense of humor regularly made him the center of attention. He liked telling people to "go home." I once heard him tell a Jew to "go home to Israel," and another time an Italian to "go home to Sicily! You haven't yet learned to take a daily shower!"

"Life *is* unfair," he said. "Let's face it: some of us *are* privileged by birth and some are *not*. There isn't pure meritocracy in this country, thank God! You're either born a gentleman or you're not."

To further confirm in the minds of others an aristocratic authenticity, he encouraged an air of decadence in himself and those around him. In his mid-twenties he had hosted what he referred to, in a specially printed five page program, as "Demolition Derby at Leighsylvania." He and at least ten friends bought dilapidated but operational cars for a few hundred dollars each. They had then raced them before a large crowd near the stables at Leighsylvania. At the time my grandparents were in London. It was an all-day event of reckless driving, loud music, and heavy drinking, at the end of which the crew from a junkyard came out and hauled away the battered vehicles. This event added considerably to his prestige but converted a fine horse pasture to mud.

Apple and my grandfather were, needless to say, generally at odds. "He's living way beyond his means," Grandad often complained. "I hope it's nothing more than a hedonistic fling. What happened to thrift and sobriety? Why not a little time for family and the community? There comes a day when we all must give up a little something for higher ideals. I don't think the Lord put us here for self-gratification only. Apple would be content to just smoke cigars in one of his clubs all day. Of course, he might stay out of trouble that way."

Apple was, indeed, a clubman. He belonged to more than he could afford. "He takes refuge in clubs," Danny Paulucci explained. "When he's in his clubs he feels above the competition, above the anxious middle class."

"We all need a sense of belonging and recognition," I offered in Apple's defense.

"Yes, because you feel a stranger to the rough and tumble marketplace. You feel incompetent out there against people with street smarts. You and Apple need the psychological boost that comes from sitting in a grand clubhouse designed by McKim, Meade and White, under massive Singer Sargent portraits, in those deep red leather couches, with a Jeeves-type stopping by regularly with another cucumber sandwich on a silver platter. It gives you the feeling that you are a *some-body*. Outside, the masses toil and you can feel superior without having wrestled in the muck.... It's obvious that Apple is suffering from some deep insecurities. His friends suffer the same way. Its roots go back a long time, well before I began knowing him. There's a missing stone in the foundation, and the house is crum-bling. The fact that he flunked out of college—never got a degree—still haunts him. But that's only part of the problem. I've got plenty of contacts on the exchange who say he's doing horribly. He's in water too deep, and he's going down. He's grabbing at WASP ritual to save his drowning ego. No one is supposed to know that his Dad bought him that seat."

Apple was coming toward the bar now and gave me an enthusiastic smile. "Tom, you're living in the area, and I haven't seen you in months! Get out of the house occasionally! Collecting bad loans can't take all your time, dear boy." He waved at the bartender.

Until that moment I had been naive enough to think he didn't know exactly how I was employed. Whenever I was dispatched by Eastern States Financial to pick up loan payments near center city Philadelphia, I was on a sharp lookout for Apple—I didn't want him seeing me knocking on the door of a dilapidated residence or coming out of a rundown apartment building and asking what I was doing. I was naturally afraid of what his perverse wit would do with my job description.

On one of these jaunts I *had* seen him—coming out of a clothing store in mid-morning. From the sidewalk I jumped down the outside stairwell to the basement of a restaurant. Fresh produce was being delivered down the same steps. A husky Italian, middle-aged, pulled a gun from under his protruding stomach. Fortunately, Apple was nowhere to be seen when, in perhaps less than a second, I was back on the street again.

"I've just returned from Gieves and Hawkes," Apple said as he was handed his drink. "A *crime* to be moneyed without style, isn't it?"

"Gieves and Hawkes? Are they friends from boarding school?" I asked.

"Not from school days, dear boy," he said as he slurped his drink. "They're Londoners. No. 1 Saville Row. The best tailors on the street."

"Oh."

"Maybe the most pleasurable experience of my twenty-nine years. First, they asked questions about my lifestyle, and what role the suit would play in my wardrobe. Meanwhile, someone is taking notes so they'll know exactly what I'll want in the future. I settled on a silk and wool mix. Six suits from Gieves and Hawkes will last twenty years if worn in rotation. That's what they'll be shipping me: six. God, I hope the market will be up when the bill comes in!" He laughed and his nose twitched like Mole's in *The Wind and the Willows*.

"I saw some of those stores when I was over in London. I remember that shop that sold nothing but hats on—"

"St. James Street. Locke & Co., No. 6 St. James Street! Founded in 1676 and still owned by the same family. Made Wellington his hats and invented the bowler! I bought a bowler from them this last visit. Haven't worn it yet."

"When do people wear bowlers these days?"

"I plan to wear mine riding…. There's a sight to behold: Lea Creswell!"

"Hello Apple! Welcome back."

"Thank you, Lea."

"When are you coming to visit me in New York again? Aren't you planning to visit Mr. Belisle soon?"

"Who's Mr. Belisle?" I asked, a little surprised by how well Lea seemed to know what Apple was up to.

"Mr. Belisle is Apple's portrait painter."

"Yes, I'm having my portrait painted! It's being done by an artist who doesn't normally do portraits of living people. He usually does scenes of eighteenth-century battles—Hamilton on the ramparts at Yorktown, Horatio Gates at Saratoga. Hussars and dragoons. I've gotten to know him well, and someday I think his work is really going to take off. So it's not going to be one of those sterile, lifeless portraits you see in board rooms—it'll be a work of excitement, of art in its own right."

"And you'll be buying a piece of immortality, so you say," added Lea. I thought she was being facetious and began to laugh, but when I turned toward her she was very serious.

"I see Binney and Dan…. Hello Danny!" called Apple. They both saw us and came our way.

"Fully invested at the end of the day, Apple? Could you believe the volume?" Danny was excited. "Hello Lea! Hello Tom!"

Binney had been caught by an old friend, vaguely familiar to me, and hadn't made it all the way over.

"Who cares about volume?" scolded Lea. "Danny, there's no money to be made following technicians. Look at the fundamentals."

"You're still trying to get through the first chapter of Benjamin Graham, Lea. What do *you* know?" mocked Apple with a large grin. "DEC another new high! IBM! Could you believe?"

The talk was of Wall Street and full of investment jargon that I knew nothing about. I felt lost and alone, and Lea seemed to have forgotten my existence altogether as I quietly slid away. I moved slowly in a zigzag through a crowd of elegant full gowns and bare shoulders. So much sex appeal. What an attractive group of people. And who couldn't look splendid in white tie and tails? I leaned against a large white column in the middle of the floor, contemplating the scene for several minutes: this *is* my crowd, and I want to be a part of it!

"You're looking just like Nathan Rothschild against his pillar at the London exchange!" exclaimed Apple. "Have you gotten the news on Waterloo, and would you mind sharing it?"

Where had he come from?

"It's time for dinner, Tom. Hello dear," said Binney as she gave me a kiss. "If you hadn't come so late there would be plenty of time to wander around in a daze. Now, come along. We're all sitting together...." The crowd, and us with it, began filing into the next room.

"You know the story of Nathan Rothschild?" asked Apple as we moved forward. Lea was listening intently. Binney and Danny had tuned out. "I took a tour of the London exchange when I was over buying my suits. There was once a certain column he always leaned against—a conspicuous place that the whole exchange could see. He got word by carrier pigeon that Waterloo was a victory but told his people to sell. The market saw Rothschild selling, and assumed that he'd learned before them the news that Waterloo was a loss. So when the whole market had collapsed, the Rothschild people bought like mad! The rest is history, Lea."

She was fascinated. He led her to a table and put her next to himself. I followed, feeling like a conspicuously forgotten parental chaperon, and took the remaining seat next to her. Binney was beside me, and Danny completed the circle. Someone else asked permission to take the sixth chair and pulled it away.

After buttering a roll, Danny wanted some fun: "If you need a loan, Apple, ask Tom!"

"Why do you always insist you're in finance, Tom?" asked Binney.

"It's a form of finance," Danny said with a wink. "Just don't forget to pay up, Apple, or you'll get harassing phone calls, or maybe a gorilla will come pounding on your door!"

"Tom," commanded Lea, "tell us why you're never quite clear about exactly who you're lending money to. We all know, and you know we know. You're not being honest with yourself."

"Is it lending or loan sharking?" asked Danny with an impish smile.

"Danny, hey! Lay off, he *is* my brother," Binney interrupted. Lea and I seldom discussed my job. I avoided the subject. When forced I generally told a few white lies, never openly admitting what I was up to. Danny seemed to know exactly what I was doing at Eastern States without having ever heard it from me.

After Binney cut him off, Danny settled down and dinner became enjoyable, except that Apple was charming Lea. I said little if anything to her the entire meal.

Around ten o'clock we were in the receiving line winding down the beautifully ornate, spiral stairwell to the Bellevue-Stratford ballroom.

"What about the cyclicals?" asked Lea.

"This bull isn't going to stop," muttered Danny.

"Ride the wild bull!" spoke up Apple. He then let out a cowboy yell that turned numerous heads in our direction. Once again talk was of Wall Street, and I was forced to stand the ten minutes in embarrassed silence.

I pulled on my white gloves as we approached the front of the line, and when we got there I bowed to the patronesses as they curtsied back. We then entered the massive ballroom alive with the music of the Myer Davis orchestra playing Johann Strauss, and walked out among the several hundred elegant couples waltzing.

It was a beautiful sight, and in a few moments Lea was finally in my arms. She remained there, thankfully, for most of the evening.

Exhaustion took us at four a.m., and I helped her to the elevator and a room reserved in my name, high above the city and safe from my predators. I was sadly aware, however, and had been so even before picking her up at her parents' Trumbauer manor house, that this would be our last night together.

∗   ∗   ∗   ∗

The following evening Eastern States Financial Services held its Christmas party. It took place in Northeast Philadelphia off the Roosevelt Boulevard, a convenient location for all the ESFS offices in the metropolitan area, at *Nero's*, a large, slightly seedy bar and restaurant with a large dance floor. The waiters spoke with mock Italian accents that seemed to disappear whenever business became a bit hectic.

I arrived by myself and a little late as I had spent most of the afternoon sleeping at Steve Van Brugh's, and when I had woken up had begun reading Livy, *The Early History of Rome*, which had left me oblivious to the time. I pulled into the lot in my Vega station wagon and parked next to Terry Dagavarian. She had just arrived as well, and as soon as my ignition was off I hurried round to help her out of her car.

Just as I got to her door, however, I heard Robert DeMille, down for the evening, snap over my shoulder, "that won't be necessary, I've got it!" Perhaps his aggressiveness confirmed the rumor: he and Terry were quietly seeing each other. Or, perhaps my good manners made him insecure about his own. Maybe the tone of his voice and his body language were saying: "Don't put us down over here in *our* territory! Save your manners for the Main Line!"

"He's just trying to be nice," spoke up Terry.

"I know...O.K., I'm sorry Tom." To save the situation he attempted some humor but without success: "Tom, is that your unassuming car? I thought they drove only foreign cars over there where you're from." He coupled this with a big smile and a chuckle. "Oh! But then I guess *old* money comes in old cars and old clothes, as they say, right?...You all set, babe?"

I followed them into *Nero's*. Inside, the room was vibrating disco through a hot and sticky orange light. One wall was a mural of ancient Rome: Romans with togas down to their waists fondling scantily clad women from all ends of the Empire. Why, in some circles, is the *orgy* assumed to be Rome's only contribution to mankind?

"Merry Christmas, Tom!" Rudy Russo extended his hand in a warm welcome.

"Merry Christmas, Rudy. How's it going up there in the Main Line office?"

"We're lending lots of money. How about Chester?"

"It's working out well. We should have a good year." We discussed business for several minutes, then Terry came by with an empty glass.

"Hello again, Mr. Main Line!" She was never without gum.

"Who are you talking to, Tom or myself?" Rudy asked.

"Tom. Sorry Rudy. You only work there. I mean, Rudy, do you and I really look like Mr. and Mrs. Cricket Club?" She turned to me: "How are you, pretty face? Looking for a one night stand?" Her voice was a sexy whisper, and she rubbed her cheek on my shoulder with a giggle. "I think we've got to do something about this boy's virginity."

It was all in fun, and I took it with a smile, but once she was on me verbally, she never let go. I hadn't learned how to shut her up, and it was not yet clear to me that such people could do damage to one's career at Eastern States. Management simply assumed that if you allowed yourself to be humiliated, you were incapable of commanding respect and couldn't be left in charge—you were a joke. Certainly this was Robert DeMille's impression: that I wasn't to be taken seriously as a long-term management prospect.

"Tom, I'm glad Terry found you." It was the voice of DeMille from behind my back. "It's good for Tom to get loosened up. Don't you think he's a little stiff?"

Unfortunately, the mere suggestion of my being stiff froze me up even more. I had been relaxed with Rudy, then was made a little self-conscious by Terry; now I was totally intimidated. I gazed down at DeMille's heavy dark eyebrows—

brows that Lea would have snobbishly called "Ukrainian." It bothered me whenever she used that descriptor, but tonight I hated those brows!

"Tom, I've been meaning to ask you, there's a youth program we're supporting, and you, of all people, can afford to give it a little money during this Christmas holiday. How about it? Can we count on you for this Christmas season?"

This wasn't the first time DeMille had asked me for money; he assumed, of course, that I had lots of it to give away. I *had* given before, but it never seemed to be enough.

"I'll do what I can," I moaned.

"You haven't squandered the family fortune, have you? I mean you *are* working for Eastern States Financial Services, so you *must* have squandered something!" Both Rudy and Terry were now on the threshold of laughter. "Connections? Education? Did you squander a *private* school education? What exactly *did* you do over on the other side of the tracks so that they threw you to us?"

"All right DeMille, just 'cause you secretly want to live in a big house on the Main Line," exclaimed Terry. "You're going a bit far—ease off."

"O.K. All in jest Tom. Hey! But Tom, don't forget about the youth program—you'll get the stuff in the mail." He yanked my tie and was off.

I was obviously looking distraught because Terry was suddenly supportive. "Tom, don't take him so seriously! He doesn't mean any harm. Get rid of that private-schoolboy sensitive disposition you've got and you'll do fine."

She and I joined Rudy at the bar, and when the dancing began, the evening got better for me. As usual I had too much to drink and several times almost fell asleep at the wheel on my way home.

*   *   *   *

The following morning, Monday, I was in the office in time to help Sue Albertini make coffee. Sue and I had a close friendship, though limited of course to office hours. She fell in with my dry humor, and when we passed in the hall we usually had a few laughs.

"I stopped in here on my way home last night and guess what I walked into?" she asked in a whisper and with an impish smile.

"What?" I whispered back excitedly.

"Robert DeMille in with Ella Colobi from the Northeast Branch…in the woman's room…on the bed they've got in there. She's living down here now. I think he took Terry home and then came over here with Ella before dropping her off."

"DeMille? I thought he and Terry were an item? How do you know?"

"I just told you. I stopped in here after the party last night to help myself to some office supplies for my kids to take to school. I opened the door to the women's room and there they were, in all their natural beauty!"

"I thought DeMille was after Terry."

"DeMille is slime! Hey, Thomas *naiveté* Lightfoot, those things happen even up in your neck of the woods. Up on the Main Line! Don't kid yourself, just because *you* don't wallow in filth." She chuckled, punched me on the arm, and walked out.

The office was filling, and I wandered out to the front room with a full cup of coffee. My desk was in the middle of a cluster of ten identical desks. The hot coffee splashed over my tongue and burned it as I sat down. Just then Dom Regula opened the door to his office behind me.

Dom, as regional manager, sat in a large, glass-enclosed office in the back of the room. His desk was up on a platform so he could see his "grunts," as we called ourselves. Dom was an ex-Marine and his operation was well disciplined; there wasn't any dallying, and some of us thought it a sweatshop.

"Tom, I've got to send you out on the *chase* today," he said as he placed the file folder of a delinquent client on my desk. The task wasn't worthy of the word, but by describing it as such perhaps some of us got through the day just a little easier.

"You've written the dates on which you've telephoned this bitch, and she hasn't sent a dime in five months. Why don't you head over there around five this afternoon and maybe catch her on her way home from work?...Probably won't be like fox hunting on the Main Line!"

A typically clumsy and unsuccessful attempt at humor from Dom. Nevertheless, we both somehow got along, and I knew he respected me for my intellect.

I spent the day trying to stay awake while fumbling through account records—still recovering from too much alcohol the previous night. Claiming that I would need the remaining light to find my way to 410 Barrow Avenue, I checked out an hour earlier than instructed.

*   *   *   *

I soon discovered that my excuse was valid: although the address was no more than half an hour from the office, I didn't find Barrow Avenue until after five. It had once been the main artery to the Northwest from the docks at Delaware Bay. Ten years before, a ramp to the interstate had been built allowing traffic to by-pass Barrow and leave this neighborhood quiet.

Potholes spread down the avenue like scars from acne. The homes were tall, old, and run down. Elegant in their day, now they were toothless, haggard, grand dames hunched forward over the street, all but abandoned.

I drove up and down Barrow several times but couldn't find 410. Parking in front of 409, I took out my frustrations by hammering the steering wheel to the intermittent pace of the windshield wipers. I grew angrier from visions of Lea Creswell talking to Apple over the telephone. They had probably been seeing each other secretly.

Across the street a dilapidated billboard rose up from the sidewalk as high as the rooftops. All that now covered its wooden planks were the few remaining paper shreds of the last advertisement:

LEARN ENGLISH IN 14 DAYS
PHILADELPHIA LANGUAGE LABS

We pressure recent immigrants to learn our language and forget their native cultures. I felt a hint of empathy for people whose culture is not respected.

Wiping moisture from the window and gazing at the billboard in the winter drizzle, I saw a hidden door suddenly open at street level near the billboard's center, and a teenage boy walk out.

410 Barrow Avenue? I hopped out of my car, breathed in the smelly air from a nearby chemical plant, and skipped across the street thinking Dom Regula was right, this *is* a chase. I knocked on the door several times before it was finally opened by a small child.

The smell of unemptied garbage was strong. The lighting was dim. A extremely obese woman sat in a wheelchair holding court in the middle of the room. Several semi-naked children sat at her feet, and three young adults were flopped on sagging couches. The television was loud but was immediately turned down when I stepped in.

"Is this 410 Barrow Avenue?" I demanded breathlessly. The matriarch nodded her head slowly with an astonished gaze. I was excited to have found the right place; I might not return to Dom Regula empty-handed.

"I'm from Eastern States Financial Services!" I announced proudly, like I was announcing a piece of good news. "You have an outstanding balance of $1,134. We have not received payment in five months. I'm here to collect payment!"

All in the room were motionless, and the children a bit frightened. Then a child began to cry, and the young adults sat up. The children climbed into their laps.

After perhaps half a minute, the matriarch broke the silence with a deep, hoarse voice: "We'll be paying our bills, Honey. We'll be paying our bills.... Don't you be coming *back*."

An odd emphasis was on the word "back." She didn't shout it. It was spoken as an eerily quiet warning, scary enough to send a little chill down my spine.

"O.K., but please make a payment." I was surprised by how weak my voice had suddenly become. I stood, and they sat, in awkward silence. Finally I reached for the door and, keeping my eyes on the group, backed out like I had once backed away from a bear and her cubs at summer camp. (I had been on a canoe trip down the Allagash River in Maine, and we hadn't hoisted our food into the air from a tree limb the night before.)

I now ran across Barrow Avenue in a daze, narrowly missing a speeding truck, and slid into my car. My hand shook as I put the key in the ignition, and I banged the bumpers of the vehicles in front and back before getting out on the street.

By the time I reached the corner light, however, I was more relaxed and rested my head on the window. I concluded that the money Eastern States had lent to 410 Barrow Avenue was as good as gone.

But that is the last thought I can recall before what felt like a baseball smashed my ear, and glass from the window, on which I was leaning my head, exploded across my face.

I screamed. My head jerked back as my foot instinctively slammed the gas peddle to the floor, and my Vega ran the red light. On the other side of the intersection I slammed on the brakes and skidded down the wet street half a block. I was close to stopping before my foot pushed the pedal to the floor again, and I swerved into the opposite lane to avoid a car.

By the end of the second block I was under control but kept moving. My neck was feeling warm. When I wiped it, my hand came away covered with blood. In the rearview mirror the left side of my head was also covered, and my shoulder and shirtfront were becoming red. I needed an emergency room but in my frenzied state could think of no other hospital than the one in which I had been born: the Bryn Mawr Hospital up on the Main Line, at least forty-five minutes away.

A policeman stopped me for speeding on my way north and, seeing my condition, radioed an ambulance.

CHAPTER 7

▼

Nothing is more wretchedly corrupt than an aristocracy which retains its wealth when it has lost its power, and which still enjoys a vast deal of leisure after it is reduced to more vulgar pastimes.

—*Alexis de Tocqueville*

...great wealth spoils ordinary human contacts. Everybody wants something. Of the Rothschilds in their pride it was said that they had no friends, only clients. Indeed, the hurly-burly of humanity, from which great wealth insulates itself, its joys and trials, is what we're made for.

—*John Train*

"You looked like a war casualty," the nurse told me when I awoke the following morning. The bleeding had been dangerously profuse. It must have been a brick thrown at the window, or maybe my assailant had used a baseball bat.

I was back on my feet again in a few days and then spent two weeks resting and puttering around Steve Van Brugh's house. He cooked my meals and ran my errands as if I were his spouse. He drove me to Leighsylvania for the Christmas party and picked me up the next day.

During my recovery I often passed his downstairs tenant, Becky, coming in and out the front door. We had tea in the afternoons, and we finally got to know each other.

Divorced and in her early thirties, Becky was attractive but tough—tough enough to make me feel effeminate. I hadn't realized that she assumed I was gay, or why else would I be living in the same house and sharing a kitchen with Steve?

"Okay, you're not gay, but you're a pretty boy from the Main Line, so why are you living here? You don't have access to your trust fund yet?" She giggled. "Did you fall off the ship and the captain wouldn't launch a rescue mission? He didn't realize there are sharks out here and you are filet mignon!" We both laughed.

"You hang onto your newspapers," I commented. Throughout the apartment there were very neat yellow stacks several feet high, evenly spaced like the exposed stone foundations to the floor of an ancient ruin.

"The newspaper is my lifeline," she answered. "I fell off the ship myself. Steve was very nice to me. I went for a year without paying him rent. But I'm working at Lancaster Pike Bank now.... You see you've got company here—Steve puts out a net, and people like us fall in. We didn't catch the ring on the high trapeze. But what happened to the Old Boy network for you? I thought blue bloods take care of their own?"

"You must have been taught that in a sociology course," I muttered. "In novels and movies you see that happening. Maybe one hundred years ago, or perhaps today where aristocracies of sorts still exist. In the seventies a British peer committed murder and his friends took him into hiding."

"Did you commit murder? Is that why they threw you out?"

"No!" We both laughed. "In these times, in this country, it's not acknowledged: the inherent social superiority of what you call blue bloods. Maybe a few blue bloods with good imaginations think they are superior, but the rest of the country doesn't think so—they're resented. And I'm probably living here because actually blue bloods sometimes have second thoughts about their own status, too: self doubt from living in a democracy. In the world of economics the aura of old money doesn't mean anything—it doesn't guarantee that the bottom line stays healthy. In business the old money image leads to disrespect because it doesn't say *entrepreneur*."

"So, it's entrepreneurs that caused you to be banished to this halfway house," Becky giggled.

"That's one way of putting it.... Indirectly, I suppose."

*   *   *   *

In just over two weeks, with time off for a quick New Year's visit to Maine, I was back in the office. My fellow workers were outwardly very sympathetic, and

Dom cut my workload temporarily. "I want to do you a favor like I did my fellow marines wounded in the Pacific," he said on my first day back.

I thought that by this comment he just meant that, until I was fully recovered, my workload would be light. But in a few months I discovered that he meant much more: I was offered the chance to work at the home office in Paramus, New Jersey—offered an entry-level position in the company's marketing communications department.

From the first day I met him Dom seemed to have blind faith in me. I knew he respected me for my intellect, but could he have also recognized some level of poise and polish that he aspired to himself, and that he thought his other people lacked? Perhaps in his growing-up years he had looked over a hedge or a wall and seen people like me dressed in white—on broad green lawns playing croquet or tennis—and been led to the seemingly anachronistic belief that there *is* an upper class, and that its members must have a special talent or knowledge that the rest of society lacks. Why else would a certain few live in such grand style? Now Dom had gotten me a position at the ESFS home office doing something for which neither he nor I were sure I had any talent.

I reported to Paramus four months after my release from the hospital. Steve Van Brugh helped me move. I had signed a lease on a studio apartment above a garage in Upper Montclair.

Steve was sorry to see me go. He envied my acceptance of the "established order," and when we parted there were tears in his eyes. He said wistfully: "Tom, you're not confused like me. You know what you want. There are no competing claims for your soul. You've got the world figured out."

"The world figured out? Steve, you don't know what's going on inside my head!"

The day he dropped me off in Upper Montclair, he was flying to the West Coast to join a bus trip through Washington State and Oregon. "It's a gypsy bus ride, a remnant of the footloose sixties. There were many buses you could take in those days that carried hippies. This is one of the last ones. You stop in the woods and skinny dip in mountain streams, take saunas, sleep as a group inside the bus where they create one giant bed. A decade ago and before there was plenty of sex and drugs on those rides. There's less of that now. But the drivers still wear buckskin and braids. It's a great way to get close to people and relive some of the good old days. It'll be a nostalgic trip for me."

*   *   *   *

I caught on to my new job quickly and was told I had "enough creativity to go places." I spent much of my time interacting with an ad agency in Manhattan. Almost immediately I came up with a promotional idea that the agency embellished and turned into what seemed to be the most successful campaign in anyone's memory. My work finally had the potential of becoming a source of pride, and I was less evasive when people outside the company asked what I did all day.

I traveled to the agency's offices at least once a week, and thus at the end of those days found myself in the hubbub of Manhattan and more often not anxious to return to the claustrophobia and loneliness of my studio apartment in Upper Montclair. During those evenings I generally wandered into one of the preppie bars on the Upper East Side. "You're bound to run into someone you know," Binney had told me after reading a list over the phone of the "right" places to go, places she had frequented during her single years.

I encountered Lea Creswell my second night on the town. Ultimately, we couldn't help but bump into each other about once a week. We met briefly for drinks a few times, but, sure enough, by summer she was seeing Apple exclusively.

I wouldn't see anyone regularly for well over a year. Binney would occasionally call and invite me to one of the charitable events she and Danny seemed to attend every weekend. Despite my promotion, such events were still expensive, two hundred dollars a ticket or more, and the crowd was generally at least ten years older.

It wasn't just money, however, that eventually led me to turn a puzzled Binney down after the first three or four; it was the thought of spending another evening with her husband. Danny seemed to be making more money than ever on Wall Street and had gotten increasingly obnoxious with each additional million. I was more respectable in his mind with my new job, but I still wasn't "worthy." He was ever more insensitive to the feelings of others and considered anyone in need of help a failure.

When not in Manhattan, I spent most evenings at the office working late to avoid returning to an empty apartment. My superiors were pleased with my dedication, and I found the work considerably more stimulating than just lending and collecting as I had been doing in Chester, Pennsylvania. One of my bigger challenges was still, however, Robert DeMille.

DeMille worked out of the Paramus office also and only one floor below me. I often had to interact with him and the regional managers to coordinate new promotional programs. Much to my embarrassment he first introduced me to his peers with: "I'd like you to meet Tom Lightfoot from the Philadelphia Main Line!"

Understandably, I was disheartened by his personal comments. They came regularly, but I never confronted him the entire time he and I worked together. Certainly others thought I should have, and occasionally someone would pull me aside and say, "You've got to talk to DeMille. He's going to hurt your career." But I never did because I was in such sore need of attention, and a side of me wondered if in DeMille's comments there was not, perhaps, a flicker of jealousy and therefore a form of flattery.

One of his subordinate managers was Carla Gubernick. Her pockmarked face was tiny compared with the confused bundle of teased hair on top. She was overweight and bitter: her husband had abandoned her and their one child years before. By the time I knew her she was mentally very tough and couldn't say a sentence without a four-letter word.

I was a target for her bitterness, and her comments got me particularly embarrassed among my own peers in the marketing department. She picked up DeMille's lines and added a few of her own: "Didn't they teach loan collecting in prep school? Is that why you got beat up in Chester?" Or: "Tom doesn't use a Rolodex; he's got the Social Register!"

Admittedly, I took it all too seriously. But my own boss was one of nine children from a poor Italian neighborhood, and to protect my career I had to underplay my privileged background or simply lie about it. The division vice president, Tommy Carey, was proud to tell everyone he was "shanty Irish," so I couldn't let him know my secret either. I was therefore uptight most of the day and earned the nickname "Stiff."

*   *   *   *

One evening, after a long day putting together a program at the ad firm in Manhattan, I took a cab up Third Avenue to the *Squandered Fortune*, my favorite barroom on the Upper East Side. I made myself comfortable and ordered a draft. People were just getting off work and the room was starting to fill. Behind me I heard some of the usual Wall Street banter: "Incredible! The momentum from Wednesday kept it chugging, and, wow, the volume! This move is deep...."

I didn't understand Wall Street jargon and would have tuned out except that a voice was familiar: Coddie Codington from boarding school? I turned slowly and sure enough it was he.

Though small, Coddie was all muscle and had been an excellent hockey player back in school and at Yale. He was also famous on the squash court for beating every varsity player our senior year, though not actually on the team. The school faculty idolized him because he so obviously played a sport to enjoy the game—winning wasn't everything, and he applauded his opponents, never argued with a referee or went to the penalty box. Such behavior, however, encouraged facetious nicknames from his fellow students. "Arnold of Rugby" was his least favorite, after the English headmaster who preached gentlemanly conduct. His teammates called him "Hobey Baker," after the Princeton hockey legend and World War I flyer who reportedly visited the opposing team's locker room after each game. That name, because of its origin, did not stay with him through Yale, but "Arnold of Rugby" did.

Now his dark hair was slicked down with a part just off center—like a character from a Scott Fitzgerald novel, or like the seniors from the twenties whose photographs had lined the stairwells in our boarding school dormitories. Women found him attractive.

Years before he had loved a girl from one of the Maryland boarding schools. But in his senior year he complained that she "lacks direction," and they split up after graduation.

He saw me and spoke up first: "Hello! Tom, my man! Hey, I'd heard from someone you were living around here. Are you living in town?"

"Hi Coddie! No, out in Upper Montclair. How've you been?"

"Great golf club out there! I played there once last summer. I'm looking to get another invite; you don't belong, do you?"

"I wish!" We were soon talking furiously about who was doing what and where from our class.

Coddie was a specialist on the floor of the New York Stock Exchange. When his grandfather retired he had given Coddie his seat. At the time Coddie was just out of college and had never even had a summer job. His great grandfather, philanthropist and benefactor of Yale, had also once had a seat on the exchange.

Though several years later his firm was hurt by the crash of '87, Coddie survived and closed out the decade a wealthy man.

But Wall Street was not where he really wanted to be. Some months later, after he and I had had a chance to really resume our friendship, we were together again at the *Squandered Fortune* when he said: "You know I've not told you this but I'm a Democrat."

"Oh? Come on, you've got to be from an age-old family of Republicans."

"No. I kid you not. My dad and his dad were Democrats."

"Hard to believe."

"My grandfather was here on Wall Street and best friends with a bunch of Wall Street Democrats who went to Washington. 'Get to Downing Street by way of Wall Street,' so the saying goes. He knew super-WASPS like Averill Harriman and a few higher-ups in the Roosevelt era, men successful in business but for whom money was not an end in itself. They saw wealth as a means of building benevolent institutions—foundations, think tanks, and so on. They were people who took *oblige* more seriously than *noblesse*. They had time to govern and were expected to…. My goal is to be like Cy Vance. Someday I'm going to get into politics."

"Will you really be happy in politics? This is a changing country. I don't read about Old Money like your grandfather running things politically these days."

"You're right. In his generation the American identity was the WASP identity. Is it still? There's less acceptance of the over-achieving WASP as a role model. We're still represented, but it's not like it was. The average WASP is too reserved to be successful in politics. He's comfortable in his narrow world, only; the ethnic hordes make him nervous…. Maybe I won't run for election, but I'll get myself appointed to some post—undersecretary of this, ambassador to that…."

They were the lofty dreams of a recent college graduate. But years later Coddie passed his seat on the exchange to his younger brother and launched his political career as the appointed liaison between the City of New York and the 1992 Democratic National Convention.

*   *   *   *

My second meeting with Coddie was again by chance and at the *Squandered Fortune*. More than a month had lapsed, and I felt flattered when he warmly called out my name from across the room.

I joined him, and we ordered drinks and chatted a few minutes. Then he grabbed the hand of a fashionably dressed girl who had suddenly walked up beside us. "Tom, do you know Posey Ludwell?"

"Posey Ludwell of Posey Hall!" We gave each other a strong hug. "How long are you in New York? I can't believe we've run into each other! What an incredible piece of luck!"

"Anyone our age and our crowd who lives in New York is going to find themselves in this place eventually," she exclaimed.

"So, you're living here?"

Indeed, she was living here. Her mother, desiring to spend time in New York herself, and looking for a way to expose her daughter to a more sophisticated life than the Maryland tobacco country, had bought a brownstone. After college graduation Posey had moved in with two other girls about her age.

Posey was to furnish and maintain the house, charge her friends rent, and have a room available for her mother who could be counted on to arrive unexpectedly. Another room was to be kept in waiting for Mrs. Randolph.

Posey, Coddie, and I spent a few more minutes catching up before I caught on that the two of them had planned to meet here at the *Squandered Fortune* for just a quick drink. They were then continuing on to dinner at a mutual friend's apartment, a middle-aged woman who knew both families, the Codingtons and the Ludwells, and who had arranged a blind date for these two "very attractive and eligible people" soon after Posey had arrived in New York. Before they left, Posey took down my number and I hers, and Coddie told me to call him next time I was in town.

I bid them farewell and settled into a large chair at a quiet table. I switched from draft beer to straight Scotch without ice and sank warmly into fantasies of Posey in my arms.

The following day I received a surprising but exciting call at the office: "Mom's going to be here with Mrs. Randolph, not this weekend, but next, and she really wants to see you," said Posey in the same happy but pleading whine Clay often used. "How about Saturday?"

"Thanks very much! Sounds great!"

"Dinner. There will be six of us."

"Tell your mother I'm very much looking forward to seeing her after so long...."

*   *   *   *

The stately brownstone façade of the Ludwell townhouse had been wonderfully restored to its turn-of-the-century elegance. The inside was, however, a shock: where were the beautiful antiques and family heirlooms found at Posey Hall—treasures of the past that confirmed the Ludwell First Family claim? The decor was contemporary and sterile. Did Posey want to keep her parents away? Was tradition and protocol too stifling at Posey Hall?

"Posey likes change," Clay Ludwell explained years later when we had renewed our friendship. "Visit that townhouse more than once, and you'll never see the same artwork. When winter comes she sells it all and buys something else that fits her mood. Then comes spring, and she's feeling differently, so she once again sells her paintings and prints and replaces them with pictures of an earth re-awakening. Come summer and then autumn and she's done it again. She sees no need to hang onto anything. She might sell an heirloom if Dad gave her one."

We sat at dinner that night at a long yellow table built in the shape of a flattened banana. The chairs were sensually curved metal tubes. At one end sat Mrs. Ludwell; at the other, Mrs. Randolph.

The latter was, of course, the same Mrs. Randolph whom I had met years before at Posey Hall. Now she was Mrs. Ludwell's full time companion. Mr. Randolph had apparently become overly content with the life of shabby gentility. He lived alone at a subsistence level on his small farm in Southern Maryland, in the run down, two-centuries-old family mansion full of flaking portraits and cracking, splintering, antique furniture. Other than farming, his only interests were histories of Maryland and Tidewater Virginia and his personal ancestry. His belief in the illustriousness of his heritage was strong enough to allow him a semblance of pride amid a life of poverty. His wife thought otherwise.

"He held onto the stocks we inherited as if they were family heirlooms," I heard her fret. "We had coal companies; we had companies that disappeared and investments that didn't keep up with inflation. We didn't sell them to buy growth stocks. No! Mr. Randolph was as sentimentally attached to the names in our portfolio as he was to the family portraits of his colonial ancestors. You *can't* sell a family portrait. But a hundred shares in a corporation is *not* a family portrait...In Mr. Randolph's mind you can't *make* money; you can only *inherit* money. It doesn't come any other way. I don't think he's ever met an entrepreneur—certainly if he did he wouldn't know what he'd be looking at! His stock portfolio came with a money manager—I think the manager was seventy years old when I first met him thirty years ago, and he never seemed to talk about the stock market when we went to visit! He never bought or sold anything for us; it all just sat in the same decrepit companies. My husband considered him part of the family, though he wasn't, and of course in my husband's mind how can you fire a relative? Finally the man died, but we still had stock in the same worthless companies years later."

Mrs. Ludwell had now taken on Mrs. Randolph's complete financial support, and the latter saw her husband but once or twice a year, usually at Posey Hall. Mrs. Randolph's position had evolved into more than just a traveling companion: she appeared to be Mrs. Ludwell's de facto, full-time maid and secretary.

That night in Posey's New York townhouse, Mrs. Ludwell was the same lively conversationalist I had known back in Maryland. The more she had to drink, the more opinionated she became and the more anxious to arouse debate or argument. She had a childish need to convince us of the soundness of her thinking, as if a persistent inner voice were saying: "I *am* more knowledgeable and insightful than people think I am, and I *am* going to prove it!" She failed to understand that an impressive intellect does not come without hard work and perseverance.

"You see Tom," she said an hour into dinner, during which the six of us had consumed four bottles of wine, "you say New Yorkers are impressed with ostentation, that the most respected people in New York are people who throw their money around and do something outlandish. Perhaps, but in this family we don't see a need for show. It is heredity that makes the *attractive* people, *our* crowd, what they are in this town and any other across America. We have been born into a certain class and there isn't the need to set about trying to win a place for ourselves."

"Well, with all due respect, Mrs. Ludwell," I responded calmly, trying hard not to sound argumentative, "if one has to be *born* into your class—"

"*My* class? Tom, you're a member too!"

"Okay, well, if one has to be born into this class, if one cannot work hard and gain entrance, are we not in danger of arousing considerable resentment from the rest of this country? And aren't we talking about something fundamentally un-American?"

"No. Our values are the traditional ones that have built this country. We represent the aspirations of the American people. Despite what you read, we continue to run this country today. Most of the important institutions—museums, foundations, the Republican Party, the world of high finance—they are all under our thumb."

"That's one opinion," I said. "But, if it is the case, that heredity *means* something in this country, and as a result we allow our organizations, clubs and institutions to be overly exclusive, resentment might be unleashed that could ultimately bring our class down. Look what happened to the aristocracies of Europe: they got their heads chopped off or ended up getting shot and stuffed down a well like the Romanovs."

"Now, come on Tom, I don't think the unwashed masses of New York City are going to erect a guillotine in front of the Plaza and get everyone who comes out!" A burst of laughter came from Posey and her two tenants; both Mrs. Ludwell and Mrs. Randolph smiled.

"I agree," I conceded, a little red-faced, "but here's another thought: if we assume that we already have a position of high status because we have been born into it, might not that encourage laziness? And as a result, if indeed as you say there is an actual upper class in this country that does wield power, might this upper class be considerably weakened because successive generations become less competent and take their position for granted? As they say: 'shirt sleeves to shirt sleeves in three generations.' In Europe they say 'clogs to clogs.'"

"Certainly, but that's exactly the reason for schools like the one you attended: the archipelago of boarding schools that stretches across New England and down to Lawrenceville and a few points south. Little islands that maintain the best traditions of this country and turn out secure young men like yourself who are leaders because they know what this country stands for and have vision about its future."

"Oh! Mom! Come on, don't flatter the kid so much," exclaimed Posey. "He's not going to be able to walk out the front door, his head's getting so big!" More laughter from herself and her two tenants.

"Well, okay. But then you're implying by that statement that we can't just sit on what we've got. We have to protect it, watch over it; it could disappear," I said.

"Yes we must. I, for example, am involved with changing the immigration laws. That's going to be my contribution over the next few years. In 1965 we opened the door again, reversing the immigration laws of the twenties. Robert Kennedy said there would only be five thousand immigrants from the Orient, and he's been proven way off. This is an Anglo-Saxon nation. We cannot loose our homogeneity—what happens if we do? Lost identity, lack of direction, lack of productivity. I am supporting groups that want to make this danger perfectly clear."

"I was in San Antonio five years or more ago and visited the Alamo," I responded. "It seems that the people who have restored the place have really glorified the Anglo heroes of the Alamo and villainized the Mexicans. It's as if they're saying to all who visit: 'the U.S. *is* an Anglo-Saxon country.' I was listening to a Mexican-American family talk. In fact, they were getting very upset with each other: the kids couldn't figure out why their Dad was saying 'we won.' This poor father was getting emotional and raising his voice."

"So what's your point?" asked Posey.

"My point is this: don't you think it will be painful for that father to see his heritage and culture disappear in his offspring? Don't you think he will suffer from a feeling of alienation from his own family? And those kids will suffer because this society has taught them that their cultural heritage is not the right one, that it's second rate."

"Now, Tom," spoke up Mrs. Randolph, "don't take things to extremes."

"Tom, Americanization means Anglo-conformity," lectured Mrs. Ludwell.

"I'm not so sure. It seems that these days someone with an immigrant heritage—Ellis Island, that kind of stuff—is seen as more genuinely American.... But, I'm not trying to argue, and I'll get off this subject now before it happens. I'm just trying to say that, as my example from the Alamo illustrates, it can be painful if you are denied your cultural identity because it's not respected, or it's unpopular or unacceptable or whatever. It's difficult when people are telling you to think bad things about yourself."

"I guess Tom's Mexican-American, or maybe he's having trouble being a WASP!" blurted Posey to another chorus of laughter. She then changed the subject, and we talked on for another hour, shifting through countless subjects with the irregularity of the spring breeze lightly gusting through the tall Edwardian windows. Around midnight I thanked Mrs. Ludwell and bid farewell to the others. Posey walked with me to my car.

"Mom isn't here much.... I want you to come back. I can tell she likes you—you'll keep me out of trouble in her book. She won't mind at all if you're over here a lot."

"I'd like to spend more evenings in town," I said excitedly. "My schedule's pretty much wide open. I mean I'd like to have you to New Jersey but there isn't much going on that I know of."

"We'll talk on the phone this week." She gently pressed my car door closed.

"Thanks again!" I called as I drove off euphorically. I sped all over Manhattan missing turns and getting lost. In my bed I lay for hours without sleep, drugged by her pretty face, her slim figure, and the knowledge that once again I would have the chance to make Posey mine. I had outgrown the inhibitions that had plagued me in the past.

*   *   *   *

Calling Posey Sunday, or even Monday morning, might appear overly anxious. I found myself spending considerable time contemplating my next move—the day and exact time I would call, my opening lines, and what I would propose we do the next time I came in town. Posey called Monday at noon, however, before I'd had a chance to put my well rehearsed plan to work.

"Can you come to the *Squandered Fortune* on Wednesday? I'll be there with my roommates, Laurie and Lois. Dinner around seven?"

Her voice was commanding. She had always been so very confident around me—spoke her mind and assumed I would do as told. Because the brothers often put me down back in fraternity days, it must have been easy to conclude that I was weak-willed. Clay had often said I was too good-natured; I wasn't mean enough, too polite.

I excitedly accepted her invitation and spent the rest of that day and the next accomplishing comparatively little—my mind being absorbed in fantasies of she and I together. Wednesday, therefore, took forever to arrive, and when it did I dressed in my best suit. The tie I selected for the evening was one I had bought for nine dollars at a Junior League thrift shop. After the purchase I had seen the same tie for more than ten times that amount in an exclusive men's shop on Madison Avenue.

Early Wednesday morning DeMille stopped me in the office coffee shop with one of his typical remarks, uttered loudly enough for our vice-president Tommy Carey and others to hear, and in a mock-British accent: "What taste you've got in clothing, young Lightfoot! Just come from your tailor? Is he in from London?…Meeting with Brown Brothers, Harriman today?"

I was at the *Squandered Fortune* by six-thirty and found a tall but obscure stool against the wall from which I could view the door. I ordered a beer and pulled Tacitus from my breast pocket. Since moving to North Jersey I had once again picked up the *Annals of Imperial Rome*. The usual unintelligible Wall Street banter surrounded me, so I managed to get through a few passages on Nero before being distracted by a familiar voice.

"Hi! Coddie!" I called, and quickly stuffed Tacitus back in my pocket.

He was dressed impeccably in what looked like a six hundred dollar suit and an Italian tie perhaps twice the price of mine as listed on Madison Avenue. On his feet, however, was a pair of black, high-top sneakers. He ordered a drink and joined me near the window.

"I'm not here for long. I'm headed to a political fund raiser."

"Coddie, come on…what's with the sneakers?" I laughed.

"What about them?"

"Going up to Harlem to play a little basketball? I don't think Averill Harriman or F.D.R. had to wear high-topped sneakers to prove their loyalty to the Democratic Party. You're too blatantly limousine liberal. Don't be so obvious. Are you a closet socialist?"

"Well, that's maybe what I am," he said combatively.

"Americans are too ambitious to be socialists—I've come to that conclusion. Secretly, the masses want to be just like you: a rich preppy. They're jealous of preppies—love-hate relationship. Americans dream about rising above the crowd. Certainly we want our kids to. So we let inequality exist in this country because secretly we like it. We just won't admit it out loud—that someone can't be special *without* excluding others."

"That's one opinion."

"Socialism is too leveling. How boring! Americans want a ladder to climb. They like dreaming about owning homes in the Hamptons."

"So, you think the masses are jealous of us? Tom, who do you think you are? No one wants to be like us. They want to burn our houses—"

"Or put a guillotine in front of the Plaza and get our fathers coming out after a few pops in the Oak Room?"

"Get in your BMW, or whatever you're driving, and go north of the Nineties. Give me a call if you come back alive," he said humorlessly.

"Come, come boys! What's the fuss," demanded Posey, her voice reminding me of Nanny Hawkins fifteen years before. She stood alone in a colorful print dress.

"I've got to be off," Coddie said. "Sorry we can't continue this. If you two are around next week, let's all meet up." He downed his drink and marched out the door ready to save the world.

Posey and I crossed the room to find Laurie and Lois already at a table. On the way over Posey murmured: "Coddie wants to rescue our souls."

"How do you mean?"

"From the evils of our class. We're a bunch of self-centered, exploitive, irresponsible, bigoted snobs. *You* know. He takes things *so* seriously. He and I have been out a few times, and now I'm afraid to open my mouth in front of him. It's like walking on eggshells. He tells me I'm to stop being snobbish; I'm to be tolerant of others. And yet, at the same time, *he* isn't tolerant—he doesn't tolerate *my* lifestyle or Mom's. Mom's over sixty, how can she change?"

We greeted Laurie and Lois and dropped the subject of Coddie. These two women aroused suspicion and didn't put me at ease. Perhaps it was the heavy make-up that rid them of all innocence. They stole my attention, and through the meal I periodically found myself interrogating them, hoping that, if I knew them better, I would become more comfortable.

Lois, I learned, had known Posey in country day school before being expelled for drugs. She had finished up at a public school and then spent two years in college before dropping out to work at a ski shop in Aspen. She had met Laurie working at the same shop.

On a trip east Lois had looked up Posey, and they spent a weekend bar hopping in Washington D.C., after which Posey invited Lois to live in her mother's new brownstone. When Lois arrived the following autumn, Laurie came with her, apparently uninvited but nevertheless accepted quickly by Posey as another welcome tenant.

Both girls had attractive figures, but they had a taste for provocative clothing and heavy make-up that I found sleazy. "Do they buy their underwear from Frederick's of Hollywood?" I later asked Coddie.

On many occasions that night, and on others that followed, I caught them staring silently in my direction. Did they find me attractive? Or, were they doing a catscan of me to determine if I would play their game? Perhaps they were contemplating the best way to dispense with me.

"We're having a party next weekend," said Lois.

"Who? Where are you having it?" I asked. Both girls looked at Posey.

"We're having it at my house," announced Posey in a proud voice. "Be there at nine on Friday night for live music. No invitations; we invite the world. We do these about once a month, so it's beginning to snowball. This one should be extra big and special. We don't think we've ever *really* announced our arrival in New York—it's our debutante ball!" she laughed.

"Then, are you wearing white?"

*   *   *   *

I took the Holland Tunnel into Manhattan late that Friday evening and met up with Coddie, who had been working a long day on Wall Street. He was dressed in another custom suit and, once again, in his black high-top sneakers bought for two dollars at a thrift shop.

"I guess if you own your own business you can wear whatever you want," I said as I drove the two of us north to the Upper East Side.

"No, I put the sneakers on after everyone had left for the day."

"The sneakers are how you let people know you have a conscience, I guess."

"You could say that. It's Posey's crowd I want to see them."

Music could be heard through the rainy air as we walked the half block from our parked car to the stately brownstone. A few passersby were gazing up through the windows, probably wondering, justifiably, whether to complain about the volume.

"Well, it's about time, Thomas Williamson Lightfoot!" yelled Posey above the crowd from across the room. "Hello, Arnold of Rugby!"

We were only about a half-hour late but the room was full. The men and women were dressed in expensive, fashionable attire.

"Ask these people what they do for a living," murmured Coddie in my ear as we made our way to Posey and she to us. "They won't have an answer because they don't do *anything*. They'll probably tell you they're venture capitalists or brokers during the week. Actually, all they're doing is recovering from the previous weekend in the Hamptons. They don't have anything intelligent or original to say."

"Posey, you *are* in white!" I exclaimed. She gave me a large kiss on the cheek. "This *is* a debutante party!"

"Yes, well it's about time New Yorkers know who I am!"

"I hope a society reporter from the *Times* is here tonight," Coddie said with a deadpan. "You should at least be able to get yourself in a tabloid."

"Hello you derelicts!" yelled Lois. "The rule is: if we don't have to carry you to a cab and pay the cabby and give him directions to wherever you live, you won't be allowed to leave here tonight!"

"Now Lois, you don't have to instruct these guys on what they know best," lectured Posey. She and Lois were then called away by the caterer.

"I see Lea Creswell and Apple," murmured Coddie, gazing into the dining room. "It's cocaine city over there." The word made me uptight—I was anticipating the inevitable peer pressure to have some.

"How do you know?"

"What do you think Apple is? He's a snowman. And what do you think of Lois and Laurie? Ever looked up their nostrils? Stick your finger up Lois's nose, and you'll probably touch the top of her skull. Why do you think they live with someone who's got money like Posey?"

I looked over at Lois. She was the one talking to the caterer while Posey merely stood and listened.

"Hey, I didn't know you knew Lea Creswell," I mentioned as the thought occurred. "And how do you know Apple?"

"Who doesn't know Apple? And I've known Lea since she moved to Manhattan." Coddie moved his gaze back in her direction. "Really into who she is...really concerned with her status in New York—uptight about it. Wants to have the same status in New York that she has down in Philadelphia, whatever that is. Do you think anything registers when she sees a bag lady?"

After a long pause Coddie laughed cynically: "Notice that we're about the youngest guys here? Lots of old men with girls one-half to one-third their age!"

People were occasionally going up and down the front stairs, and Coddie and I wandered up after them. On the second floor landing we could hear the sound of commotion and the Grateful Dead drifting down the stairwell, so we followed it up another flight.

Up there a large dark bedroom was thick with marijuana smoke. The only source of light was a small black and white television showing a porn film, and someone had just laid out lines of cocaine on a glass tabletop. Empty bottles and trash—fast food wrappers—littered the floor. Perhaps ten people were collapsed on the many sofas shoved against the walls around the room. A couple stood up and went into a bedroom across the hall. We stayed a few minutes before wandering back down.

"I think the third floor party's been going all day," Coddie surmised. He introduced me to a few new faces, and Posey and I managed to speak off and on. But neither Coddie nor I were happy with the crowd, and the party was still very strong when we left around midnight.

"It's a self-destructive group she's fallen in with," he lectured as we walked up the street. "I'm not sure the Ludwells understand what can happen to a rich girl like Posey in New York—they end up in a drug dry-out center in Minnesota, if they're lucky. Someday maybe she'll learn: happiness isn't just having money; you've got to achieve and create. Want to see my place?"

Four blocks away we rode up the thirty floors to Coddie's spacious apartment. It was full of New York memorabilia: campaign posters of all eras, large prints of Alexander Hamilton and John Jay, newspaper pages nicely framed announcing major events in the history of the city, and a host of objects that would have aroused the jealousy of the trustees of The Museum of the City of New York.

"Quite a collection," I told him.

"I'm working on it. Do you want 100 year-old port?"

He brought out a bottle, and we sat before a beautiful view of the city skyline.

"So…she told me you were her brother's roommate in college," he said as he poured me a glass.

"Yes, Clay Ludwell. We haven't really been keeping up. He's out west on a family ranch."

"Yes, one of the many family holdings. The mother's got the money. Certainly, I know of the family. There's a cousin or two in New York." He swished the port around his mouth.

"And the grandparents are here," I said.

"Yes, they give money to various museums and what not around town. I've seen their names engraved on brass tablets here and there…. You know that's the thing about Posey."

"What?"

"Money. Posey comes to New York thinking the whole world knows about and is interested in her family because they're rich and they're Old Money. But there's already a lot of money in this town. Admittedly, her mother's family is a well-known name in American industry. But it's not a New York name, and it's not New York money, and you know we old New Yorkers view everyone else as provincials who—"

"But, nevertheless, you are all *smitten* by anyone with money," I interrupted. He put his drink to his mouth and ignored me.

"Furthermore, her last name's Ludwell," he continued. "And who's heard of Ludwell unless you're a member of the Society of the Descendants of the Lords of Maryland Manors, or some such silly society?"

I laughed. "Well, she's probably changed some since I knew her as a college freshman…. Clay is not really like that, though. He's responsible. He's not self important at all. He's a really good guy."

"The problem is the family office."

"Family office?" I asked.

"Yes, they've got a family office like the Rockefellers have Room 5600 and the Phipps family has the Bessemer Trust. The son of the original family patriarch, Posey's great grandfather, I think, set it up for his descendants. It handles all their investments, collects dividends, makes distributions, and so on. But where it gets the family into trouble is when it also gets Posey a limousine if she wants one. Or it acts like a travel agency—she just calls and tells them where and when she wants to go. It will make airplane and hotel reservations, get a table at a restaurant, hire a party caterer, walk the dog, find a cleaning lady, balance check books; you name it! Ultimately, it's kept most of the family members from growing up—they act like children."

"Clay never mentioned a *family office….* But I'm not surprised."

"Since Posey's been here in New York I've been out with her a few times and gotten to know her. She thinks people automatically want to do whatever *she* wants them to do. Wealthy families like hers generally have a lot of hangers-on—people flock to them like royalty. I've seen it in my own family, even though we don't have anything close to the Ludwell empire. There are people out there who get totally enamored by other people with lots and lots of money. I guess it's because so many people with no money and no imagination lead very mundane, dull lives, and, when they get in with someone who's loaded, their lives suddenly speed up and get a lot more exciting. These two girls Posey's got as roommates, Laurie and Lois, total losers. Rejects…. Posey's giving them a taste of the good life. Meanwhile, she's become addicted to the power of money. Laurie and Lois do anything Posey wants, at the snap of a finger! They'll cancel whatever plans they have if Posey includes them, even at the very last minute, in hers. They follow her around like the Queen's maids-in-waiting.... Posey also seems to think she can have any guy she wants because her family's got the bucks."

"I saw some of that in college, but is it really just the money?"

"Well," Coddie laughed, "it could also be because she's on her back pretty quickly and almost every night.... Here's another Posey trait: she thinks she's gaining status by being irresponsible. Only people with big money can be that irresponsible. So, being blatantly inattentive to other people's feelings and to life's many details, and laughing about it, is a way of boasting.... She is used to having people bow down to her. What, does the family still have slaves down there harvesting their tobacco? It's these hangers-on that she picks up so easily whom she can treat like dirt. And there must have been some guys in her life who've been enamored by the whole idea of someday being on Easy Street and who have screwed up her mind. She seems to think every guy out there is wanting to eat out of her hand."

"You know...I guess I really don't know her anymore. It's been awhile."

"To be blunt about it, I get disgusted over there. Posey never has anything original or intelligent to say. And her mother! She's in another world...."

*   *   *   *

Posey called my office in the early part of the week. I thanked her for the party, and she asked why I had left so early. She wanted me to stop by again, on Friday. I said I couldn't make it the next weekend but could the following. She was sorry it would be so long.

My father had called Sunday morning to remind me of my grandfather's birthday. There would be a party for him the next weekend and someone had to represent the grandchildren. "What about Apple?" I asked. "Doesn't he live in Philadelphia?"

"I can't find Apple, and his mother's out of the country."

The following Saturday morning I therefore found myself driving south through ninety-degree heat on the dreary New Jersey Turnpike—my grandparents were expecting me at eleven. My four windows were down, yet I remained damp from the high humidity. The low clouds above the smoking oil refineries were a painting of dirty dripping water. When I pulled in the long driveway of Leighsylvania, my immediate plan was to dive in the pool.

I went in the servants' entrance—oddly quiet—and hurriedly up to a second-floor bedroom to change. I did think briefly about how quiet the house was; *no one* seemed to be around. Nevertheless, in seconds I was in my trunks and selfishly jogging to the pool.

I recall passing that familiar ugly tree—the tree that didn't sprout branches skyward in graceful "Y's," but rather from spots in the bark. Like hair from a mole on a person's skin, thin wispy branches sprang from these spots in all directions. The tree stood outside the window of my grandmother's studio.

Years before the wind had blown a strange seed high into one of the four chimneys of the house. It germinated and ultimately became a five-foot sapling, causing damage to the stonework before my grandparents had it ripped out and the chimney repaired.

But just before they took it down, it must have dropped a seed to the ground outside my grandmother's studio. The following summer we noticed a sapling of the same species, and it grew into the ugly tree I was now passing.

"It's come to tell me something," my grandmother often said. "I've never had to live with anything ugly. It's time I did." She never had it removed.

I jogged on to the pool. It had been built in the thirties and didn't have a filter. Every few weeks my grandparents would drain it and fill it with fresh water from the estate well, so the temperature was usually in the low to middle sixties. Swims were generally not long.

Today was an exception. The water hadn't been replaced in several weeks, and daytime temperatures had been breaking records. I therefore dallied in the water. I even got out twice and dried off, only to dive in again.

But blaming what happened on the water temperature is just another attempt to ease my conscience.

My grandfather was at one of his usual board meetings when I arrived, and the household staff was out doing errands for the evening event. The last member to leave was told she could go at eleven because one of the grandchildren would be arriving at that time, if not before.

I arrived, however, around eleven thirty and spent at least an hour swimming and reading a magazine. When I finished I began wandering the house to announce my arrival, but by this time my grandmother had been alone since sometime after eleven and been suffering from a stroke. If treated earlier, it may not have ultimately led to her death.

When I ascended the front stairs, I found her at the edge of the second-floor landing on her hands and knees. I had an ambulance outside in minutes, and I and several of the help spent the afternoon and most of the evening in the hospital waiting room.

She was back at home in a week with a full time nurse, but she never fully recovered. When she spoke during her last weeks she was embarrassingly candid, telling us thoughts she would have never confessed to before. She was dead in less than a month.

The week before her death I had one last opportunity to be with her alone. She was propped up on an embroidered chaise in her studio—apparently a fixture there for weeks, though the stroke had put to an end her great skill as a landscapist. Most of what she said I couldn't really follow, didn't see the logic behind. But I do recall one lengthy sermon.

She was talking about some cousins—cousins of whom I had never heard. Was she talking nonsense again? I thought I knew all our relatives. There weren't many close cousins to know, or so I thought.

"You look surprised when I mention these people," she lectured. "But they're related to you. The same blood flows in their veins as flows in yours. I'll tell you the reason you don't know about these people: they don't have any money.... And you see money is all it boils down to in this country. Your grandfather has told you otherwise and has told me otherwise for more than half a century.... You've never known a part of this family because they don't have any money. It's not *who* you descend from. You're no one special because your family began at Jamestown or signed the Declaration of Independence or rode with Stonewall. That's buncombe!...When a family makes a lot of money, its members go digging around to see what kind of illustrious ancestry they can come up with. They don't want other people thinking they've just arrived.... You know we descend from King Edward III and the barons of Runnymede? How silly! So do thousands of other people, probably everyone who's ever seen the Thames. But try telling your grandfather that. He says our ancestry gives us a mission. What, to exclude his cousins because they don't have any money? What you *accomplish* in this world is all that counts. Don't go living your life thinking family history means anything. It fertilizes the imagination; your grandfather's was ready for the harvest long ago. There *is* an aristocracy in this country, but it's a natural aristocracy based on virtue and talent...."

I sat listening—never said a word. She didn't give me the opportunity and, given her mind at the time, would not have listened for long. It was the last time I saw her alive. We buried her in the family plot on the Fourth of July.

*   *   *   *

On weekends Posey would insist I meet her in town. She had a spare room and empty bed. I had thought that soon enough I would be regularly sharing *her* bed. Occasionally I did, but I was not the only one. I had also thought that over time something would develop between us. It did, but I was only the youngest of the many men in her life.

It did not take long to know the new Posey. Perhaps she had been the same back in college days, but if so my high regard for her brother and her family had prevented me from seeing it.

Now I discovered that if someone didn't know the source of the family fortune, Posey was quick to make it clear. I observed how Posey was compelled, by virtue of having nothing else to point to about herself, to let everyone know to whom she was related and what super-ordinary things members of her family had done or were doing. She had the compulsive need to tell about the twenty thousand acre ranch in Colorado, the museum wing named for her family in Pittsburgh, or about Posey Hall. She was forever talking about a cousin or an uncle who had just sailed a single-handed trans-Atlantic race, or who was climbing the Matterhorn, or a taking a rafting trip down the Amazon.

Illustrious ancestors were readily claimed and thrown in, though her knowledge of these well-known historical figures was very limited, and she regularly put them in the wrong century.

The knowledge that others were aware of her family's glorious exploits, its magnificent properties, and its incomparable contacts and heritage provided the shallow foundation for her ego.

After weeks of listening I became amused by the ample reinforcement for this talk about her family. Her peers were unable to make any comparable claims: they were not from similar means or were too young to have achieved anything of significance themselves. Furthermore, they had not yet won enough self-assurance to publicly belittle someone boasting of an inheritance like Posey's. When new initiates were awed, I was amused to hear them excitedly teach others about the Ludwells, and amused by how very proud they were to be in the know.

The many permanent hangers-on were the "Posey Pack." Coddie considered me one of them. As the weeks passed I recognized the larger picture, and considered the designation unwelcome.

The Pack flattered Posey and her mother by never ceasing to show its fascination with the exploits of the wealthy and well connected. It was the rotten residue remaining when the people of substance had stopped listening. Its members were content to rely, perhaps eternally, for life's excitement and better moments on handouts from a wealthy patron. I recalled incidents in history when this species had achieved real power, and then put it to corrupt use by exploiting and ultimately doing-in the naïve benefactor.

*   *   *   *

Such were my observations and experiences by the time I arrived in Las Vegas, Nevada, the following winter. Posey had persuaded me to join Lois and her by convincing me that there was indeed a part of America I hadn't seen.

Clay Ludwell surprised us with a telephone call the early evening of our first day: "In some ways Las Vegas has not changed in a hundred years," he said. "The difference is that today there are several million light bulbs. Back then there was gambling and prostitution and the Wild West, and today there's gambling and prostitution, and it's still the Wild West."

"But it all seems so temporary. It's life for the moment," I complained. "Is there anything worth saving here? If someone dropped the bomb on this place, would there be anything to regret losing? I mean, what is there really worth saving here?"

"There may not be anything worth saving there, but I'm just trying to tell you that it does have a heritage. It's the product of cowboy days and the Wild West. You're thinking the whole thing's just some developer's dream."

"Okay, but this is certainly an extreme. It's for people who aren't concerned with yesterday or tomorrow, only the present. It's American hedonism at its best. I think this country allows such a place to exist only because it's in isolation; there's desert in all directions for hundreds of miles. You can't just wander here; it takes some effort.... Hey, I've got to go. Your sister wants the phone. Be talking to you!" I passed it back to Posey, grabbed a towel and went to the shower.

Clay was calling from Colorado. After college he had moved west and would ultimately remain there about ten years helping manage his grandfather's ranch in the Rockies. For the moment no enticement seemed to make him want to move back east, to my regret.

The shower water felt slimy. I forgot to unwrap the bar of soap before getting in. The wrapper quickly became soggy, melted off the soap and clogged the drain. But the hot water relaxed me, and I stayed in for twenty minutes thinking thoughts of Clay and the Ludwells.

Clay had so much going for himself back in Maryland. Why wasn't the family's tradition of civic mindedness pulling him back? I thought he had such strong attachment to the land that had been in his family for three hundred years. Maybe there wasn't room for both he and his father? Yet Clay was his father's son—his father *would* make room for him. But, in the case of Posey, certainly she didn't feel a call to duty from the Potomac River Valley.

"I'm sure you know that family history doesn't inspire any sense of duty in Posey," Coddie had warned. "It simply provides justification for her acting superior. But in the case of both she and her mother, superior airs mask some deep insecurities that make them unable to deal with anyone who's not their own upper-class caste. So, they retreat into their money. When they feel the least bit insecure, they dial the telephone and call in the money like the infantry calls in helicopters: to pick them up from difficult situations and bring them back behind the lines."

I finished my shower and quietly dressed while Posey remained on the phone. A knock at the door and in walked Lois from across the hall. She was in her typical attire, a very short, tight-fitting dress. Admittedly her figure was impressive.

"All set?" I asked and continued dressing. Lois went to the far corner of the room and emptied the contents of a silk purse. I saw her begin laying down the first, neat, white line on a small mirror. I immediately retreated into the bathroom.

We took a cab to another hotel for dinner. On the way I saw a sign that proclaimed:

CANDLELIGHT WEDDING CHAPEL
IMMEDIATE WEDDING
and services
Notary 24 hours

Get it done with as little effort as possible! Abandon tradition; make it short and easy—instant gratification. No wonder Posey was attracted to Las Vegas!

I was reminded of Coddie's description of Posey trying to hold down a job on Wall Street: "She would be tremendously excited one day; then the next she would be on to something totally different, oblivious to other people's work or feelings." Apparently, the hours were long and too difficult, so she was on the phone constantly with friends discussing men and clothes. She called limousines when asked to go out on assignment or to get to and from work. She didn't bother to cash paychecks—money had no meaning.

Lacking the patience and discipline to see projects through, she was pushed out of four or five jobs within two years of college. Finally, even her family was afraid to give her the names of new contacts.

"Because of my heritage and family name, my place is really above economics," she once told me in an attempt to rationalize her failure to hold down a job. "Someone has to let the world know what the good life is. The working classes have to have a lifestyle to fantasize about. If people like me didn't exist, wouldn't the world be terribly dull? And why should I dirty my hands groveling for money? I have the opportunity to lead a life of beauty. I have the privilege of making my life an art. I have no need to be practical."

Posey had bought Lois's and my round trip airplane ticket to Nevada. Lois didn't mind me coming because she had long since learned I wasn't going to prevent her from making Posey's decisions. I was only *one* of too many men available to Posey, and my credentials were not particularly impressive. I was just interested in not being lonely—a harmless hanger-on.

We had a fun dinner and then went back to our hotel and the tables. I watched Posey at a two-hundred-dollar blackjack table lose more than five thousand dollars in less than half an hour. She managed to recover about a third of it by three in the morning, when she quit. Lois played roulette with an allowance from Posey. I was also offered money to buy chips but declined.

After an hour watching Posey, I found a two-dollar table where I stayed until midnight, when Lois came by. She was going up to her room; did I need anything?

I followed her up to get out of my tie and into more comfortable clothes. When I was done, I walked across the hall and knocked on her door. Her room smelled of marijuana.

"Here. Have you ever had any?" she asked. I didn't like her thinking me so naïve and squeaky-clean. Yes, I had smoked dope on occasion in boarding school and college.

When we got back downstairs and had found Posey's new table, I felt the effects of the drug coming on. It seemed considerably more powerful than what I remembered smoking in the fraternity.

"I'm going out for some fresh air," I told the two women.

Out on the street, the drug swept me away—lights, sound, and motion passed through me like rolling ocean waves.

Up the sidewalk I saw a grand entrance of white columns, marble steps and fountains seemingly unconnected to a building. It appeared to be a grand and glorious doorway to nowhere, within which stood the statue of an ancient

Roman on horseback sculpted in what looked like marble but was actually fiberglass. I innocently wondered whether it was Caesar after defeating the Helvetii. I walked up the steps among gushing fountains, circled the Roman, and stepped onto a moving conveyor belt that I discovered went out the other side.

This moving walkway was in the open air with just side railings and a roof over top. There were several turns and at each turn I was forced to get onto another long conveyor; there were no walkways going in the opposite direction to take me back. Where was I going? I became wet with sweat as the drug brought on a terrifying paranoia.

I soon discovered that the glorious entrance I had passed through actually belonged to a casino some distance away. This entrance, and several others like it, acted as long tentacles that sucked people up off the busy streets and brought them into the casino's gaming rooms.

The moving walkway dumped me out into a massive hall lined with slot machines, amid which stood more statues of ancient Romans. A live centurion in tunic, crested helmet, and muscular breastplate greeted me. He asked several questions, but I stood without answering, staring at him a good minute in disbelief before wandering among the gambling tables and naked Romans in statue and painting. I passed a wall mural of scantily clad senators and emperors probably fresh from an orgy and found a bust of Tacitus watching over a $500 blackjack table. Pliny the Younger stood among the slot machines, and Cicero's head was mounted above the men's room door.

I was now hopelessly lost, and the drug's effects were not receding. I wandered in and out of other casinos following the crowds. In one lobby two beautiful women, identical twins with exquisite breasts, captured my imagination, and I stood staring. They were bronze and well polished, so couldn't flee my drooling gaze.

How much time passed, I don't know, but when the drug began to subside, I was looking at tigers in the Mirage Hotel and Casino. They were beautiful, white tigers—white because in the Ice Age the breed had lived in snowy surroundings. Now several were housed in a massive pen in the Mirage atrium. They paraded their majestic beauty back and forth along the edge of a pool, and a hundred spectators jammed the rail in awe.

But beautiful white tigers in a hotel lobby? No, it was not an illusion—and I *was* coming down, finally.

Years ago I had looked at Posey and seen beauty. Now I understood that I hadn't been in love with *her*. I had fallen in love with her family lineage, her family seat—Posey Hall, and her mother's money and famous family name. Her money and heritage had given her a special beauty, grace, and style. They had clung to her like the sweet smell of soap. Now that sweet scent was gone.

The drug had worn off, and soberly I went searching for a cab.

CHAPTER 8

▼

What is called family pride is often founded upon the illusion of self-love. A man wishes to immortalize himself, as it were, in his great-grandchildren.

—*Alexis de Tocqueville*

Family portraits. The member of the council by Smibert. The great merchant uncle by Copley, full length with a globe by him, to show the range of his commercial transactions. A pair of Stuarts. I go, other things being equal, for the man who inherits family traditions and the cumulative humanities of at least four or five generations.

—*Oliver Wendell Holmes*

"Our divisional vice president doesn't want you," said Terry Dagavarian quietly over lunch on one of her monthly trips up to the home office. We sat in a gourmet deli in Upper Montclair. A year had passed since I had been to Las Vegas with Posey.

"What do you mean Tommy Carey doesn't want me? How do you know?" I asked in shock.

"I was up here on one of my usual trips, and he wanted to know what's happening at the branches. He had me to lunch, and we had a few drinks. He started getting sloppy—telling me things I shouldn't know. He said: 'There's going to be some reorganizing, and we don't need Tom Lightfoot.'"

"Don't need me for what? Does this mean I'm about to be fired?"

"There are no grounds to fire you. No, he'll keep you, but I suspect he's going to find a way to stuff you in a dead-end job from which you can't go anywhere in his division. You'll have to take a lateral move into another part of the company or leave altogether if you want to climb the ladder."

I felt like crying. Should I believe Terry? Could Terry have really heard Carey correctly? Or was she telling me this to make me want to quit so that perhaps she or someone else could take my job?

"Are you saying that I have no friends here?" I asked in a panic. "Do you or someone else want me out of the way? Terry, why are you telling me this?" I didn't mind sounding snobby when I said defiantly, "I was raised to believe that you speak well of someone behind his back or you don't speak at all!"

"Hey, calm down! Don't come after *me*! I'm actually doing you a favor because I think a lot of you. I think you'd better get out of here because you're very talented and don't deserve to be stuck in the mud. This is what's in store for you: you'll stay in the job you've got now, or Carey will reorganize you into something less interesting. You'll always be told you're doing a decent job, but you'll just never get anywhere. They'll lead you on by giving you cost-of-living increases and an occasional slap on the back, and you'll wake up twenty years from now realizing you've never gotten anywhere. You'll work damn hard between then and now because you'll have innocently kept the faith. You've been raised in a trusting environment where, when you're asked to do a job, you can assume the request is not an attempt to exploit you, and it's therefore expected that you'll fulfill your duties to the very best of your ability.

"But you're too trusting, too loyal. You were raised to adhere to a sort of anachronistic gentleman's code of high ideals—loyalty to God, King and Country…Sir Thomas Lightfoot…. Can loyalty exist in the jungle? Maybe the one in Africa in days of empire, but not here in North Jersey. You're going to be a victim if you mistakenly think Eastern States Financial has good things in store for you. Mark my word: you'll never get promoted, and, most tragic of all, you'll never reach your full potential. They'll have quietly *stolen* your life away, and when you leave or retire you'll be forgotten quickly. Don't assume the people around here have a sincere interest in you…. Look at Rudy Russo. He's been up here, what, less than a year now, from the Main Line office? A lot less time than you, and he's already a level above you."

"That's been a hard one to deal with," I confessed. I was embarrassed that Terry was aware of my not being promoted from coordinator to supervisor like my peers. "There are a few other guys besides Rudy who came into the home office at about the same time I did, and every one of them has gotten some kind of a bump. I *am* feeling it. But what have I done wrong? Why me?"

"You're from a different environment, one that's not appreciated here. You're not appreciated for what you have. You're not someone from the streets. Your accent and the way you talk makes them think you're soft. They probably think you go home every night and call your nanny. You're a WASP blue blood."

"…And as such I've been trying to unlearn the moth-eaten assumptions of my forefathers. Did I cross Tommy Carey the wrong way? If I did, I wish someone would tell me when and where!"

"Tom, don't raise your voice. I really *am* trying to help. Don't be mad at *me*! Let me just remind you of one thing that I'm sure you know about Carey: he started out a poor boy. He never had anything growing up, never got on an airplane 'til he was in the service; went to college on the G.I. Bill. *You* know that whole line he occasionally gives us in speeches. He likes his people to be the same."

"I'm not his type. I know it," I said wistfully. "I guess everyone thinks I've got money, and people who already have money are soft and limp, naïve, can't get anything done! They're not tough enough to compete. They could never be cut-throat. You must all be asking: 'What is Tom Lightfoot doing *here*?'"

"Yes, Tom, and they also ask: How can someone at the management level you're at live here in Upper Montclair? You should be in Clifton or Hackensack. This town is for someone who's at Carey's level or higher. You're not out in Far Hills with Malcolm Forbes, but you are in a place that more than a few higher-ups have their sights on, and they're wondering why you're here twenty years before you should be."

"Now, Terry, you and I have had some heart-to-hearts before, and I've told you I *don't* have any money. I'm *not* sitting on a trust fund. I'm just living in a studio and barely manage to do it on the salary they pay me. I'm really not doing anything wrong."

"You're not doing anything wrong, but the fact that you have the audacity to live here says something. Some people are saying: 'He's not from the New York area, how does he even know about a place like Upper Montclair?'"

"Look," I pleaded, "this neighborhood is not what it was twenty years ago, ten years, five, so on. Newark is taking over. Go down Bloomfield Avenue: every week the war zone moves up a few yards as store owners and small businesses get scared and pull out. People with money are going further west or to Long Island or Connecticut. This place isn't what it used to be."

"Now, come on, Tom, it's got a reputation that's way above Clifton or some of the other neighborhoods Eastern States people live in. If you don't want to believe me…well, it's your future…. They don't feel sorry for you for that incident that put you in the hospital awhile back. You were stupid to have gone into that place to collect the money—we all drove by to have a look. They think you don't have street smarts. Your having gone in there in the first place is further evidence you're just a naïve pretty boy who's not from the streets. You *have* to be from the streets to run this business. Living in a town like Upper Montclair, with its preppy stores, isn't going to give you the smarts you need…. If you want to be a part of Eastern States, why don't you wear different clothes? Your jackets should have belts on the back and flaps on the breast pockets. Don't dress like you've just strolled away from your yacht. The only leather *you* wear is belts and shoes."

"Look at Robert DeMille. He copies me! He comes in wearing what I had on the day before."

"DeMille can get away with it. They all know where he's from, and he sure ain't from the Main Line. There are one or two other people who occasionally dress like you in these offices—it's just that everyone knows they don't come from the Main Line and don't live in Upper Montclair. Some people want to look like they come from the Main Line, but they're fooling no one, not even themselves. You're the only genuine specimen here and you don't belong…. You're tall and good-looking. We're all squat and ugly…. Your manners are too good. Why, when you eat, does your left hand *always* have to be in your lap? No one in this office has manners like you—you won't make it in this business being polite. The thing about manners is: people without them feel insecure around people with them—you and your manners are a threat. The guys here consider elaborately cultivated manners unmanly…. And you speak too well—the same thing applies: people who don't speak English as well as you feel insecure around someone who knows the language. Why do you have to pronounce every *l-y*? Can't you just say *real* instead of *really*? And you're sure to pronounce every *i-n-g*. You should say *gonna* like the rest of us, not *going to*…. You don't swear! You're not crude enough…. You see what I'm talking about? You're suffering from the envy of those who think you're too rich, too handsome, too well educated. You're tall, good looking, and therefore *must* be snobbish. Tom, get out of here or you'll never reach your full potential!"

*   *   *   *

The next morning I was sulking around the office when my father called. Since the previous day at lunch, my mood swings had been dramatic: mad and irritated, ready to march in and knock Tommy Carey's head off, then depressed, convinced Terry was right, thinking that I really had no friends here after all, they were just people I spend the day with. I had put in so much hard work at Eastern States—was it all for nothing? At times I was mad at Carey, then at Terry, then at my family for making me who I am.

The sound of Dad's cultivated voice over the phone made me mad at my family, so I expressed no regret when he said, "Your grandfather is dead...cardiac arrest." He must have been puzzled by my lack of emotion because he immediately put Mother on.

She was upset. "The world is worse off, today," she wept—in what was for her an unusual display of emotion. "He was the patrician ideal; one of the last true gentlemen.... He set a fabulous example for this family. He was a brilliant man, and he was everything that's good about this country...."

My father eventually got back on and told me Aunt Beale, Apple's mother, had been with Grandad when he died. "She is attending to all the arrangements and has let me know that she's trying to get everyone to come, even your Aunt Binney in Europe."

Aunt Binney lived in Paris. She and her husband had been there for the last twenty-five years. Their one child had been educated in the United States but now lived in the South of France. Conventional wisdom had it that Aunt Binney didn't live in this country because America was too "vulgar."

"Why don't you head down there tonight?" Dad pleaded. "Mother and I can't leave Maine until the day after tomorrow because I've been sick, as you know. I really wouldn't mind you there to represent me. Can you take tomorrow off? Danny happens to have been in Philadelphia on business, so he's at Leighsylvania already. Your sister plans to get a train. I've left a message on Henry's answering machine...."

Needless to say, I was only too happy to get out of the office for the rest of the week, and by seven that evening I was packed and driving south through the usual heavy humidity and high heat of August.

I was surprised to see the house almost completely dark when I drove up the long driveway and swung around to the servant's entrance in the rear. I had called ahead to let Clara know I would be in around ten, and I therefore found it odd that a light had not been left on for me at the door. I stumbled through the pantry and pushed into the dining room.

My anger had shifted direction since talking to my father in the morning: I was now mad at Tommy Carey and the whole Eastern States management team! When I pushed open the dining room door and saw that the spotlight was not on above the portrait of William Williamson Lightfoot, I grew even angrier.

I dropped my suitcase to turn it on. The high white collar and wind-swept hair caught my imagination as usual, and I stepped back to gaze and conjure up images of the first Confederate ironclad. Maybe if I were a war veteran I wouldn't be having difficulty at Eastern States Financial.

Then, suddenly, loud obnoxious music shattered my quiet contemplation. It was coming from the library, and it wasn't a befitting classical sound. It was something contemporary and a threatening intrusion into my grandparents' house. I stormed through the living room to see who could have forgotten so quickly all that my grandfather had stood for.

Danny Paulucci sat with his shoes on my grandmother's needlepoint ottoman, smoking Grandad's tobacco from an ornately carved, antique, ivory pipe that would eventually find its way to the Atwater Kent Museum in Philadelphia.

"Danny, you're trespassing!" I yelled, venting all my frustrations from work.

"So, the heir is here to claim his lordship," he snickered.

"Don't give me your crap!" I grabbed the pipe from his hand and banged out the ashes. "You have no business making yourself at home like this!"

"Aren't I part of the family? I guess you don't think so with a name like Paulucci. Well, I was headed up to bed anyway. You stay down here and contemplate the world you've lost. Lament it. The world of your imagined inheritance has now vanished."

He held a document in his hand that he mysteriously pushed into a pile of dusty papers. He then turned off the reading lamp, and I herded him to the stairs.

*   *   *   *

The following morning the well-trained platoon of servants scurried about doing all its ritualistic duties as if Grandad was still roaming the house and grounds. I was reminded of Japanese soldiers still serving the emperor in the jungles of the South Pacific long after the surrender.

By early afternoon Henry had arrived, as had my sister Binney. Aunt Binney had wired from Paris the previous day, informing Beale and Dad that she and her husband would not be coming. Her daughter, Nicole, would be attending in her place.

I informed Olga that there would at least be four for dinner and maybe five—Nicole.

"Then that means maybe seven," she said. "Apple is coming with his fiancée, Lea Creswell. You heard the announcement?"

Yes, I had. It had not been a surprise. Apparently Apple's mother had suggested he join his cousins for dinner and bring Lea, as she would soon be a member of the family. Like the rest of us, both Apple and Lea would eat and sleep at the house until after the funeral.

"Hello, Count!" Ole had snuck up behind me as I was talking to her grandmother. Now at the University of Pennsylvania Law School, she carried an air of sophistication that I hadn't seen before. Her outfit was especially attractive, as though she had just stepped out of an expensive specialty shop on the Main Line. "It's Laura Ashley," she answered to the question posed by my eyes only.

Unlike the rest of the staff, she seemed to have quickly abandoned the trappings of service to my grandparents and discarded (hopefully burned!) the white uniform and nurse's shoes.

"Olga, make that eight for dinner," I said, casting an admiring smile at Ole.

The heat was unmerciful, and we all spent the afternoon in the pool. From the diving board I saw a limousine coming up the driveway around four o'clock. In a few minutes Nicole, whom none of us had seen in years, stood on the terrace. She was even more ravishing than I remembered—slim, blond hair down below the middle of her back, dressed stylishly, and very tan from a summer on the Riviera. Her only time in the United States had been the four years spent at a New England boarding school.

We gathered for cocktails at the usual six-thirty, and, in an unplanned show of respect for my grandparents and the help, were all in ties and jackets or dresses. The heat had still not let up. "Grandad doesn't believe in air conditioning," my grandmother had complained over the years. Ole came in and out with plates of hors d'oeuvres and a variety of teasing comments. The mood was not sad, though certainly not celebratory. It was ripe with anticipation.

After a few drinks, Binney quietly passed the word: Danny had found a copy of the will in the library.

No one, however, made an *immediate* move in the direction of the library. The will was not our business; our parents would let us know about it.

But perhaps a little more vodka was intentionally poured than would have been otherwise, and in the merciless heat our inhibitions vanished when we looked toward the library again. Apple moved first. He said later that his intention had actually been to open a terrace door. Nevertheless, even a small move in the right direction was read as a move to the library, and as a group we were soon on the way to have a look at Danny's find.

I recognized it as the document that had been in his hand the night before. Was it the real thing or an early and discarded version? We were not entirely sure, but later events confirmed that the final document differed on only a few minor points.

Nicole picked up the dusty copy, sat in my grandmother's chair and began to read. But her voice was not solemn enough for the occasion. Rather, it was an insulting voice of rising and falling cadences more appropriate for reading an adventure story to children. The feeling was obvious, from this disrespect, that she had not been close to our grandparents and to Leighsylvania, and I was suspicious of her motive for showing up now.

Meanwhile, the rest of us stood in silent curiosity—as motionless as the hot and humid August air.

"I always hoped that my children and grandchildren would carry on the best traditions of the family to the best of their abilities," the will read. "Are the members of my family in a position to carry on these traditions effectively? Or, will inherited wealth lead to a parasitic existence that will betray the efforts of our forebears and be destructive to my heirs and to society? Will the fragmentation of our fortune reduce the family name? Will the Lightfoot name loose its strength and disappear from its place of distinction in America? It is with the desire to insure the future excellence of the name Lightfoot that the significant share of my assets be passed into the Lightfoot Family Foundation."

A "Lightfoot Family Foundation" was to be set up and receive eighty million dollars in cash and blue chip stocks and bonds. This foundation was to dispense funds to schools, colleges, and universities in Pennsylvania and Virginia. It was also to "act as a guardian of the national heritage" by dispensing funds to historical societies across the nation and to provide grants to scholars of American history. A board of directors was to be set up that would include my father, his two sisters, and us grandchildren. Several prominent outsiders were also named, among them a member of the faculty at Harvard.

Leighsylvania and all its contents were left to my father and his two sisters. $25,000 was left to the Society of the Cincinnati. Enough money was to be set aside to allow Ole to finish law school. None of the grandchildren were mentioned except as members of the board of directors of the new Lightfoot Family Foundation.

"And that's basically it," said Nicole with a forced smile as she skimmed the last few pages of legalese. In disbelief Binney reached toward her and plucked the will from her hands. Apple looked over Binney's shoulder in a panic to verify what Nicole had just read.

A few minutes later the group wandered silently, like a dazed and wounded platoon, through the living room and across the front hall to the dining room—all of us contemplating Grandad's reasoning and the long-term personal implications.

Like a galleon of old, this new foundation would sail intact through the ages, its cargo holds full with the bullion of our heritage, protecting it and the Lightfoot name perhaps forever from the rocks of family incompetence, dispute, and irresponsibility.

*   *   *   *

The Civil War table had been set in its ultimate glory: eight massive candle sticks stood like an old-growth forest of silver over a ground cover of China-trade plates. The plates had arrived in a Donald McKay clipper well over a century before. Each place setting included seven silver utensils and several pieces of delicate crystal.

Perhaps the staff had decided that they themselves wanted to see the table in all its glory one last time, as it was doubtful our parents would be in a mood of celebration. Or, perhaps the staff had also secretly read the will and by their actions were saying: "We'll throw you one last extravaganza; after this it's the cold, cruel world. We want to show you what you'll be missing!"

Danny was already in the dining room. He knew what the will said and hadn't stayed around. He was waiting behind Grandad's chair at the head of the table.

"Binney," I said softly, "I'm single tonight, so I've invited Ole." She quickly nodded her approval, and I sensed that she, like I and some others in our small group, felt we were finally righting a wrong. I went through the pantry to fetch her. She was in a colorful print dress and wore a happy face.

When we arrived back in the dining room, we found Danny now seated with Nicole on his right and Lea Creswell on his left. At the opposite end sat Henry. I put Ole on Henry's left; Binney was on his right. Apple and I sat across from each other in the middle.

Other than the clink of silver on china and the occasional ring of crystal, the room was quiet when Ole and I took our seats. No one was ready to speak his or her mind until the help had served the cold vichyssoise and retired to the pantry.

We were all picking up our large King's Pattern soup spoons when Danny looked at me and asked with his usual condescending laugh, "The past is the only comfort left for you, Tom. Where will you go to re-create your lost world? Are you prepared to join the unwashed masses?"

"Danny, I've been trying to join the unwashed masses for several years at Eastern States Financial but without success," I said calmly. I won laughs from Apple and Binney. Danny even gave me a wink.

"But what a shock," mumbled Apple. "What a mystery!"

"It's not a mystery," spoke up Henry. "It's very obvious to me."

"How can it be so obvious?" puzzled Nicole.

"I'm sorry you've come all this way from the South of France for nothing. You should have given me a call," deadpanned Henry. "I would have told you not to come."

"The master sleuth speaks. Oh! Sage of the ages, tell us why your grandfather sold out," pleaded Danny.

"Out with it, Henry!" commanded Apple.

"…Partly, it was conscience…my friends."

"Would there be any other response that could possibly have come from Henry's mouth?" muttered Danny into his wine glass. "I suppose you're going to tell us the Lightfoot money is tainted money—from the Opium Wars, or it's from the corpse of the Confederacy and therefore slavery!"

Henry expanded: "You know that ugly tree outside Grandmother's studio window? The one that came down from the chimney? You pass it on the way to the pool. The one she used to talk about so much in her last, senile years? Well, it was symbolic of her conscience coming to the surface. She used to say the tree was coming to get her. Actually it was her guilt coming to get her. 'I like having to look at something ugly all day,' she told me. 'I've never had to before, and now I feel better about myself.' Grandmother had to do something about these guilty feelings so she got Grandad to do what he's done."

"What on earth, Henry, was she so guilty of?" asked Lea.

"The extravagant lifestyle. Furthermore, Grandad wasn't really the man he pretended to be and the man she wanted him to be."

"What do you mean by that?" asked Apple.

"There are the Ledbetters. First cousins of Grandad's who live right here in Easton, Pennsylvania. He seemed to want nothing to do with them because they are as poor as church mice and don't fit the family ideal."

"Who?" asked Apple and Nicole in unison.

Henry ignored them, "And Grandmother died still upset about the many years Grandad supported the Vietnam War. She also couldn't stand the way he was forever coming out with statements like 'the Kennedys are shanty Irish,' or 'blacks wanted to fight for the Confederacy.' I remember him referring to someone from China as a 'nonassertive coolie type' and as a 'passive Confucian.'

"But it wasn't just our grandmother's idea. Leaving everything to a foundation fit nicely with Grandad's desire for self-glorification and immortality. He wished to perpetuate and immortalize himself and the family name. He'll get *Lightfoot* over dormitory doorways at a few colleges in Virginia, and there'll be more than a few chairs in history to have the Lightfoot name."

"I know I'm the pot calling the kettle black, but aren't you being a little cynical?" asked Danny. "I see somewhat of a contradiction here. Your grandfather seemed to believe in family so much, why not insure the continuance of the Lightfoots? The family's finished now. When the money's gone, well-known families disappear in this country. Money's the foundation of social standing; without it, you'll disappear into the unwashed masses."

"Social standing is *not* as simple as just dollars," lectured Apple. "First, it's not the quantity of money; it's the age of the money—inherited money is better than self-made money. But, also, it's who you know, where you went to school, where you work, the way you dress, the language you speak. It's your family history, your heritage, and that's something you're born with. In fact, maybe Grandad is saying by his will: 'you don't need the money to maintain the family identity because social and cultural capital are more important than economic capital.'"

"Apple, wishful thinking. Impeccable ancestry plus zero money does not equal high social status in this country," Danny emphasized.

"Even without money, we *are* looked up to! It's *our* class that elevates this country as a whole!"

"Apple, your heart is arguing, not your mind. Those days are over, if they ever did exist. You treat the Social Register like it's a copy of Burke's Landed Gentry. You think some ultimate genealogical society, high on a misty mountaintop, decides who gets listed. As soon as you were born your name was in it, so God must have had something to do with it, right? Wrong! The sad fact is that the Social Register is nothing more than someone's business; Malcolm Forbes owns it."

"Apple," asked Henry, "didn't you leave out another dimension that defines an upper class? How about charity? Noblesse oblige?"

"Why aren't you a minister?" snickered Danny at Henry.

"Well, if you don't include that dimension in the definition, it might be mis-interpreted to include some of the high-society followers of Nancy Reagan—lux-ury without responsibility."

"I agree with Henry," I spoke up. "To add to what he's saying, aristocrats feel a sense of duty and are not on the make. I'm thinking of Clay Ludwell's father. Aristocrats are therefore less corruptible. They pursue government in a disinter-ested, selfless way. They have *character*! I'm also thinking of the Founding Fathers and our ancestors, the Lees of Virginia. I'm thinking of the Roosevelts. An aris-tocracy can give us order and continuity in a changing world."

"But is there really a well defined aristocratic class in this country?" asked Nicole. "Do you really find such a homogeneous group of people over here who share the same way of dressing, acting, speaking, etc.? Would anyone in America instantly recognize someone with an upper class heritage? I don't—"

"We *don't* have an aristocracy over here in America," interrupted Binney. "But we *do* have Old Money—that's Old Money spelled with a capital 'O' and capital 'M'."

"…Yes," resumed Nicole, momentarily caught up in Binney's comment. "But I don't think heritage plays any role over here; in America someone can break into the upper echelons in one generation, and, therefore, a homogeneous class, connected by blood, has never developed. Furthermore, the right to your heritage is not God given over here like it seems to be in Europe. I call it 'divine right' over there. It sounds like we have some unknown cousins who are examples of what I'm trying to say: the Ledbetters?"

"I disagree!" argued Apple. "It exists over here the same way it exists in Europe. Grandad betrayed us; he betrayed his class. Isn't the primary goal of a true aristocrat to make sure that his line continues, that the heritage is not forgot-ten, that the family continues to maintain its position or status in society and keeps getting stronger and more powerful and influential? Doesn't Grandad's money belong also to the generations yet unborn? Each generation should be allowed to use the dividends and interest—and trusted not to spend principle. Isn't there a partnership between those who are living, those who are dead, and those who are not yet born?"

"Apple," answered Henry, "you're missing the point. Don't think so selfishly. The Lightfoot Family Foundation will insure that our heritage will not be forgot-ten in the face of institutions and laws in this country that would otherwise wipe it out. This country long ago eliminated primogeniture—I think the only place it ever existed over here was in Virginia during colonial times—and we've got inheritance taxes. Our laws and institutions pretty much eliminate what exists only in the minds of a few people in this country who like to play make believe that they are something special—aristocrats or something else really special. They pretend they were to the manor born, or part of only a small minority born with blue blood and divine right."

"During the Middle Ages," spoke up Nicole, "Spain had a substantial population of Moors. Apparently, the white Caucasians were keenly aware that blue veins are visible on lighter skin people, only. Thus the origin of the term."

"Today," continued Henry, "there are plenty of white-skinned people with very visible blue veins among the great unwashed here in the USA. The *American Dream* is not just a materialistic dream of automobiles and houses for everyone. It's also a dream of a social order in which men and women can reach the full potential of which they are innately capable, and be recognized by others for what they are, regardless of their heritage—ethnic, socio-economic, whatever.

"Tens of thousands of people descend from the Mayflower passengers, but how many of them know it? And if they do, most of them have enough sense not to care because that and fifty cents will get them a cup of coffee. People don't start trying to dig up an ancestor who came over on the Mayflower until they've made a few bucks. Then the anxious middle class in them takes over, and they want to let other people know they're not nouveau riche. Robber barons recruit genealogists to find a real baron in their family tree."

"Pigs in clover! Codfish aristocrats! Upstart crows in our feathers!" exclaimed Danny. "For once I *think* I agree with you, Henry, though I had thought democracy to you meant the leveling of all versus opportunity for the individual. This country worships the self-made man. And that's where we really differ from exhausted Europe, Nicole. Britain was more dead than alive until Margaret Thatcher somewhat restored the entrepreneurial spirit. But before Thatcher, disrespect for the self-made man meant that in England the right energy was lacking—the energy that renews society. Hereditary aristocracy doesn't try hard because it's born knowing it's already won. In countries where ancestor worship is practiced, the rest of society emulates those to the manor born and the end result is a lazy population because those to the manor born are a lazy bunch. America has done well not because of our natural resources. Russia has more natural resources than we do. America has done well because Americans respect hard work, individual initiative, success."

"And that's another reason the will reads as it does," argued Henry. "Our grandparents saw what inherited money does to people: it makes them cowards; it's something they hide behind. When things get a little too challenging, the inherited rich aren't forced to tough it out; they just call in the money—"

"Like the infantry radios in helicopters," I said pensively.

"Very good, quiet Tom," said Danny. "And, what do we have? Unproductive, unhappy people. Money subverts the talents people are born with."

"I disagree," complained Apple. "Money *can* do good. And why should Grandad have the right to be the one family member who gets to give all the family money away? Why not one of us? Did the family vote to elect him as the one to become…immortal, as you say, Henry? I call it selfishness."

"Again you're missing the point, Apple," argued Danny. "*You* will be giving the money away. *You* will have the opportunity to be on the board of the new foundation."

"If I may put in my two cents," spoke up Ole timidly, "shouldn't we be asking who made the family money, and did the family money maker have a larger purpose for the money he made other than to simply pass it on to future generations for their comfort?"

"Ha! Here's the person with the real inside!" roared Danny. "We know why Grandad kept Cinderella around."

"Don't be rude, Danny!" scolded Binney.

"I'm sorry."

"I'm just asking: do we know the history?" Ole's voice was shaky, and her face bright red.

"Tell us the history," commanded Apple.

"If you know the history, you're more Lightfoot than any Lightfoot here," lectured Danny, pointing at her. "Apple, if you don't know the history, then you have betrayed your grandfather more than he's betrayed you."

"Back off Danny Boy. Some of us don't know the *complete* history—Ole, what can you tell us?"

"Okay…," she said nervously. "You see that portrait behind Henry? I think that gentleman's at the root of this."

"William Williamson Lightfoot?" puzzled Apple.

"The man whose character triumphed over catastrophe…ill fortune nobly borne," I mumbled to no one.

"You know, when I first began working for your grandparents, I would come walking through this room each night after everyone was in bed, and the spotlight above William Williamson Lightfoot was always on. I would instinctively turn it off and go on up to bed. It was several weeks before word got to me that you grandfather was asking who was turning off the spotlight. I was told I'd better not keep turning it off…. I did a lot of talking with your grandfather over the past several years, especially after your grandmother died and he was alone. I may have been the person he was closest to in his final days. We got to know each other *very* well."

"Yes, I bet a lot better than any of us ever knew him," suggested Binney. "Our emotions always got in the way."

The soup was cleared and the main course served as Ole looked at the portrait, then back at us, and told all she knew. I chose not to speak up, though I was familiar with all her facts and in considerably greater detail.

*   *   *   *

Our Great-Great-Great-Grandfather, William Williamson Lightfoot, was born into a family that could trace its roots back to Jamestown and counted the Lees of Stratford, the Byrds of Westover and other first families of Virginia as ancestors. He had married Penelope Benbury MacDonald of Eatontown, North Carolina, in 1838, the same year the portrait was painted. Penelope's family had instigated rebellion in North Carolina in 1776.

A career naval officer, William Lightfoot sailed with Commodore Perry to Japan in 1853 and was an admiral in the United States Navy when the first shots were fired on Fort Sumter. Though a Southerner, Lightfoot did not believe in secession, but like Robert E. Lee his loyalty was to Virginia first.

Among other accomplishments as a Confederate naval officer, he and his command designed, built, and installed the engines in the Merrimack. And, at the height of the war, he made a miraculous journey to England by way of the Caribbean to assume command of a warship being built at the Liverpool shipyards. After his arrival there, however, Ambassador Charles Francis Adams informed the British that if that warship and others like it were allowed to follow the C.S.S. Alabama as a marauder on the high seas, there would be war with the United States.

William Lightfoot never took command of the ship and ultimately returned to Virginia at the War's end to find his wife and daughters living amid devastation.

His son, Tom, was my grandfather's grandfather and an early graduate of the Naval Academy at Annapolis. As a young lieutenant in 1861, he was on cruise in the Mediterranean. His ship entered a Spanish port and was greeted by the naval attaché from the American embassy in Madrid. The captain was informed that the United States was at war, and that the officers and crew were to "once again swear an oath of allegiance," as Grandad explained it. "No one but the captain knew for a month or more that the United States was at war with itself."

Tom Lightfoot, therefore, spent the war years on a northern naval vessel. As Grandad wrote me at boarding school, "there were plenty of opportunities to join his fellow Virginians, but by the time Tom understood the magnitude of the conflict and that his father had resigned his commission in the U.S. Navy to join the Confederacy, he also understood the preeminence of the Northern might and, as important, the North's intentions."

Tom was aboard the Hartford at Mobile Bay with Admiral David Farragut. He was in charge of the engine room, and as such, family legend has it, was the direct recipient of Farragut's famous order: "Dam the torpedoes, full speed ahead!"

In 1866 the younger Lightfoot sailed into Hampton Roads and went on leave up to Charlottesville where now lived his parents and three sisters. The tone of his reception in Charlottesville can be understood from a description Grandad gave me verbally: "Shades were slammed down. People crossed the street rather than pass him on the same sidewalk. There was bitterness to extremes that has not healed for generations. The residue of the Civil War still resides in me, your grandfather."

The bitterness between father and son would never completely disappear. "I deprived myself of honor; I am the guilty party," the younger Lightfoot is supposed to have uttered at the end of his long and fruitful life.

Nevertheless, the two men apparently did grow closer as the years passed, and the son supported his parents financially until their deaths in the 1890's. The elder Lightfoot spent those post-war years tending to the needs of disabled veterans—"ill fortune nobly borne."

Tom Lightfoot remained in the United States Navy and, like his father, also achieved the rank of admiral. In his late forties he resigned his commission, however, to devote his time to business and charitable interests.

For most of his adult life Admiral Tom was the only source of income for his family living in Charlottesville. His three sisters were never to marry as "all eligible men had either been killed or maimed in the war or were discouraged from matrimony by the poverty the war had created," wrote my grandfather.

Admiral Tom had a son, William Williamson Lightfoot II, whose ambition was to follow family tradition with a career in the navy. He matriculated at Annapolis and served in the Spanish American War. Tragically, he was killed just as the war came to an end when a depth charge misfired.

Prior to his death William II had married and had a son: my grandfather, another Thomas Williamson Lightfoot. William II's young widow and my grandfather moved into Admiral Tom's large house in Washington D.C. in 1901.

Born in 1895 and living with Admiral Tom from an early age, Grandad was at the receiving end of countless Civil War stories. Veterans of both the North and South were constantly flowing through the house, and he grew up with a very deep understanding of the tragedy on both sides. When he was in his nineties, more than one hundred and twenty years after the war had ended, we could readily see a sense of inner turmoil when discussion turned to the Civil War. Before family dinners at Leighsylvania my father would regularly tell brother Henry and myself that the Civil War was off-limits as a subject of conversation.

Grandad was only one of a number of family members under the care of Admiral Tom after the turn of the century. As a boy Grandad had two spinster aunts and six spinster great-aunts with which to contend, all living in the same large house.

Admiral Tom also felt obligated to several black families that had served the Lightfoots since the days of slavery. The murder of a member of one of these families in the basement of the Lightfoot home received front-page headlines and was the subject of considerable talk around Washington in 1906.

The mother of the murdered man had cooked for the Confederate William Lightfoot since before 1860, and her grandson was the playmate of my grandfather when both were boys.

The latter two lost contact with each other around 1920, but thirty years later recognized one another on the Pennsylvania Railroad. Grandad was on his way to a board meeting in New York, and his childhood friend served him breakfast in the dining car.

"I was with your grandfather on that train ride," Dad recounted. "Just before we left the dining car, I watched him write a check for $10,000 and attach it to the bill."

Admiral Tom was not only a successful naval officer; he was also a shrewd businessman. The exact details of his moneymaking have never come down clearly, but we do know that with his admiral's pay he bought farmland throughout the South at very depressed, post-war prices and supplied raw cotton to mills in the Northeast. He eventually bought mills in Reading, Pennsylvania, and in his old age possessed a considerable business empire.

Along with his growing wealth came an ever-greater capacity to do good deeds, and his admiration for his father led to the deepening personal guilt over the war-ravaged South. He volunteered, therefore, to join the boards of charitable causes from Virginia to Florida, and he immersed himself with people and ideas that he thought would heal the nation.

In 1907 he accompanied the younger Charles Francis Adams to the Lee Chapel in Lexington, Virginia. There Adams delivered the seventy-page oration that elevated the reputation of Robert E. Lee to the sublime status it has enjoyed since in the mind of the American public, North and South. Out of Adams' oration, some have said, came a re-born Union.

When my grandfather came of age, Admiral Tom sent him to Harvard and then to the Philadelphia Textile Institute. The Admiral's interests had turned exclusively to business and charity during the previous decades, and, with the death of his only son in the Spanish American War, he was not anxious to have his one grandson make a career in the military.

Nevertheless, in 1917 my grandfather couldn't be dissuaded from volunteering for military service and was off to France with the regular army. Despite a particularly rough time in which he participated in three major American offensives and received several minor wounds, he arrived home healthy in 1919.

In the early twenties Grandad bought a small home in the western suburbs of Philadelphia. At the very end of the Main Line, he could be close to the Philadelphia business hub and also within commuting distance to Admiral Tom's textile mills in Reading. He married my grandmother in 1924, a woman from an old Philadelphia family with Quaker roots.

When Admiral Tom died, Grandad inherited all: the business empire of textile mills and real estate and the accumulated charitable responsibilities. He stepped into board seats left vacant by Admiral Tom and for the next half-century was pursued by educators, foundation executives, and non-profit organizations in Virginia, Maryland and Pennsylvania.

Grandad remained a staunch Southern Democrat to the end. These political leanings were but *one* manifestation of his loyalty to the South. His accent was Southern (both generations of his offspring, though all Northerners by birth, still drag out the "e" in *bed* and *red*), and when his friends went north to their sailboats in Newport and Mt. Desert Island, he went south to ride and buy horses in Middleburg, Culpeper, and Charlottesville. When he learned that my brother and I were applying to northern prep schools, he offered to pay tuition and living expenses at Woodberry Forest or Episcopal. Though we did not end up at either of those schools, various members of the family, including myself, received undergraduate or graduate school educations in Virginia.

In my university days Grandad often came to visit, and he and I traced the family history on Revolutionary and Civil War memorials and tombstones, at historic homes, and in historical society libraries. On many autumn weekends we cruised the red and yellow Virginia valleys in his large, comfortable Jaguar exploring and, for him, rediscovering the Old South. He and I laid to rest the last of his great aunts, born nine years after the end of the Civil War, whom he had supported for decades in a Richmond nursing home.

*   *   *   *

"So, you see," said Ole as she finished her abbreviated version of the story, "your grandfather may have inherited his riches, but he also inherited a mission. 'Lots of money can be dangerous if there is no grand purpose,' he often told me."

"Didn't he think any of us could have used the money constructively?" asked Apple. "Isn't our class the hereditary custodian of what is best in America? Why is a foundation a better custodian?"

"Yes, you all are being deprived of your primary mission," agreed Lea.

"Would you have been faithful to it, Apple?" asked Henry.

"Cinderella, you've figured it all out," exclaimed Danny in the direction of Ole. "Become a family shrink. Quit the law! Do what you do—"

"Let me cut off my rude husband!" began Binney in a loud, authoritative voice, "and tell you all what I think played a part in our *abandonment*, as some of us here might be tempted to refer to it.

"We're all aware of how our grandparents argued through the years. The will was a final attempt to mend their relationship. It was also an attempt to heal the rest of the family. What about my own mother and father? They moved to Maine because they were taking sides in the war our grandparents were waging. And there are also a few tug-of-wars going on in our generation that we are all aware of. According to the will, each of us is supposed to be invited to take a seat on the board of this new foundation, and we will have to work *together*. From the grave our grandparents will force this family to be whole and no longer dysfunctional. Grandad's last will and testament may finally heal this family."

Through the main course and fabulous dessert, the discussion never moved far from my grandfather's will. The estate would ultimately be appraised at almost one hundred million dollars.

*   *   *   *

The older generation was not posed questions about the will immediately. After all, we were not supposed to have rummaged through my grandparents' personal papers to find a copy and then read it out loud. When our parents were finally asked, it was months later and on an individual basis.

My mother interpreted Grandad's will in light of *her* family, the Clafflins of Boston. Lee Clafflin was one of three financial founders of Boston University. There was also Clafflin University for blacks in Orangeburg, South Carolina.

"Old money, inherited money: it's not any one person's possession," Mother instructed Binney and me that fall. "We are only its steward. Its trustee. Harvard University wouldn't be what it is today, with the largest endowment in the country, without people like your grandfather. There is a strong Boston tradition of public service that seems unusual to your materialistic yuppie generation. *Ask not what your country can do for you, ask what you can do for your country.*"

She spoke these words to Binney and me in the Great Room, watching the crew from Christie's box a Newport highboy. "Don't you really mean, Mother, that withholding money serves the Protestant ethic—we're supposed to avoid pleasure and self-indulgence?"

"That's right, Tom, be a Puritan: don't take pleasure in anything and make sure no one else does either! No. You know I don't mean extremes like *that*! You know what I mean—"

"We're not so sure!" Binney laughed. Mother smiled.

"Well, we must remember that your grandfather was raised by Victorians. Admiral Tom who raised your grandfather, his sisters and his father the Confederate—all these people were Victorians. Victorians were of the opinion that man was not put on this earth for the sole reason of gratifying himself. Such was the credo of the people around your grandfather when he grew up. Self-sacrifice, devotion to duty, honor, hard work, temperance: this was the Victorian code, and the one by which your grandfather lived his life. And, of course, he was obsessed with Robert E. Lee and the example he left behind: devotion to duty, the triumph of character over catastrophe, ill-fortune nobly born and all that."

Not until the following spring did Dad share his thoughts on the will. He and I were on an evening walk at Leighsylvania the night before the land was to be sold. The air was cool and the sky clear. Dad quietly contemplated the moon's path across the pond, sighed, and wistfully said, "Your Grandad and Aunt Binney in Paris never got along…. Aunt Beale goes through principal, though she *is* the loser if any of us are…. Grandad had mercy on me. You see if he had left the money primarily to me, it would have come with strings that I become a semi-public figure like himself. Your grandfather would have expected me to move from Maine to a major urban center, join a dozen boards, perhaps become politically involved, get invited to a governor's mansion or maybe even the White House, and a bunch else."

He chuckled but through a hollow smile. It was the laugh he often used to hide disappointment.

"Grandad knew what his son wasn't," he concluded.

*   *   *   *

After that final glorious dinner at Leighsylvania before our parents arrived, we grandsons and granddaughters finished what remained of the cognac, and then one by one drifted up to bed. Ole and I were the last, and I gave her a kiss before we went our separate ways.

I've never slept well on a large meal with lots of alcohol. Furthermore, I was used to air conditioning, and the warm humid air refused to move. The nervous chatter of insects in the Pennsylvania summer night was exaggerated in my semi-consciousness.

Around three a.m. I decided to try some reading. But before turning on the light, I walked over to the window and sat on the sill. I was sadly contemplating the few remaining months that Leighsylvania would remain in the family. Then, across the patio at the far end of the pool, I made out two figures in the hazy light of the moon.

I stopped breathing and swallowed dryly, a little spooked. Burglars? No, they were sitting and dangling their feet in the water.

In a few moments I regained my composure. Then, still in my boxers, I scurried through the hall, down the backstairs, and out the pantry door. I crept round the house and peered through the boxwoods to where I thought the two figures were sitting.

No one was there! My heart pounded while I waited at length among the mosquitoes, hoping to hear or catch a closer glimpse of my prey, but to no avail. I walked to the pool's edge, stood for a moment, then slipped in naked for a refreshing, nighttime swim.

*   *   *   *

This uniform was worn by me in the
Great War, and the stains upon it are
my blood.

I read these words out loud from a note pinned to my grandfather's World War I uniform. It was the morning after our final glorious dinner, and I had been snooping through an upstairs hall closet when I came across it. I brought the uniform downstairs and unfolded it on the floor before my siblings and cousins.

"As you know, Grandad was a great admirer of Justice Oliver Wendell Holmes," I reminded everyone, all curious spectators looking for stains of blood as I smoothed out the arms and legs against the rug. "When Oliver Wendell Holmes died," I explained, "his friends found his Civil War uniform and attached to it was a similar note." I knew this from a conversation with Grandad after he had read a Holmes biography.

We stood quietly round the uniform for several minutes. Then Apple, detecting a mood change in our small group, announced the beginning of what he promoted through the day as "the Great Leighsylvania Treasure Hunt." With the knowledge that we had been all but abandoned in the will, and motivated by what our grandfather's Great War uniform symbolized (that he had been in war and none of us had nor done anything else so noble, and we had therefore been lesser beings in his mind), Apple's treasure hunt ultimately became for some of us a raid of vengeance. Beyond the plainly visible antiques, of which the house was full, we all knew there were significant hidden treasures to be found.

Led by Nicole and Apple, we began opening closets, cabinets, chests, and drawers that none of us had felt at liberty to look inside before. We found silver of every shape and form: flatware, candlesticks, trays and bowls, many carrying dates prior to 1900 and many the names of major horse shows. There was Irish crystal and China-trade plates, platters, and urns. In a bonnet-top Queen Ann highboy was a collection of small ivory carvings of human skulls, skeletons, snakes, tigers and figures that were half man, half beast. Bookshelves were crammed with volumes from the 17th through the 19th century. Various chests contained yards of lace and silk and some dresses from the ante-bellum South, found virtually intact. Glass cabinets held ancient snuff boxes and miniature portraits of our ancestors. Hidden behind a couch were three paintings wrapped in brown paper that Christie's would ultimately auction for $100,000 each. A marine painting by Thomas Birch—*A China Trade Ship Greeted by its Merchant Owner and His Family*—was found in the basement, and in the attic was found an oil of a steamship by Antonio Jacobsen. Some fine pieces of furniture were discovered in a forgotten storage room above the garage, among them a Sheraton tester bed and a Federal sideboard.

Before lunch we were all at separate ends of the house. I was wandering down a second story hall and stopped in front of Nicole's half-opened door. I knew she was in the Great Room but stood motionless outside to confirm no one else was near. Nervous that perhaps Ole would somehow catch me snooping again, I very cautiously pushed the door open and tiptoed in.

I felt protective of Leighsylvania, and Nicole seemed an interloping stranger.

In the middle of the room sat a steamer trunk. I recognized it as the one I'd seen in the basement: dusty and dented but sturdy, it had probably been used forty-five years before to pack my father or his sisters off to boarding school or summer camp, or perhaps it had accompanied my grandparents on one of their many trans-Atlantic voyages aboard the *Ile de France*. It was empty when I lifted the lid and looked down in, but why had she dragged it all the way up from the basement? That evening I mentioned what I'd seen to Binney, who became as suspicious as I. Unfortunately, we did not ask questions until it was too late.

In the afternoon our curiosity about the contents in a safe was satisfied after decades of speculation. The safe had been built into a wall in my grandparents' bedroom, and was now hidden behind an 1858 oil painting of a New Bedford whale ship. When we were children, there had been wild rumors of this safe containing gold doubloons.

Apple had somehow found the combination in our grandmother's desk in the library—the desk that a Christie's representative later identified as a "Queen Ann walnut, slant-front desk" and appraised at sixty thousand dollars. Apple came into the Great Room breathless, calling everyone to come quickly. We followed him up the stairs and down the hall and excitedly watched him make several tries at the dial before the door opened.

The safe was full to its ceiling. After a frozen moment during which I hoped even Apple and Nicole might ask themselves if they weren't trespassing, we began pulling out the contents. In all we counted at least 300 pieces of silver flatware. There were twenty-four diamonds, including one that would sell at Christie's for over $50,000. In an ancient wooden box was one of the more interesting finds of the weekend: a collection of letters to our ancestors from various notables. There was a letter to Henry Lightfoot, a Virginia tobacco farmer, from Thomas Jefferson. There were letters from E.I Du Pont de Nemours, Princess Eugénie the wife of Napoleon III, Marshall Foche, and, of course, Robert E. Lee. There was a $400 check paid to the impoverished Lafayette on his triumphal return trip to America in 1824, reimbursing him for the funds he had supplied the family in 1785 to set up a publishing business.

The treasure hunt came to an end in the late afternoon when Dad and Mother arrived, followed within the hour by Aunt Beale and her husband. Nevertheless, the presence of the elders did not prevent the secret late-night plunder by Nicole of many of the smaller and more valuable treasures in the house. When a large limousine came for her the day after the funeral, Binney and I noticed the steamer trunk already sitting on the floor of the passenger cabin when we and the rest of the family came out to give her a farewell hug.

"Does the family exist for the individual, or do individuals exist for the family?" asked Binney, a year later when the house had been sold and its contents auctioned off or split up. "I think it used to be the latter, but Nicole has proven by her act that the Lightfoots are no longer a family, just a collection of individuals....

"Those ancient little treasures were a very important part of the house," Binney lamented. "It's not just a question of their value at auction. Collected by so many previous generations, they were the fine detail by which I thought of Leighsylvania and shall remember it. They had helped us define ourselves.

"I think it was the visible presence of that collection of ancient little treasures that mislead me over the years. They were in this house for my entire life and contributed to the family's aristocratic mystique. It was a mystique implying eternity: individual family members live and die, but the family never dies. It keeps going on its own momentum, generation after generation, sometimes for centuries like the old families of England who reside in stately homes, never losing their coherence or particular status. But how incredibly fragile a great family can be in this country! How quickly it can disappear—blown away like a...handful of dust."

*   *   *   *

The evening of the arrival of my parents and aunt and uncle, we poured just one cocktail each and right after sat down to a considerably more modest dinner than the one served the younger generation the previous night. Conversation, needless to say, never touched on the will; it covered a range of less interesting but more practical topics such as the funeral.

Late in the evening, just before bed, we cousins were once again in the cold, spring-fed pool. Sadly, it would be the last time I would feel that invigorating water; water that made our hair clean and silky and that cooled our bodies enough to get us to sleep. When we climbed out of the pool we wrapped ourselves in the blanket-size towels, custom-made for my grandmother. They covered my entire six-foot frame yet were still long enough to drag on the ground behind.

I was in bed around midnight and soon fast asleep. But by 2:30 the heat had assaulted me, and I was floating in and out of a sweaty consciousness like the night before. I went to the bathroom and stopped to look out the window. The two ghostly figures were back! I shivered and stood paralyzed.

A minute later I went down the backstairs and round the outside of the house through the ever-present pungent smell of boxwoods. The house lights were out, but again a dull moon filled the haze. Once more my heart was pounding and my body dripping. I lay on the cool grass, waiting for a splash or a voice to rise above the chattering insects so as to set my bearings. It came in the form of a barely audible sigh and whisper. I slithered through the boxwoods and stopped atop a mound, perfectly motionless, head up, eyes and ears in extreme concentration like a reptile.

In the gray light and erotic heat, secret lovers were silently embracing on the edge of the pool, and I relaxed somewhat after confirming there was no threat. In a few minutes they rose up and walked away from me to an opening in a circle of shrubbery—in the middle of which I knew existed a small garden and open patch of grass.

I never mentioned what I had seen to Binney. Apparently Danny, whom I could recognize by his height, had never been discreet, and my sister seemed to have ample evidence to force him out a year later and get a divorce.

The woman was Nicole. Unlike the other women in the house, only Nicole's hair fell below the middle of her back.

*   *   *   *

As I parked at the funeral two days later, a large Harley Davidson pulled in beside me. Climbing off the bike, with full beard and black leather from neck to toe, was the grandson of one of my grandfather's first cousins—a member of the Ledbetter family mentioned by Henry at the table several days before, and mentioned by my grandmother after her stroke. I had remembered to ask my father about this branch of the family during casual conversation the previous evening.

This cousin's name was Dominick Cuomo and, like the rest of us, was a descendent of various old Virginia families. When I learned his name I was reminded of people living today with names like John Quincy Stallone and Nathan Hale Steinberg.

After the turn of the century two Ledbetter sisters, impoverished by Reconstruction, had come up from Virginia and settled in the coal regions of Northern

Pennsylvania. They taught school and ultimately married men working in the steel mills.

Dom Cuomo and I shook hands in the parking lot and talked after the funeral. Apparently his mother had read Grandad's obituary in the newspaper. Since her son was on his way south before a cross-country bike trip, she had persuaded him to stop by to satisfy her curiosity.

I concluded that his family harbored no ill feelings toward my grandfather and had never expected anything from the Lightfoots. He had known of our existence but little else when his mother had passed him the newspaper clipping. When he later saw Leighsylvania, he asked a few questions but clearly had no knowledge of, or interest in, the family history. Within an hour of his arrival, this descendant of the Lees of Stratford was gone, ultimately riding his Harley west to harvest the old-growth forests of Oregon.

*   *   *   *

More than a hundred people attended the funeral, an impressive number for a man over ninety years old. Among those in attendance were a university president, an ex-governor of Pennsylvania, and a retired United States senator from Virginia.

Only family attended the interment in the Gothic clutter of Laurel Hill Cemetery. It was an overcast and gloomy day in that haunting necropolis above the Schuylkill. My grandfather was placed in the family plot beside his wife, her parents, and various Philadelphia ancestors. The tombstone, to be put in place several weeks later, would read:

THOMAS WILLIAMSON LIGHTFOOT
1893–1987
Château-Thierry, St. Mihiel, Argonne

With my grandfather's interment the plot was thenceforth full—family members alive today must go elsewhere. Cast adrift by our forebears, we shall lie eternally in some distant, lonely field.

CHAPTER 9

▼

Amongst democratic nations, new families are constantly springing up, others are constantly falling away, and all that remain change their condition; the woof of time is every instant broken, and the track of generations effaced. Those who went before are soon forgotten; of those who will come after, no one has any idea: the interest of man is confined to those in close propinquity to himself.

—*Alexis de Tocqueville*

Only in one particular collective guise do today's descendants of the once rich, well born, and powerful patricians survive in the public mind: as the self-styled and self-promoting guardians of what they like to call the national heritage.

—*David Cannadine*

For I agree with you that there is a natural aristocracy among men. The grounds of this are virtue and talents.

—*Thomas Jefferson*

We have it in our power to begin the world all over again.

—*Thomas Paine*

Atop the Brandenburg Gate the four-horse chariot driven by the goddess of Victory glows gas-blue in the floodlights. It is after midnight, yet a small band of the curious still lingers among the gate's Doric columns and in the central passage once reserved for carriages of the Hohenzollern Court.

The Berlin Wall is down, and pieces of it have been crushed into pocket-size fragments. We wander past tables covered with the graffiti-colored concrete chips now for sale as souvenirs. Alongside are piles of uniforms of the old East German army, now also for sale to tourists. A young man under twenty, pulling his army coat tight against the fall wind, discovers that we are from America and keeps us in front of him for a quarter hour with questions about the West. His eyes sparkle and he speaks with hope and excitement. He has heard of Minneapolis, Minnesota, the city in which I now reside.

I have been sent to Berlin by my present employer, an electronic components manufacturer. I am the firm's advertising and communications manager.

Coddie is with me. I mentioned over the phone that I would be attending Funkausstellung, the bi-annual consumer electronics show. The trip was an opportunity he had been waiting for—the chance to visit Berlin in the company of friends now that the Wall has come down.

*   *   *   *

For more than three years Coddie and I have been apart geographically: I am living a block from a lake and in view of the skyline of Minneapolis. Despite the long distance, Coddie and I have remained in touch. I stay with him when I'm in New York, we talk on the phone, and I recently got him elected to the board of the Lightfoot Family Foundation. He is already a very active participant. "How appropriate," Danny is reported to have jealously told Apple, "Arnold of Rugby on the *board* of the Lightfoot Family Foundation."

It is four years since my grandfather's death. Four years that have passed so quickly, and yet the words of my grandparents are now merely distant echoes.

I am a happier man now. I feel a new sense of freedom. At the office I talk very openly and at greater length than ever before to all my fellow workers, and in the neighborhood I am active and have been elected to represent the ward at various political caucuses. My inhibitions have crumbled, and I view the future with excitement and optimism that I had not previously known.

My boss is a native Minnesotan. He and the others in my office find no significance in my accent, one that Eastern States employees found snobby and fun to imitate behind my back. No one knows anything about the Main Line. My boss and everyone else at the office are oblivious to the baggage I carried in the East.

"I bet life is easier here and more productive because there's less concern about social status," hypothesized Coddie on a weekend visit to see us in Minnesota. "When people move here, I bet their prejudices fade away…and that's because there is, comparatively, greater homogeneity racially, ethnically, and economically. This city isn't at war with itself."

We were on an evening walk when we had this discussion, along the lake near my house.

"I heard on the radio recently that Minneapolis is still ninety-two percent white, second only to Salt Lake City among major metropolises," I responded.

"Exactly what I'm talking about. That's evidence for what I'm trying to say. The population of Minnesota *is* overwhelmingly Northern European. Furthermore, the blue-collar worker is a small minority; the poor are not visible. The homeless bag lady, common to the streets of New York and whom I must step over when I walk down into the subway each morning, is non-existent."

"And here's more evidence for your hypothesis," I suggested, "whereas back East you might attend private school because of your parents' desire to raise you apart from the unwashed masses, one of the premier Minnesota private schools boasts consistently of its ethnically and racially diverse student body so as to attract candidates."

"Okay—just what I'm saying. The exception proves the rule. Contrast what you said with the fact that many of the exclusive Eastern boarding schools were founded when waves of immigrants were flooding onto our shores, and this country was becoming increasingly heterogeneous."

"Here's another fun fact," I murmured as we parted our way through weeping willows. They sit on the lakeshore there like shaggy dogs. "The Minneapolis-St. Paul Social Register, first issued in 1907, was discontinued twenty years later due to lack of interest, never to be revived."

"Haa *Ha*! I *am* a sociologist!" he roared excitedly. Just then the elegant lamps along our path lighted up in unison, burning like a ring of birthday candles round the lake. Coddie rambled on, continuing to postulate about social status and Old Money in Minnesota versus Old Money in the East. I thought of Binney's comment: "America has no aristocracy, but it does have *Old Money.*"

Politics is now Coddie's full time vocation. He's left Wall Street and works for the Democratic National Party—for one dollar a year, I'm hearing from sources in the East. I enjoy Coddie's company; many tire of him quickly. Word from the East is that all our old friends are sick of his non-stop theorizing on social issues.

"Blue bloods are permissive of liberal thinking here because they aren't threatened by race and ethnicity," he announced loudly over the expanse of the evening lake. "Civic involvement is not beneath the Minnesota patrician because, if he must rub shoulders with the masses, it's not so dramatically obvious that those shoulders are the shoulders of the great unwashed. He won't think he's getting his hands dirty."

"I suppose you could be on to something," I mused, but he had lost my attention. Now at the windward end of the lake, I was captivated by the whitecaps splashing toward us under a red, mackerel sky.

*   *   *   *

Our hotel is in the old East Berlin. It is a beautiful, luxurious hotel, built by the Communists for Western visitors only. The bellmen, waiters, and busboys are in their early twenties and tell wonderful stories of the first morning they passed through the Wall and spent a day in the West. "They're all so excited," said Coddie. "A chance to begin the world all over again."

We are wandering back from the Brandenburg Gate to our hotel. A sinister bust of Lenin behind a wrought iron fence has yet to be torn away. We pass an Aeroflot office—two letters in the neon sign are out, and the inside is a wreck.

"Hey, a friend of mine is buying a place at Leighsylvania!" Coddie suddenly exclaimed, breaking the silence between us. "I forgot to tell you!"

"Not surprising," I replied. "The developer has been building homes every half acre…. It's sad my father and his two sisters didn't find it practical to keep…. My grandparents' house now sits on just three acres, resembling a luxury liner tied to a dock for a rowboat. The road leading up to it has been called *Manor House Lane*, and the new owner made a fortune in computer software. He's trying to re-invent himself as a member of the country gentry and keeps bugging Dad for stories about the house—so he'll have an ideal to follow, I suppose."

We walk on in silence. My thoughts linger on Leighsylvania and its rolling green hills that have now disappeared. Centuries ago it was a place of flintlock and silk stockings. A hundred years ago: top hats and waists made slim with corsets. And in my grandparents' day: jodhpurs, thoroughbreds, collies, and large meals under Sully portraits and absorbing discussion by the library fire. It is now over a hundred backyards full with brightly colored plastic children's toys and the smell of hamburgers on charcoal.

The fieldstone walls that remained of the farmhouse built by our first Quaker ancestor in America, Baldwyn Leigh, the ancient ruin that my grandmother had so poetically incorporated into her English garden, has been bulldozed and buried. The developer failed to see its potential charm next to the sterile structures he was building.

"This is what's so distinctive about Americans," spoke my disappointed mother one fall day on a return visit to Leighsylvania that we have since regretted. A lover of history and gardening, standing in the red and yellow autumn leaves where the ruin had once been, she shed a tear but nevertheless had strength enough to rationalize the developer's misdeed with the words of Thomas Jefferson: "I like the dreams of the future better than the history of the past."

"Americans are ever anxious to start over, to make things new," she continued, after a moment of thought with Binney, Apple, and me as her audience. "It gets us out of a rut, and we're not depressed because we can be free of the past, if we choose. Re-inventing ourselves lets us maintain the optimism we Americans are so well known for. Long ago we severed our roots and came to a distant shore."

Apple had a few poetic words of his own on that occasion, as he gazed across the changed landscape: "Our family's sail is now but a spider web billowing in the wind."

"But remember that the Lightfoot Family Foundation does provide at least some level of cohesiveness and immortality to the family," I responded in an attempt to cheer him up and encourage greater participation on the foundation board. In one respect he was right, however: we are all across the country now.

Henry is in California and works in college administration. He recently drafted a position paper, signed by his college president, rejecting an endowment gift for yet *another* chair in European History. Henry's words and phrases were quoted nationally. They have been challenged in some indignant right-wing newspaper editorials and by an outraged radio talk show host.

The incident was further evidence in support of my grandmother's observation, twenty years before, that Henry is heir to that streak of Leigh family thinking that began with our Quaker ancestors three hundred years ago. "We've had someone like your brother in every generation," she wrote me. "My uncle left his land in Maine to the Penobscot Indians. Our family were abolitionists long before it was popular. Some of us were sent into exile for being pacifists during the American Revolution. We knew George Fox, and we brought his thinking to the new land with William Penn. That thinking has been a force in this family and in this country, and it has found refuge in your brother. May it continue into future generations, ever evolving for the good of America, as it has in the past."

Henry is an active participant on the family foundation board. He has not yet re-married, but he and Lea's sister, Mary, may have resumed their relationship, dormant for nearly two decades since their time together at the University of Virginia. She is a Senate staffer in Washington, D.C. They were talking non-stop at Apple and Lea's wedding. Can it really be just her *job* that takes her to the West Coast so often?

Binney and Danny are, thankfully, divorced. Binney is in Maine, married now to a Bowdoin College professor of history and son of an Episcopal minister. She has a daughter and is the hardworking, conscientious secretary of the family foundation. She is also a fanatical collector of English Staffordshire figurines.

"How much is a lot of Staffordshire?" I asked her.

"Just a little more."

"Binney, are you trying to keep the *special relationship* alive single-handedly?"

"No, I'm just trying to replace what Nicole took."

Danny is still on Wall Street and single. "Danny was hurt because we didn't appreciate him for his net worth," Binney suggested. "It also might surprise you that now he's sorry he's no longer part of the Lightfoot family. Maybe that's why he occasionally writes you, Tom. He's feeling a little guilty, at last."

"Danny drove a hard bargain at work and a hard bargain at home," said my father. "Everything was a question of power; he was always competing."

"It's the *third* generation makes the gentleman," commented Mother.

Danny travels regularly to London where he shops for clothes—"all made of the finest cottons and wools!" Apple has exclaimed. Apparently he is never seen with someone who's *not* in the Social Register.

Apple's and Lea's wedding was perhaps the most extravagant the Main Line had witnessed in more than a generation. The parties leading up to it drifted on for weeks.

Apple and Lea now live serenely in the fox hunting country of Middleburg, Virginia, supported entirely by Lea's trust fund. They buy expensive clothes and give extravagant gifts to family and friends. Apple has acquired a strong interest in heraldry and spends considerable time charting the family tree on his personal computer. It is rumored that on that same computer he also keeps meticulous graphs of his bowel movements.

"I hope he sends the graphs to American Standard," quipped Ole.

Apple is a disinterested member of the board of the Lightfoot Family Foundation. He attends all the meetings—perhaps because we pay for travel and accommodations. Or perhaps because we hold them at places like Stratford, ancestral home of the Lees. We also pay a small sum beyond travel and accommodations to each member who attends. "We *should* be paid every time we attend," Apple concurred. "After all, the House of Lords pays an attendance allowance."

Henry regularly complains about them after our board meetings: "Apple and Lea never have anything particularly interesting or original to say. Do they know anything about anything except horses and heraldry these days? Certainly nothing going on outside their own charmed world troubles them in the least. And the people with whom they hang out are just as indifferent to the feelings of the rest of the world. It's a cult of leisure. It's a life of privilege without power, although somehow they think they're in the crowd that sets the example for the rest of the country. Amazing! On the surface Apple does have a certain charisma; I'll grant him that. But the clothes, the nice cars, the horses and other accoutrements of old money convince some people to respect him for what he is as opposed to what he does, which is nothing."

I am the receiver of Ludwell family news through Coddie, and Clay and I talk several times a year.

Bored easily and lacking the self-discipline to take on a project and see it through, Mrs. Ludwell wanders the world aimlessly with Mrs. Randolph. Clay describes them as "space travelers. Weightless like astronauts."

Clay and his mother never speak. "I got to be thirty years old and realized Mom isn't the mother I thought I had. I'm old enough to recognize that she doesn't live up to the ideals by which I thought we were raised. I feel she's betrayed us or let us down. It now seems as though I no longer have a mother— as if she's no longer living—and I miss having one. My life is a little emptier."

Clay has returned to Maryland to be near his father. "Dad wants me to manage the farm and wants me to run for the legislature when he retires in a few years."

Posey Ludwell is still in New York. She had a seizure from cocaine several years ago and attended Hazeldon, the drug rehabilitation center in Minnesota. Her father managed to bring her home to Maryland but only for a year. After that she was back to her old ways in her New York brownstone.

Lois still lives with her. *She* apparently makes the regular forays down to Manhattan's Lower East Side in Posey's BMW for drugs. Lois herself, however, has totally dried out, according to Coddie. *She* runs the house: orders the food— most of the meals are catered, recruits cleaning women, hires the help and music for parties, and, most importantly, acts as Posey's secretary—paying the bills and communicating directly with the family office. "Don't ask me why the Ludwells don't know what the *hell* is going on!" Coddie exclaimed. "Lois wears beautiful clothes and seems to be driving Posey's BMW up and down the East Coast whenever she damn well pleases! What is the source of her income other than Posey's checkbook?"

My parents move between Castine in the summer and a house on the ocean in Georgia during the winter. My father's spirits shrank after the break-up of Leighsylvania. "Like a balloon left in the cold," lamented Mother. About three years ago, in extreme depression, Dad tried to asphyxiate himself.

"He was not a success in your grandfather's mind, and therefore his own mind," Mother complained to me in the lobby of an expensive psychiatric hospital. She turned and gazed through a large window. She put her hands on the sill, leaned forward and sighed. "How could anyone in this day and age think he could hold onto a place like Leighsylvania?" she rationalized. "You can't pass a suburban estate, as massive as that one, on to the next generation intact!...A hole opened in his life—he said he felt empty. He told me a part of him vanished when he could no longer smell the hay at Leighsylvania, when he couldn't be refreshed by that cold spring water in the pool, when he couldn't work with his mother in the sweet smelling soil of that garden around the stone ruin left by Baldwyn Leigh.... I guess in short he didn't feel there was a home to come back to. I thought we had created *something* in Castine. Obviously not. By definition I guess an exile wants to return home."

We were both silent for several minutes. "I wish Grandad hadn't by-passed Dad with those portraits," I finally murmured. When the official will had been presented by Drinker Biddle and Reath, we were surprised to discover that the portraits of William Williamson Lightfoot and his wife Penelope were to go directly to me.

In Minneapolis I have proudly hung them on opposite walls; they face each other silently. The tense eyes of both follow me wherever I move about the room. The oil paint on both portraits is cracking with age, and, as such, both images appear to float in a ghostly way bellow the surface.

William Lightfoot, in black jacket and high collar to his ears, with heavy brows, wind swept hair, and handsome visage, inspires my dreams. He urges me on to greater things.

"I shouldn't have asked Dad for that $3,000," I confessed to Mother in the hospital lobby. "It really rubbed something in."

Soon after I received the portraits, I took them to the Minneapolis Institute of Arts for a cleaning and was informed that I must immediately spend three thousand dollars in conservation. Someone, perhaps seventy-five years before, had put liners on their backsides. These liners were now separating from the original canvas, which was now bubbling and beginning to crumble. Would I loose another connection with my past? Dad sent me the $3,000. I wasn't aware how it hurt him that the portraits hadn't been willed to him.

As the years have passed Dad's condition has improved. He severed all ties with the world of investments and went to art school to perfect the already impressive talent he had inherited from his mother. Today his impressionistic landscapes are fetching high prices in Bar Harbor and Newport. A gallery in New York is becoming ever more persistent for a one-man show.

Dad acted to pass management of the Lightfoot Family Foundation to the younger generation early on. At the second meeting he nominated me foundation president. The family voted me in unanimously for an indefinite period. "Tom understands the family: its past and present, and the future that Grandad envisioned," he told his sisters and the assembled cousins. "I think he understands how his grandfather would have wanted the family money spent."

*   *   *   *

Coddie and I wander into our Berlin hotel and look for my wife. She has spent the last several days sightseeing with Coddie while I attended the electronics show. I spot her writing postcards at a table near the grand staircase—a grand and glorious staircase reminiscent of the one at Posey Hall.

Coddie was my best man, and Clay Ludwell and brother Henry were the ushers. It was a small but fun wedding in Bethlehem.

Danny attended, uninvited. Before leaving he told us: "I'm so glad Tom's finally married Jane Eyre."

"Reader, I married him," replied Ole with a happy face.

Soon after Ole finished law school, an advertising executive, with whom I had once worked in New York, recommended me to a client who had a job opening in Minneapolis. I was hired, and we moved west. Ole is now an associate in the city's largest law firm.

"We've talked to a lot of emotional people today," she says as we sit down near her. "Families being re-united after decades."

"We're here in Berlin at the right time. I'm glad you came with me," I reply.

"I had to get away from all that silver!" she winks at Coddie.

"That's the problem, you never help me out, no matter what brand of silver polish I get!"

"I don't think there's a brand of silver polish in the entire world that we don't have a sample of. Is there room for anything else in our house?" she winks again at Coddie, and we all laugh.

Coddie is well aware of my silver collection and enjoys teasing me about it too. I like the attention. The collection came from Leighsylvania, of course. Most of it is family pieces from the nineteenth century and some even earlier.

On Sundays, about once every month and a half, I switch off the flat roar of professional sports, and in the yellow light of the declining afternoon, polish this silver. Removing the tarnish lifts my spirits and restores my sense of belonging to the Lightfoot family, once again.

AFTERWORD

It is with great sadness that I inform you, the reader, that the final paragraphs of what you have just read are *not* true. Regretfully, Tom Lightfoot is no longer living; he was killed by a drunk driver. Not by a drunk driver in another car, but by the driver of the car in which he was the passenger. The driver was one of Tom's employees.

Although Tom, Ole, and I did visit Berlin, the turn of events referenced in the final passage of Tom's autobiography were, simply, Tom's wishful thinking. He and Ole had spent time together, and he was certainly in love. But the two never married, although I know he proposed.

There was, and always will be, a place in Ole's heart for the Lightfoot family. But Ole was frustrated with Tom. For most of her life she had successfully played in the rough-and-tumble world that Tom had spent his life trying to come to terms with. She has now made a name for herself as a Wall Street lawyer and achieved most of what she's done on her own. She did not have the patience for Tom. For her the future is everything, while Tom loved the past.

I found pieces of a rough, autobiographical manuscript when Tom's parents and I visited Minneapolis to sort through his possessions ten years ago. I assembled the pieces, along with facts from my own memory, letters, and extensive interviews to create the story you have just read.

The driver in that fatal automobile accident, someone who worked for Tom, did not survive either, and in this afterward I will refer to him as "Jim." Jim had been through treatment for alcoholism but was back to his old ways when he took Tom and himself off the road at over 90 miles an hour.

Why was Tom in the car in the first place? My theory is: because he had been too nice to say "no," and because he still possessed the innocence that years before had allowed him to collect bad loans in dangerous neighborhoods.

After a company dinner the drunken Jim had demanded that Tom get a lift with him back to the office parking lot to fetch Tom's car. Tom had felt obligated to accept the lift because Jim and he had been battling each other for more than a year, and the ride would be a chance for reconciliation. Managing Jim had been a challenge.

Tom was generally seen by the fellow workers and employees I interviewed as very knowledgeable, insightful, thoughtful, pleasant to be with, and trusting of others to an extreme. He harbored no prejudices and demonstrated great respect for all around him—of any race, class, or ethnic background, rich or poor, male or female. But this acceptance of others was a trait that infuriated Jim, who had been growing ever more insecure as women and minorities had made headway in the workplace. Jim's humor was funny only at the expense of others, especially women and minorities—and of Tom.

Tom had been too polite to turn down the offer of a ride from the drunken Jim. He had probably seen the ride as a chance to connect with Jim and repair the relationship—a chance to bring Jim around and perhaps encourage him to again seek treatment. Tom's graciousness and desire to help led to his own demise.

Jim had driven a landing craft during Macarthur's Inchon invasion of Korea and was therefore considerably older and, he felt, wiser than Tom. He was near retirement and frustrated that in his final days he had been placed under the management of someone so much younger and lacking the street smarts that he, Jim, thought he had in abundance. He couldn't stand Tom's "style." He saw Tom as "wimpy" and referred to him as "The Gay."

Jim was single, had been divorced twice, and had sired five children, none of whom were close. His savings were minimal and retirement apparently appeared bleak.

My interviews with Jim's co-workers revealed that they thought he'd had had enough of living and that the crash was *no accident.*

We all cried at Tom's funeral, Ole included.

Tom had a short will in which he stipulated that the money from his estate be used to fund portraits of faculty retiring from our boarding school. Very appropriately, a teacher of *two* generations of boys, an instructor of Roman history and Latin—of Virgil, Marcus Aurelius, and Cicero—was first to be painted. The portrait was unveiled with great ceremony and thanks were given to Tom. It hangs proudly in the school's eloquent dinning hall. Students who ask about this schoolmaster are told of his dedication, self-sacrifice, high integrity, and passionate desire to have generations of schoolboys and girls understand ancient Rome as well as did America's Founding Fathers.

Tom was buried in Castine, Maine. His parents will someday be buried alongside. Thankfully, he was not buried in a "distant, lonely field."

978-0-595-31611-3
0-595-31611-5